DEADLY
DEPTHS

Also by John F. Dobbyn

Neon Dragon

Frame-Up

Black Diamond

Deadly Diamonds

Fatal Odds

High Stakes

DEADLY DEPTHS

A NOVEL

JOHN F. DOBBYN

OCEANVIEW (PUBLISHING
SARASOTA, FLORIDA

ISBN 978-1-60809-622-0

Published in the United States of America by Oceanview Publishing

Sarasota, Florida

www.oceanviewpub.com

10 9 8 7 6 5 4 3 2 1

A great portion of this work of fiction is based on researched historic fact, but the truest statement of all is this: Without the inspiration, excitement, faith, and deepest love of the most wonderful person I have ever met, thank God, my partner in everything, my Lois, it would never have been begun, let alone published. She is my first editor of every word, always author of our titles, and the one I've loved in the extreme from the moment I met her through every God-given year of our marriage.

CHAPTER ONE

"HEY, GUYS! No class today! The old man died!"

The student who yelled across campus to his classmates was just a blur. But, to me, it stung—a dismissive epitaph for the man who had become like a father to me. Professor Barrington Holmes—the man responsible for enticing me out of a career in the criminal courtroom and into one in the law school classroom.

This was my third jarring brush with Professor Holmes' death that morning. The first was a "breaking news" television report that shocked me so profoundly that I had to replay it to absorb it.

The second brush was a cryptic call ten minutes later from the university president.

"Matthew. My office. Right now."

"This is about?"

"Start driving. Turn on the radio." *Click.*

Wishful disbelief had descended into unwilling acceptance by the time I reached the president's door. I'd have knocked, but a command beat me to it.

"Get in here, Matthew."

I did. Cecil Connely, phone in hand, cut short his pacing behind his desk to nod at a chair. He mouthed the word, "Sit."

I expected his next word to be "stay!"

I'd given up jumping to orders when I left the intelligence branch of the Air Force eight years earlier. I made an exception. The president was visibly strung tighter than piano wire.

I sat through a series of his one-word responses into the phone. "Yes . . . when? . . . No . . . Never." Then a muffled, "He's here now."

He set down the phone and lowered his rigid frame onto the front half of his chair.

"Hell of a morning, Matthew."

"I heard it on the news. No details."

"Yeah, well, whoever said the devil is in the details was a psychic."

"You mean a 'prophet.'"

He gave me a blank look. "What?"

"Nothing. You summoned. I'm here, Cecil. At seven o'clock in the morning. I'm as shocked about Professor Holmes' death as anyone outside of his family. But why did you . . ."

"You two were close, weren't you?"

*   *   *

That question set off more than I was ready for. So many thoughts at once. I'd been one of those college students who casually slid down the prescribed pipes, cruising from summer vacation to fall break, to Christmas break, to spring break, and back to summer.

Then for no good reason I can remember, I took Professor Holmes' basic course in Archeology. It was the only course that fit into my schedule with no early morning classes.

First lecture. About twenty-five students. I was the first one he called on with a question about the preassigned reading. I tried a little dance around a wild guess and struck gold. He smiled, nodded, and said, "Thank you, Mr. Shane." I nearly threw my shoulder out, patting myself on the back.

As we walked out of class, the professor casually walked out beside me. He put his arm on my shoulder and gave me a warm smile. I returned the smile. Clearly my bluffed answer had snowed him.

"Mr. Shane. You're a bright lad."

"Thank you, Professor."

"You've got a good reputation around here."

"How do you . . .?"

"Nothing personal. I do a little research on all my students. Archeology is not overwhelmingly popular. I like to analyze why my students take the course." He spoke in a quiet, soothing voice.

The smile continued. I followed up on the buddy approach. "The enrollment's full. Maybe it's the reputation of the professor."

The smile broadened, and the arm on my shoulder held me close enough to whisper. "Oh my, Mr. Shane. I believe you and I are going to have to take this from the top next class. Here's the lay of the land. Archeology is not an interest with me. It's not a subject to teach. It's not even a way I make a living."

"It's not?"

"No, Mr. Shane, none of that."

"Then what—"

The arm on my shoulder stopped us. He turned me to face him eye-to-eye, still smiling. "It's my life. It's totally absorbing. And more, considerably more, it's occasionally . . . quite dangerous. Do you believe that? Probably not. No matter."

"If you say—"

"Take this to heart, Mr. Shane. If you ever spend class time—my time—again with the unmitigated bull-crap you treated us to today, which, I might add, is unworthy of you, I'll take personal delight in bouncing your unprepared rump right out that door. Yes? Have we got that locked in? Good."

The warm smile continued as he peeled off out the door.

From that day on, I put twice the effort into his class that I put into any other. He became my advisor, first reader for my senior thesis, and, after three years in Air Force Intelligence, the first one I sought out to discuss my decision to go to law school. In practice, I chose a law firm that litigated criminal actions related to stolen antiquities. The choice, I'm sure, was largely a reason to keep in close touch with Professor Holmes.

After three years in the courtroom, the seed he planted back in college grew into an impelling desire to teach—to teach the way he did. He backed my application to become a professor at Hawthorne University's law school. Over the next four years, we met at least once a week at the faculty dining room for lunch.

*   *   *

My mind was still a logjam when the president said it again. "I said, 'You two were close, weren't you, Matthew?'"

"Close . . . yeah."

I'd never said it before to anyone, even to myself. I said it now with conviction. "I deeply love that old man."

I could have added "like a father," but Cecil Connely exuded the kind of chilled aura that stifles any personal inroad. I sensed I'd already gone deeper than he cared to pursue.

"Well, be that as it may, we have matters to discuss."

"We do? Why?"

He walked his little scooter step around the desk and came closer than I had ever seen him come to another human being. "Because I'll be damned if I'll let this university be drawn into a scandal."

That set me back. Even any local newspaper would be hard put to find anything in Professor Holmes' life to warp into a scandal.

"I don't follow."

His voice was down to a biting whisper. I noticed tiny beads of moisture on his forehead. "This goes no further. He was found in his office by the cleaning crew. It was about five a.m. They called the police."

"You mean 911."

"No. Dammit. The police. He was clearly . . . dead."

"Why the police? He had a heart condition. He's been hospitalized twice. I wondered how long he could go on those antiquities expeditions."

"It wasn't his heart."

Cecil's secretary, Carol, knocked and opened the door enough to speak. "The police detective's here. He wants to speak with you."

Another wipe of the brow. "Tell him I'm . . . Give me a few minutes."

"If not his heart, what was it, Cecil?"

"His wrist was slashed. He'd bled out."

That one cut my breath short. Cecil railed on, but I wasn't getting it. "Cecil. Stop! Go back. What did you say about his wrist?"

"Just that. The police came. They went right to his office. They saw the . . . body. They're calling it suicide."

Now my mind was racing at warp speed. Everything I knew of Professor Holmes' passion to wring every drop out of every moment of his life screamed that suicide in the same breath with Professor Holmes was an oxymoron.

"Matthew, focus here. I need your attention."

"I'm here. How did you hear that? About the suicide?"

"The police called me at home. It was about six. I came right over."

"Did you see Professor Holmes' body?"

"Of course not. I came to my office. They met me here. They asked me questions, but I couldn't add anything."

"And then you called me. Why, Cecil? I probably know less than you do."

"Weren't you an investigator or some-such with the Air Force? I remember from your application."

"Yes. Intelligence unit."

"And you were a criminal trial attorney in practice."

"Also, yes. So what? The university has an attorney. General counsel. Ets Reagan."

He waved a dismissive hand. "She knows about contracts, fundraising. I need someone from the trenches."

"For what? Even if it were a suicide, which, by the way, would stun the living hell out of me, it is what it is. What more can I say? To the police or to you?"

He took another deep nervous breath. "It may not be, as you so glibly put it, 'what it is.'"

"Whatever the hell that means."

Carol poked her head in to say that the detective was becoming more insistent.

Cecil waved her off. "A minute! A minute!"

He ran in his little prancing steps back around his desk. He took something out of the center drawer and pushed it into my hands. "Read it. Quickly."

The single sheet of Professor Holmes' university stationary looked like it had been folded in a rush.

"Read it. Read it!"

I'd always had difficulty deciphering Professor Holmes' left-handed scribbling, but this took double the effort. As nearly as I could tell, it said:

Matthew. Sorry. No other way.
Maroon file—

Nanny Town
Tell Monks all
No time

An ink line ran slanting down the page from the last letter of "time" to the bottom right corner.

"How did you get this, Cecil?"

"The cleaning lady, Myra. She found it under his desk. She brought it to me. I'm assuming the 'Matthew' meant you."

"Have the police seen it?"

"I don't think so. I told her to keep it to herself."

"And that's why you called me?"

"That's part of it."

"And?"

"The police officer, the detective, he asked if you'd be on campus. I told him he could meet you here."

"What's his name?"

"Something like McCane, McLane. I'm not sure. Listen to me. There's just one priority here. There will be no scandal. No sensationalism. The papers would love it. Our donors, one in particular, would not love it. You know about these things."

I walked over to hand the letter back to Cecil. He pushed it away like it carried a virus. "You keep it. I don't want it around here."

"This could be evidence. If there's more to this than—"

"All the more reason. You handle it. I want you to take the lead on this. Beginning with this detective."

"Hang on, Cecil. Let's be clear—"

I still felt as if I were bouncing off walls in a pitch-black room. This was no time to imply that either Cecil or the university or anyone else was my "client," with all of the obligations and attorney-client restrictions that word would instantly produce.

I never finished the thought. Cecil pushed a button. He rasped into his intercom, "Carol, send in the officer."

Mac McLane had been a detective since long before I went into practice as criminal defense counsel. That alone should have put us instantly and irrevocably in enemy camps.

It's hard to explain, but from the moment I first met him as the arresting office, testifying against my client in an antiquities theft prosecution, there was something in his crusty, up-front manner that struck a rare chord. I couldn't put it into words, but during that cross-examination, we looked each other in the eye. A faint message seemed to flow both ways. Contrary to expectations, it said to each of us, *This one has no hidden agenda. This one is real.* That initial impression was fertile ground for a trust that just continued to grow deeper.

It was an unlikely match, but over the years, Mac and I met a number of times, well out of the public eye, each to pick the brain of the other when a case ran one of us into a brick wall. More than once, a fresh look from the other's perspective had produced a chink in that brick wall that led to either a justified plea of guilty or a dismissal of charges. That trust grew into a friendship that defied the odds.

*   *   *

Cecil greeted Mac at the door. He quickly ushered him over to me. Mac and I gave each other our usual simple nod of recognition.

"Hell of a morning, Matt. I'm sorry. I hear this time it's personal."

"It is, Mac. In spades. Were you the first one in?"

"No. Detective Flynn took the call."

"Have you seen it for yourself?"

"I just came from there."

"First impression?"

He rubbed his forehead. Not a good sign. "Right now I'm thinking something you don't want to hear."

"So I'm told. You can guess my opinion on that."

"That's without seeing the body."

I shrugged.

I knew that would be a heart-twister. It also seemed unavoidable. I stood up and headed for the door. I let Mac go first, while I turned back to cut the cord that could affect my discussion with the police. "Cecil, two things. You may have to talk to the police again. I don't know where this is going. One piece of advice is all you need from me. Tell the truth, all of it. No shading. No omissions. If you don't, it'll sure as hell come back to bite you. Then you will have a scandal on your hands."

He padded over closer and whispered. "What about the . . . you know, what I gave you?"

"The truth. All of it."

"But . . ."

"Dammit, Cecil, all of it. Second thing. Call university counsel. Now. She needs a heads-up."

He seemed flummoxed and in need of one more push. "Tell her everything. She's your lawyer, Cecil, not me."

CHAPTER TWO

I'D WALKED DOWN that corridor to Professor Holmes' office hundreds of times, and each time in anticipation of meeting my mentor—the one person I knew would always be solidly in my corner—even more so since the passing of my parents.

But not this time.

The door was open. The uniformed cop standing a few feet up the corridor from the door waved Detective McLane past. He used the same beefy hand on my chest to stop me cold. "Not you."

Mac turned for a quick, "He's with me." That got the hand off my chest but not the smirk off his face. Mac caught the look. When we passed the blockade, Mac asked in a whisper, "A little history there, Matt?"

I kept it to a whisper too. "Some years back. I was in practice. Your Officer Sacher threatened the family of a sixteen-year-old kid I represented 'til the kid confessed to a rape that occurred six blocks from where he was at the time. During Sacher's testimony at the trial, my cross-examination was less than delicate. The charge against my client was dismissed. Sacher caught a suspension and a lot of heat. I guess all is not forgiven."

Mac looked back at the glare on Sacher's face still aimed at me. Again, a whisper. "I've heard stories. We have a few bad apples. He's at the top of the tree. We'll weed him out someday. I can sit on him here, Matt, but you might do well to stay out of his way."

"My every wish."

He nodded to the office. "Shall we?"

He let me go through the door first.

I thought I was ready for what I'd see. Not even close. I felt every nerve and muscle in my body freeze. I forced my eyes to take in Professor Holmes' lifeless body.

He sat slumped over his desk. The enormous void I felt was the absence of that aura of vitality that always radiated, not just from his eyes, but from every inch of his body. The truth of what I was seeing finally overwhelmed my compulsion to repress it. My old friend was somewhere else, somewhere better—but not here.

Mac gave me a minute to manage the emotional side and focus on cold details. If I were just looking at a photo of the scene, my snap assumption would have been classic suicide. His left arm rested on the desk beside his closed eyes. The gaping slash on his left wrist was at the center of a crimson circle.

His shirt was open at the collar. There were no visible signs of neck or head trauma. No evidence of bullet, stab, or blunt force wounds.

"Take a minute, Matt. You knew him. You know the room. I want to hear what you see that I don't."

I used the minute to scan and think. Then I nodded toward the uniform at the door. "Can we close the door, Mac?"

He did. "Okay. What?"

"I could have told you it's not suicide before we came in here."

"Based on what?"

"I know him too well. I mean I really knew him."

Mac rubbed his chin. "I'm not dismissing that, but could you set it aside for a minute? What are you seeing here? Objectively."

I looked at Mac. "How good is the detective who reported this as a suicide?"

He gave it a second before wavering the palm of his hand to indicate mediocrity. "Ignore that too. What do you see?"

"The first thing that grabs me says, 'No way.' His left wrist is cut open. That's a problem."

"Spell it out."

"Professor Holmes was left-handed. Very left-handed. He'd have used his left hand to cut his right wrist, not the other way around."

"Yeah."

"And if I could say so, your Detective Flynn should have picked that up. Look at the arrangement of everything on his desk. His desk-phone. His pen holder. The different wear on the drawers on the two sides of the desk, the position of the screen of his computer. This whole setup screams of a left-handed user."

"Granted. And yet, not totally conclusive. There's no evidence of a struggle or any physical compulsion. Nothing directly suggests anyone else was involved. What else?"

"Look at the round circle of blood under the cut wrist. If he had slashed the veins and arteries himself, the blood would have gushed out in a much different pattern. Right?"

"So it would seem."

"Which says he was already dead when his wrist was cut. That blood should be checked to see if it's even his blood."

"I'll make a note."

"And if he was already dead, what killed him? No evidence of external force. This is another question for the medical examiner."

"Noted. Anything else?"

"Yeah. My guess is that he died right here. It's unlikely anyone would try to carry a body of his bulk from outside, especially with cleaning crews in the corridors all night."

"That would be a challenge. Is that it?"

I took the cryptic note out of my pocket. I spread it open on the desk. "The cleaning lady who found his body found this under his desk."

Mac looked at it without touching. Then he looked at me. He had the lines in his forehead that I expected. "How the hell did you get it? This shouldn't have been touched."

"She must have read it and thought it should go to the top. She brought it to the president's office. He gave it to me."

Mac held a folded edge down with his pen, not to add yet another set of prints to the evidence. He mumbled the words on the note.

Matthew. Sorry. No other way.
Maroon file
Nanny Town
Tell Monks all
No time.

He looked up. "What about the handwriting?"

"It looks like the professor's hen-scratching, but I'd stake my life it's not."

"Why not?"

"For one thing, look at the fallaway pen line right after the last word, 'time.' Makes it look like he died right at that point. No time to even sign it."

"Yeah. I see what you mean. It runs left to right down the page. Whoever wrote it used their right hand."

"Not possible for him."

"How about the words themselves? Anything familiar?"

"No. None of it. No connection. I know the professor went on antiquities digs every summer. All over the world. In fact, he was gone a few days last week."

"Where?"

"I don't know. He usually tells me. Not this time."

"Did you ask him?"

I nodded. "And that was unusual. I asked him before he left. He just said 'Somewhere I've never been.'"

"Did he—"

"Another thing. He was always like a kid waiting for Christmas before leaving on one of his expeditions. Bursting with excitement about what he might find."

"This time?"

I shook my head. "He seemed to be dreading something. I started to ask what it was, but he cut off the question. He just got back four or five days ago. I hadn't seen him since before he left."

Mac's cellphone took him away from the conversation. I could see the lines creeping across his forehead as he listened. He barely breathed into the phone. "I'm on it. Where?"

I tuned out while he continued to listen. I walked to the window to get my mind out of overdrive. Unwelcome thoughts were pounding on every side of my brain.

I was looking out the window across the campus when Mac walked over. His hand on my shoulder startled me. He looked at my face. "What is it, Matt? You look . . . something."

"I just had the damndest feeling. Like nothing I've ever felt before."

His puzzled look asked the question.

"Mac, this is eerie. It's suddenly beginning to feel . . . very personal. To me."

"I'm sorry, Matt. I know."

"No, not that. In a different way."

"What are you talking about?"

"Just listen. Whoever set this up carefully laid out a scene that would convince a detective at the end of his night shift, who wouldn't mind minimizing the paperwork, that it was a straight suicide. Case closed. That could have been the end of it."

"Keep going."

"And yet the killer left enough inconsistencies to convince someone who looks beyond the obvious, someone who knew the professor well, that the professor was murdered. Could be just sloppy work by the killer, right? Or . . ."

"Or what?"

"Maybe the inconsistencies were deliberate."

"To accomplish what?"

"To send a message."

"To whom?"

"That's the eerie part . . . to me. Personally."

He gave me a look. "C'mon, Matt. I know the note mentions your name. But . . ."

"There is no 'but.' That assures that this so-called suicide note would somehow pull me into it. Suppose the killer, or whoever sent him, knew that I'd pick up on the left-handed clues. More likely than anyone else. Suppose this whole setup was intended to send the message directly to me that the professor was murdered."

"And why you?"

"I don't know. Maybe the strongest way to suck me into following up on whatever the words of the note mean without tipping it to anyone else."

I could see disbelief written all over Mac's face. "I think you're too close to this emotionally, Matt. If it is murder, the killer might have just wanted to make it look more convincing as a suicide. Therefore, a suicide note. Why to you? Because he somehow knew you two were close."

I shook my head. "That's what's got me on edge more than anything else. I'd swear to you, Mac, if it ever really came to taking his own life, not a question in my mind, the professor's first and last thought would be of his wife, Mary. Not me."

I could see he was at least thinking about it.

"And how about that last line in the note? It says, 'No time.' *No time for what?* If the professor were trying to bleed himself out, that's not a quick process. It doesn't square with that cryptic note."

He didn't answer, but the lines were back on his forehead.

"You want it straight, Mac?"

"Always."

"God forbid. I think this whole heartbreaking mess, including the murder, could be a message."

"To you? From whom?"

"Damned if I know. But whoever it is knows I can't walk away from it 'til I find out."

CHAPTER THREE

No matter how close we became over the years, it was always "Professor Holmes." It wasn't a formality. It was what it implied—a respect that ran to the depth of my soul.

But from the day I met her sometime in my junior year of college, his wife was always "Mary" to me. Somehow it passed between us early on that my own mother had succumbed to an illness when I was in grammar school. Maybe that had something to do with our slipping into first names early on.

She was at the door at my second ring. She looked—what can I say—like I felt.

"I knew you'd come, Matt."

The hug must have lasted a full minute. The earth had fallen away under both of us, and we were hanging onto the only constant that hadn't changed.

"Did you hear what they're saying, Matt?"

I couldn't say that word either. "I know it's not true. So do you."

"But they're saying he cut his own wrist. If it were his heart, I think I could . . . I've almost been expecting it. Those archeology expeditions of his. Actually, they're probably what's kept his heart going this long."

"Maybe that . . . and you."

Her voice stuck. She took my hand and led me to the kitchen. It was a sign of the closeness of the three of us that we never sat anywhere but in the kitchen.

"Have you talked to the police, Mary?"

"Someone, a Detective Flynn, I think. He was here. He left just before you came. He was asking inane questions. Was Barry disturbed? Was he bipolar? Did he suffer from depression? Good Lord."

"What did you say?"

"I told him if he had half the drive my husband had on his worst day, he'd get his tail out of my house and find out who killed . . . My God, Matt. I'm just realizing it. Did somebody kill Barry? Is that even possible?"

I think the thought just hit her like the same steamroller that hit me in Cecil's office.

"I don't know. What I do know—and what I promise—is that someday I'll come to you with the answer."

A tear came loose, and she just nodded.

"Can I show you something, Mary? It's a little jarring. Are you all right?"

"Sort of. What?"

I took out the photocopy Mac let me make of the paper that had been found under Professor Holmes' desk. I opened it up. I could see Mary doing a quick search for her glasses.

"I'll read it to you. It's in what looks like the professor's handwriting."

"Scrawling,"

That brought half a smile. "For sure. Here's what it says, nearly as I can tell. 'Matthew. Sorry. No other way. Maroon file. Nanny Town. Tell Monks all. No time.' That's it. No signature."

She sat in silence.

"The cleaning lady found the note under his desk early this morning. Does it make any sense?"

Without a word, she got up and poured two cups of coffee, both black. She put one in front of me and sat down.

As if there had been no pause, she simply said, "Maybe. Did Barry ever mention a group he called 'The Monkey's Paw Society'?"

I had a flash back to the cryptic words in the note—"Tell Monks."

"No. He never mentioned it."

She shook her head. "I called them 'The Society of Wishful Thinkers.' Five of them, counting Barry."

"Who are they?"

"They're an eclectic collection. Four people about his age. One time or another, I guess they were each bitten by whatever insanity sends people into the armpits of the world after hidden treasure. They apparently came upon a map or something, leading to some kind of pirate treasure. I'm surprised he didn't mention it to you."

"So am I. Did he ever go after pirate treasure before?"

"No. That's another surprise. He'd get excited about turning up a thousand-year-old cracked urn or some Stone Age club in an excavation. But never anything like gold or silver."

"So why this group?"

"I can only tell you what Barry said. The other four are from places all over the map. They'd meet at conventions. The last time was in Cairo. Barry came home talking about some object a pirate had stashed on an island in the Caribbean. This group had something that was supposed to lead to it."

"What was the object?"

I could see her sorting out memories while she refilled our cups. She was still puzzling when she sat down. "I don't know. Usually, Barry would spout more details than I needed to hear about cave-pictures or whatever he was going after." She shook her head.

"This time he was not into details. There were phone calls over the next few weeks. Then he packed up and flew to someplace in Jamaica."

"Just like that."

"Like that. I asked him for details, but he just kept saying leave it to him. This was going to be our retirement fund. You know, even that was out of character. Barry never gave a damn about money. And retirement? It'd kill him in a month."

"When he got home from Jamaica, what did he say?"

I could see on her face that this part was troubling to recall. It took her a minute. "We shared everything, Matt. You know that. Every detail of those archeological jaunts. He couldn't wait to get home and tell me about it."

"I know."

"Not this time."

"Like what?"

"He had nothing to say about it. He was gone a few days. When he got home four days ago, nothing. He wouldn't say a word."

"You asked?"

"Of course. He just kept everything inside. There was a tension about him every time I'd mention it."

She seemed lost in thought. I broke the pause. "Strange. Whenever he'd get home, he'd call me for lunch and a talk. I never heard from him this time."

"Until that note." She hesitated a few seconds with new wrinkles on her temple. "He loved you like a son, Matt. You know I do too. But . . . I can't help wondering . . ."

I knew what she was thinking. Why a note to me and no word to her?

"Mary, he didn't write that note. I'd bet my life on it."

"Then who?"

A shrug was the best I could do. "Tell me about this Monkey's Paw group. Was that his name for them?"

"No. That's what they called themselves. I have no idea why."

"Did any of them go with him to Jamaica?"

"Matt, I'm telling you. He told me nothing."

"Did he hear from any of them after he got home?"

"Yes. Yes. A note came yesterday."

She jumped up and went into the professor's study. She came back and handed me an envelope. The letter inside was on plain lined paper. The only words on the note were in a handwriting I didn't recognize. "COME FAST. IT'S HAPPENING."

There was no signature and no return address. The postmark was "Bayou Ste. Germaine, Louisiana."

"If it was so urgent, why didn't he email or text or phone?"

She just shook her head.

"Mary, do you have the names and addresses of the other members of that group?"

"No. Maybe in Barry's files."

Another thought occurred. "Did the professor ever color code his files?"

"Why?"

"That note I showed you. It mentions a 'maroon file.'"

She went back to his study and went through his file cabinet. She came back with a light in her eyes and a file folder marked simply "Maroon."

We opened the folder to find just one sheet of paper. It had four names with cities on it in the professor's scribbling. One name jumped out because of the postmark on the letter. "Rene Perreault. New Orleans, Louisiana." The other three names had a city beside each of them: Montreal; Port Royal, Jamaica; and Bridgetown, Barbados.

"May I take this?"

"Of course."

I stood up for one more hug and a very indefinite, "I'll be in touch."

*   *   *

It was summer break at the law school. With no summer classes, I had no ties. Tenuous as it was, the best thread I had to the group that seemed to be pulling the professor's strings was the Bayou Ste. Germaine postmark on the note, most likely from Rene Perreault.

It felt like slipping into an old pair of shoes to be back in investigation. The intelligence work I did in the Air Force gave me a sense of the process. Oddly, I felt a kick of adrenaline to be back at the game.

A three-and-a-half-hour flight to Louis Armstrong New Orleans International Airport got in at about six p.m. As an inveterate jazz fan, I had the first lift of spirits in two days in seeing proclaimed everywhere in the airport the name of the man most responsible for fathering the American art form in its infancy. Appropriately, he was known to those closest to him simply as "Pops."

I checked into the Hotel Royal in the *Vieux Carre* a block off Bourbon Street. I was flying blind, but one theory had served me well in the past. The two fastest ways to tap into a salable source of unpublicized information about any city, particularly one with New Orleans' thriving underbelly of vice, was to pay the dues up front in cash to any cab driver or concierge over fifty. Of the two, the latter had led me up fewer blind alleys than the former.

On that theory, as soon as I had checked in, I waited behind a semi-sober group of tourists at the concierge stand. When they moved to the side with a map, I quietly passed a hundred-dollar tip to the aging concierge with the name tag MARCEL for the name of the best Cajun/Creole restaurant in the Quarter. The tip bought me the name of K-Paul's on Chartres Street, home base to the incomparable but deceased Chef Paul Prudhomme. It was information that I'd known from experience for at least ten years and could have had from any shoeshine boy for a buck. The implication was clear to us both that I'd be back for information on the more dicey side when there was no one else within hearing. It also implied the need for the level of discretion that is frequently their stock-in-trade. I was painfully aware that what started this odyssey was the violent murder of my closest friend.

I left the few things I'd packed in my room. I went down to the lobby. This time I had Marcel to myself.

"*Oui,* Monsieur Shane. I can serve you in what way?"

The accent was deep New Orleans Cajun, which raised my hopes. He had checked on my name in anticipation, which raised them even further.

"I need to make contact with someone in Bayou Ste. Germaine. I just have a name. Rene Perreault. How difficult will that be?"

Some slight wrinkling of the skin around his eyes triggered an alert I wasn't expecting. His tone was low.

"*Eh, Monsieur.* That could be a bit difficult. That bayou, you know, it's a very . . . mmm, private place. Very insular people, could we say. They have not exactly laid the welcoming mat out for strangers, those people."

I sensed a brick wall until he added, more quietly, "Unless, of course, you have contact with the right person."

The slight smile that raised the ends of his moustache like little flags restored my confidence. It also conveyed a revaluation of the information. Another note of like denomination passed under the shelf of his stand. It was absorbed like a bill in a slot machine.

"And tell me, Marcel. Do I have the good fortune to be talking to the right person?"

The smile remained. "Will you be dining at K-Paul's this evening, *Monsieur*?"

"If I can get a reservation."

He raised his hands and shoulders slightly in a typically French gesture. It clearly meant that he would make a call and my path would be greased.

I smiled back.

"I'm certain you'll find everything you wish. All to your liking."

"I would be most grateful, Marcel."

"I'm sure of it, Monsieur Shane."

That had the ring of another revaluation. No matter. I hadn't come this far to lose hope. Another note fed the kitty.

I started to leave. Marcel came around his stand and held my elbow. The smile had faded. "The name of this person in Bayou Ste. Germaine." He bent close to my ear. "It's not one to be spoken lightly, that. Be careful, *Monsieur*. I believe—"

Just then another hotel guest approached Marcel with a New Orleans map in his hand. His smile returned and his tone rose. "I believe you will enjoy your dinner, Monsieur Shane."

CHAPTER FOUR

It was coming up on seven-thirty p.m. when I left the Hotel Royal. I turned down the doorman's offer of a taxi for the comforting pleasure of walking under the late shadows of Ste. Louis Cathedral in Jackson Square. Another time, the jugglers and sidewalk artists would have slowed me up. Tonight, my mind was on other things.

Dinner at K-Paul's began as I'd remembered. The welcome was enthusiastic when I walked through the door. My name brought a gracious smile from the hostess. The name of Marcel of the Hotel Royal brought immediate seating at a coveted table close to the kitchen.

If anything on earth could put the weight of my mission briefly on the back burner, it was that first taste of Paul Prudhomme's chicken and andouille gumbo.

I learned years ago that the chef briefed the waitstaff nightly on what had come in fresh that day. It would have been criminal negligence to disregard the waiter's recommendation of the blackened Louisiana drum fish.

Difficult as it was, I rationed the amount of wine consumed with dinner suspecting that the rest of the evening would be a bit of a crapshoot. But there was no reason to abstain from Paul's signature

bread pudding and hard sauce. Neither did I refuse the chef's tradi-
tional gift to any lone diner of an after-dinner cordial.

The check was delivered and paid. I was about to stand, totally at
a loss for my next move, when an older Black man with deeply
weathered skin in a tropical white suit was beside me at the table.
Something between a smile and a grin seemed like a fixture. I
remembered casually noticing him standing outside the door when
I arrived. His accent was deeper than that of my concierge, Marcel,
and a clear mongrelization of pure Cajun.

"You have enjoyed your dinner, *Monsieur, oui?*"

"*Magnifique, merci.*"

"*C'est bon.* And now, perhaps, you'd wish a ride? You'll follow me,
yes? There's a door behind the kitchen. We can avoid the crowd on
Chartres Street. Shall we? . . . Now, Monsieur?"

An alarm went off. I first chalked it up to his slightly grating insistent manner. Then I flashed back to a recollection of the two he was
standing with outside the door when I arrived. My immediate mental reaction had been "God forbid we ever meet in a dark alley."

And now I was being "invited" to the dark alley behind the
restaurant. I made no move to stand.

I said it quietly. "Did Marcel send you?"

He said, "*Oui, Monsieur.*" But there was an instant of hesitation
that said he didn't know Marcel from Bugs Bunny.

I continued to sit. My hesitation did not go over well. The smile
became less of a fixture. The tone became less permissive. "I think it
would be well if you came this way now, you. The door. Just there."

My comfort level was down to three and descending as rapidly as
the graciousness of my companion. I still made no move to stand.

"I'd like to hear more about this ride before I accept."

The face of the man in front of me turned to stone. He glanced
over at a Black man I had noticed dining alone at the table beside

me. A slight nod and the man rose from the chair to what looked like six inches above my six foot one. He was beside me in three steps. His face showed scars that I assumed had been left by people who had previously disagreed with him.

I felt a hand the size of a slab of pork ribs under my arm. Refusing the invitation to stand was no longer an option.

The man in the white suit opened his jacket enough to clear the butt of what I assumed was a blade of some proportions. He whispered quietly but emphatically, "You should look around here, you. Nothing but hungry tourists. No one gonna fight your battle if you make noise. We agree? Good. Then we leave."

The alley behind the restaurant was as dark as I had imagined. I walked half a block with my elbow gripped in a five-fingered vise. A car—the rear door open—stood waiting. I was propelled by the iron fist into the back seat.

My two fellow travelers took the front seats. We began winding through the less touristy streets of the city.

The scenery went slowly from urban streets to swampish, steaming wetlands as we covered miles in what I sensed was a southeast direction. Within less than an hour, the light of a half moon was outlining a lane-and-a-half of crudely paved road. It wound through dripping cypress trees that rimmed a black, mist-exuding expanse of water.

The sounds had gone from a cacophony of Cajun, country, zydeco, and Dixie bands, blaring out of small clubs and strip joints, to a different cacophony of frogs, insects, and whatever bayou creatures came out at night to eat each other and brag about it at the top of their lungs.

The fact that I was allowed to see the route played havoc with my imagined prospects of a return trip to the hotel. I'd have actually welcomed a blindfold.

The human silence was broken only by occasional orders or directions spat out by the white suit to the giant behind the wheel. Since it was all in a language I'd never heard, I was still in the dark in every conceivable way.

The pavement soon became gravel. A mile or so later, in one quick right turn, it went from gravel to a rutted dirt path that led over a low log bridge that could loosen the teeth of an alligator. The black water on both sides of the bridge was dotted with beady pairs of shining eyes that seemed voraciously alert to our crossing.

The ruts led from the bridge to what might generously be called a cabin. The light in the window suggested that we were expected.

The driver pulled open the car door. He gripped me by the arm. Within seconds we were up the three creaking steps, across the porch, and into the single room.

Mounds of crushed Jax beer cans and unlabeled jugs littered the floor behind a plank table with a bench and two chairs. A rumpled bed filled one corner, and a faded, spotted, overstuffed chair, back to us, filled another. An aroma of spicy cooking hung heavy in the fetid air.

The grip on my arm let loose. A voice came from the direction of the chair. "Leave us be. Wait outside, you."

It was just a few words, but the accent was in no form of Cajun I'd ever heard. Yellow light from a kerosene lamp lit the sweat-beaded features of a Black face that could have been anywhere from fifty to ninety. When he stood, the arthritic movement of bone-thin limbs said closer to ninety.

"You can sit." His voice was raspy. It was followed by a coughing jag that went on for half a minute. In the midst of it, he replaced words with a gesture toward one of the chairs. I felt myself slipping back into a frame of mind to take orders. I sat.

He moved in jerking steps to a cardboard case on the floor. He pulled out a half-empty bottle labeled "Jack Daniels." He scooped two semi-clean glasses off a shelf by the sink and took more jerking steps back to the table. He poured a liquid that looked lighter than anything I recalled being distilled by Jack Daniels. He half-filled each of the glasses and painfully steadied himself on the back of the other chair.

He held his glass up to me as if making a toast. I followed the invitation and raised a glass with him. He coughed a bit more, and said softly in perfect Irish, "*Slante.*"

I still held my glass up in front of me. "Before I take you up on your toast . . ."

He laughed a soft laugh. "No, no. You're thinking right. Mr. Jack Daniels did not brew this fine liquid. But I assure you, its pedigree in these bayous goes back just as many years. I say it again, *Slante.*"

I re-weighed the wisdom of touching my lips to whatever dried greenish-yellow crust rimmed my glass. Under the circumstances, I came to the default conclusion—what the hell. I clicked my glass with his. "*Slante.*"

That first sip had a kick that could lay low a moose, but it was also as smooth as anything flowing out of Mr. Jack Daniel's fine distillery. I found myself taking a second sip, and a third, before nodding approval to my host.

He smiled in acceptance of my compliment. He took another deep draft of the liquid before enduring the pain of lowering his angled frame into the chair opposite me.

He refilled each of our glasses and raised his with just a nod before consuming half of it. I took another swallow in certain assurance that the fire in the liquid would knock out anything that lived on the rim of the glass.

I set my glass down and waited out another coughing jag. When it ended, he took a deep breath and looked me dead in the eye. "Mr. Shane. I could apologize for what I can imagine was the . . . insistence . . . with which you were brought here."

I stated to speak, but he cut me off. His voice was a bit stronger than his physical condition would suggest. "But you're here. There are more important things to say. And little time. So to hell with it."

For lack of a better answer, and with little choice, I nodded acceptance of the non-apology. He nodded back.

"You came down here, I mean New Orleans, because of the suicide of your friend, Professor Holmes. We can start there."

That went too far. "No. I don't know where you get your information. It was not suicide."

His voice came up three notches more than I thought he had in him. "Suicide? Murder? To hell! He's dead! We can agree on that?"

I was a bit stunned. To move it on, I simply said, "Go on."

"Good." He was back to a normal tone, and I was on notice of who was in control of the conversation.

"You came all the way down here to see Monsieur Rene Perreault. Why?"

"I have only one interest here. I want to prove to myself and everyone else that it was not suicide."

His impatience flared. He shook his head and waved a feeble hand in a gesture of dismissal. "No! Listen to me! Murder, suicide, accident, it's not worth a tinker's damn! It makes no difference! There is one important thing here. Do you know what Holmes and Perreault were doing? And those others? And more important, where they were doing it? You have one chance. I want the truth, or by damn—" The cough caught him again in mid-sentence. I let it subside before answering. His eyes were boring back into mine.

"No. I don't know what they were doing. Or where. And unless it explains Professor Holmes' death, I don't give a damn."

His breathing was heavy. The coughing had worn him down. His tone was low. "That's not very reassuring, Monsieur Shane."

"I'm totally in the dark here. I have no idea who you are or what you want me to say. If you want the truth, that's it. All of it."

His eyes were boring into mine looking for more. He must have come to a conclusion. His eyes fell back on the table. "Then I'll tell you all you need to know here. And then I'll have your word."

"My word on what?"

"Listen first, you. Your friend Holmes, he was destined to die. By murder, suicide, accident, no matter. He was a fool. They were all fools. And not without warning."

"Warning about what?"

"They were after that thing. Those fools. It meant more to them than their lives. They were told about the curse. She made the curse. She laid it down centuries ago. She still lives. She gives it power."

"Who?"

"The Mother of Us All. She is Obeah woman. The curse can't be broken."

"I have no idea what you're talking about."

"Then I tell you what I told them. Listen to me. The curse is this. If you people, you outsiders, you *bakra* set your foot once on our most sacred land, your life is over. You will die by some disaster. And it won't be long coming. They wouldn't hear me. Their greed made them deaf. They came. And now, as it was certain to be, your friend is dead."

My expression must have combined confusion and basic disbelief. He looked deeply into my eyes. He seemed to find no resolution.

"I give you one chance, Monsieur Shane. Will you swear to me by whatever is holy to you—no matter what you hear from Perreault or the others—you will go back to your home? That you will never touch our sacred land? Swear it now, by your life."

His eyes seemed to be penetrating my thoughts. I had sworn before. I had sworn to Mary that I'd bring her the answer to Professor Holmes' death. How could I swear something now that might prevent me from ever finding that answer? The best I could give him was simply silence.

I could see a cloud cross his face. He seemed resigned to a conclusion. "So you'll see this Rene Perreault. If you don't get your answer from him, you'll go to Montreal. Then to Barbados. These Monkey's Paw Society fools. And if none of them can satisfy you . . . you won't stop 'til you go to my Jamaica. You'll go, and you'll desecrate the most sacred place on earth." His voice became calm. "And that will be on my head."

His eyes were scanning my face. The truth left me no room to hide. "Perhaps so. If that's where I'm led."

He closed his eyes. He forced his body to stand. His words had a finality. "And perhaps not."

He called in a voice louder than I thought he could summon. "Ander! In here, you!"

The door opened. The giant who had dragged me into the shack was there. The old man simply said, "Now!"

Before I could rise out of the chair, the big one had his arms around my chest like steel girders. He lifted me like a sack of grain. He carried me through the door, down the steps, and back down the path—back to the log bridge and the still, black water.

CHAPTER FIVE

BY THE TIME he hauled me to the log bridge, those mammoth arms had nearly crushed the breath out of my lungs. I'd have given a rib for just one gulp of air.

We finally reached the center of the bridge. He dropped me like a dead goat. I gasped, and thanked God for the breath.

I caught a look into the steamy liquid below. What was smooth as a pane of glass before was now roiled by the flailing tails of alligators, fighting each other for the best position to catch what was about to drop from above. By all odds, that would be me.

The cries of gators whose parts fell in the path of snapping jaws launched an instant cloud of birds' wings into the air. I was still frozen to the spot. The only thing my body could do was strain to fill my lungs with air.

The giant was also apparently winded from the exertion. I could hear his rapid breathing over the din. It gave me a moment to think. In that moment, I could do nothing but pray.

The moment passed quickly. Those steel arms locked around me again just under the ribs. I could feel myself being hoisted above the low railing.

Fear was now into full-blown panic. Moonlight flashed on teeth grinding like tree shredders.

I said my last word to God. I closed my eyes and braced to be plunged into the sawmill.

It came. But instead of hitting churning water and teeth, my hip fell back on the solid logs of the bridge. The steel arms were gone. I was lying alone on the bridge.

I recalled a single sound above the din at the instant I expected to be hurled over the railing. I could swear it was a rifle shot.

I got to my feet as fast as I could. I looked over the edge of the bridge. The moon lit a tumult of slimy, writhing green bodies, scrambling over each other and tearing at something large that was rapidly disappearing.

I was still gaping, stunned, seconds later when a Black man with a rifle ran up beside me. He shouted over the din. "You all right? Can you walk?"

"Yeah. I think."

"Then let's get outta here."

He was nearly the size of my attacker. He took my arm and pulled me for the first few steps. I found my footing and ran to keep up with him. It was a hundred yards to his car. The motor was still running. In seconds, we were on the road, spraying dirt and then gravel. When we hit the paved road, he turned on the headlights and slowed to somewhere around the speed limit.

I had questions, but I held them until we were well on the road back to the city. He said it first—what we were both thinking. "That was about as close as you could cut it. You sure you're all right? I could stop if you want."

"No. Don't stop 'til we get to Canada."

He smiled. "I guess you're all right. You do take up with strange playmates."

"My mother warned me about that. Could I ask you about a dozen questions?"

"Like?"

"Like how did you know? Who sent you? In fact, for a start, if you don't mind, who are you? Then I have about ten more."

He laughed a soft laugh. This time I caught a slight accent more African than Cajun. "I'll be taking you to someone who can answer all your questions better than I can."

I just nodded. I settled back in the seat and gave in to a weariness like I'd never known before. I think I dozed off without answering. The last thing I remember before sleep was something I saw when I looked back at that shack just before running for the car. It was framed in the lantern light of the window. The ice-cold expression on the face of the old man.

*   *   *

I was gently jarred awake by my driver. I took a quick look out the window. A calming wave settled over me when I saw that we were at the entrance to the Hotel Royal. My driver nodded to the front door.

"We're here, Monsieur Shane."

"So I see. I haven't thanked you. I never had to thank someone for saving my life before. I most surely do now. *Merci*. And I do mean *Beaucoup*."

He smiled and just nodded. "You're safe now. For the time being. Be careful, *Monsieur*."

"Whatever it means to be careful, I'll try. I still have those questions."

"I know." He reached over and opened my door. "Go in now. Tell the concierge who you are."

I took that as the best answer I could get for the moment. I walked into the lobby. The clock behind the reception desk said half past midnight. The young man at the concierge desk was not Marcel, but I followed directions. I simply said, "*Bon soir*. My name is Matthew Shane. Do you have—"

I could see him reach under the stand. He handed me an envelope. "Is this from Marcel?"

"I believe it is, Monsieur Shane. Sleep well."

It was my every wish. I waited until I was in my room, door locked and bolted, to open the envelope. A piece of hotel stationary had a brief handwritten message and the signature, "Marcel."

I went out to the balcony facing the inner courtyard to read it: "Breakfast at nine, Willa Jean's. Take Cab 47. No other."

*   *   *

I was awake at six, shaved, dressed, and hiking the few blocks to the Café Du Monde on Decatur Street. Did that qualify as being careful? Maybe yes, maybe no. Whatever "careful" meant was trumped by a crack of dawn yearning for a couple of the world's most irresistible beignets smothered in powdered sugar and several mugs of their deep dark coffee with chicory.

I was back at the hotel by eight. Marcel was still not the concierge on duty. I settled into the morning *Times-Picayune* on my room balcony. At eight forty-five, the room phone rang. It was the concierge on duty.

"Monsieur Shane. You have a cab waiting at the entrance."

I had a flashback to the episode of the night before. "Can you tell me? What number is the cab?"

"Monsieur?"

"The number written on the side of the cab."

The voice came back in about twenty seconds. "Monsieur. Number forty-seven."

That did it. In three minutes, I was in the back of a cab, cruising through New Orleans streets for which the word "quaint" must have been coined.

In fact, we cruised for fifteen minutes. After four blocks on Ste. Philip St. up to Dauphine St., he took a left on Ste. Ann, and then another left back to Chartres. I said to the driver, "Interesting route. Did I mention Willa Jean's on O'Keefe Ave.?"

He smiled back to me in the mirror. "No worries, *Monsieur*. I'm not boosting the fare. It's already been paid."

"Really? By whom?" After the previous night's escapade, I was suspicious of free rides. It might have shown in my tone.

"By a gentleman who asked me to see that you were not followed."

"Interesting. And who might that be?"

"He's waiting at the restaurant. I'm sure he'll tell you all those things."

*   *   *

Willa Jean's was a sweet choice for at least two reasons. It was well out of the French Quarter, west of Canal Street in the Warehouse District. That meant it was easy for a savvy cabbie to lose even the most determined tail. Secondly, the chef could drive a confirmed dieter to a calorie binge with southern creativity—even on breakfast.

I added a tip to whatever my host had advanced the cabbie for a truly elusive itinerary. The young lady who greeted me at the door of Willa Jean's picked up where the cabbie left off. "Monsieur Shane, I believe."

I nodded and returned the smile.

"The gentleman is waiting."

I scanned the tables for a single of roughly Professor Holmes' age. No contact. Instead, I saw a man in a trim light beige suit and tie looking in my direction. He stood up at a table toward the rear of the restaurant. He could not have had more than five years on my thirty-two.

After the previous night, I walked back to his table playing mental "What's My Line" with the customers I passed. No alarms, until I walked between two singles at tables flanking my supposed host. They were male, molded for speed, with bulges under loose clothing that could only be weapons.

I joined the man standing with a handshake. "Could you be Rene Perreault?"

His smile seemed genuine. "I'm afraid not. I'm his grandson. He asked me to meet you. Would you join me?"

I tried to hide my disappointment. "I'd be delighted, but . . ."

"But you came a long way to talk with my grandfather, yes? And you shall. I'll take you to his home on Bayou Ste. Germaine. We have some time yet. Perhaps you'd enjoy a bit of Willa Jean's breakfast first? We can talk before you meet my grandfather."

"I'd enjoy both."

When he ordered the classic shrimp and grits with a poached egg, there was no need to ask if he'd been to Willa Jean's before. It seemed like eminent good sense to order the same.

Coffee, hot, dark, and rich, was poured into hefty mugs before the waitress went back with our order. My host had a gracious manner that contrasted with that of my previous night's companions. "I'm sure you have questions, Monsieur Shane. I can answer some of them. It will save time for my grandfather."

"Please, make it 'Matthew.'"

He nodded. "Maurice."

"So, questions. Where to begin? Maybe with that whole episode last night. Did you . . . ?"

"Yes, I heard. I'm sorry you went through that. You might want to know that Kwame, the man who fortunately arrived in time, he was sent by my grandfather."

"Thank God. But why?"

"Your concierge. Marcel, he's from our Bayou Ste. Germaine. An old friend of my grandfather. He called us when you said you wanted to see my grandfather. We assumed that you were sent by Professor Holmes, yes?"

"In a way, yes."

"*D'accord.*" He leaned forward. "My grandfather is also well aware of the, shall we say, eccentricities of the old man who brought you so close to death last night. Kwame is a close friend of my grandfather. He arrived at K-Paul's to pick you up just as he saw you leaving, perhaps under duress. He had you in sight from that moment on. The rest you know."

"Not all the rest. You mention the 'eccentricities' of that old man. He talked about some woman, the mother of someone, some curse."

"Ah yes. Good place to start."

Our waitress arrived with plates of steaming hot delicacies. Maurice's smile was back. "As I say. We have time. My grandfather's occupied until this afternoon. Shall we first . . ." He held his hands out in a clear invitation to eat first, talk later. I could hardly disagree.

Twenty minutes later, our plates were removed and coffee mugs refilled. After a few words in Cajun French from Maurice, our waitress withdrew.

Maurice sat back in his chair. "Now then. You mentioned a woman. How much do you know about the Maroons?"

"I recently saw the word." I thought of the cryptic note under Professor Holmes' desk. "No more than that."

"Then let's start there. I have to go back centuries. This much is fact. When the Spanish ruled Jamaica as a colony, they brought African slaves over to work the sugarcane fields. But the slaves they brought were unique. They were from the Ashanti tribe in the area of Ghana on the west African coast. They were brought west to Koromantee in Ghana, then shipped in slave ships to the east coast of Jamaica. These Ashanti Africans were known to be so fierce, so rebellious, that they were actually banned as slaves in the French colonies.

"In 1655, the English conquered Jamaica from the Spanish. The British first set the slaves free. These former slaves went north, into the high Blue Mountain forests. They settled there. They formed their own colony. The English called them 'Maroon.' It came from the Spanish word *cimarron*, meaning 'fugitive, gone wild.'

"The British later found they needed slaves to work the sugar crops. They brought over more Ashanti slaves. They were still hard to hold. There were slave rebellions. Many escaped. They joined the other Maroons in the mountains. For eighty years, with only guns they could steal and not even a steady food supply, these several hundred Maroons held off attacks to recapture the slaves by thousands of well-armed English troops."

"Impressive. How?"

"I'll give you two answers. One will make sense to you. The Maroon village was at the top of a mountain. They chose well. There was only one steep, rocky path to the village. Room for just one English trooper to pass at a time. Heavy bush and tree growth on both sides. The Maroons used guerilla warfare, counterattacking from ambush. Over the next eighty years, thousands of English were killed. Less than a hundred Maroons."

"Clever. They must have had good leadership."

"Mm. Now you cut to the heart of it. Would you excuse me?"

He looked up. One of the men from the adjacent table approached, leaned close, and whispered to my host. I could only gather that it was in Cajun French, and not trivial.

His expression went suddenly dark. He stood. He looked at me with what I could only interpret as urgency. "Please, Matthew. Come now. We can talk in the car."

The man at his side whispered again. Maurice tossed his napkin on the table. He followed the man toward the back of the restaurant. I followed close behind.

In that order we marched at quick time through the kitchen, out the door, and into the back seat of a waiting Lexus SUV. The man in the lead took the front passenger seat. Doors were scarcely closed when the car was in high gear.

Maurice was on his cellphone speaking in short bursts in Cajun French. I could hear short bursts coming through from the other end. Each of them deepened the lines in Maurice's forehead.

When he snapped the phone shut, he stared at the back of the seat ahead of him. He seemed to be wrestling with emotions while he was pulling thoughts together.

I gave him the time in silence, feeling like an intruder on some family catastrophe. In a few minutes, he seemed to reach a resolution. He glanced over as if he were just becoming aware that I was beside him.

"Matthew. I'm sorry. I didn't mean to catch you up in this."

I had no idea what to say. He tapped our driver on the shoulder and gave an order. It became clear when the driver's foot grew heavier on the gas pedal.

Maurice looked me in the eye. "Actually, you were caught up in this thing when you stepped on that plane to come down here. You must have realized that last night."

"Maurice, as you say, I'm in it. And totally in the dark. Could you tell me what just happened?"

His voice caught for a second. "My grandfather has had a serious accident. We're going there now."

I almost didn't dare ask. "Is he going to be . . . ?"

"I don't know."

CHAPTER SIX

WE FLEW AT a clip that made me thank God for a straight paved road. Both sides fell off into blackish swamp water. Cypress trees with gray beards of hanging moss stood like macabre sentries over a cemetery of rotting oak trunks. I blocked imagining what venomous life-forms lay under the surface.

For miles, the silence hung as heavy as the moss. I finally made an uncertain attempt at a break.

"Maurice, I'm sorry. Something happened to your grandfather. Can you tell me what?"

He answered without looking over. "An accident." There was a pause. "I don't know. Perhaps not an accident."

"I'm so sorry. Is he . . . ?"

"Alive? So far . . ."

He stopped mid-thought as if something suddenly connected. He looked at me directly for the first time since the drive started. "Your friend. Professor Holmes. Is he well?"

"No. He's not."

His tone was insistent. "Tell me."

"He's dead."

It seemed to hit him as a personal jolt.

"Tell me how."

"There's a question. The police think it was suicide."

"And you don't?"

"Not at all."

"Then what?"

"I'm sure he was murdered."

"My God." He barely breathed it. What color was left drained from his face.

"I'm sorry, Maurice. I'm lost here. Did you know Professor Holmes?"

He came out of his fog. "No. I never met him."

Touchy as it was, I needed some answers. "Maurice, I hate to press it, but I'm floundering. You seem—I don't know how to put this—unusually affected by Professor Holmes' death. If we could talk, maybe we could help each other."

He looked over. "Perhaps."

"Let me go first. Maybe these tragedies connect. We'll never know if we don't talk to each other."

He just nodded, but I still had eye contact.

"Professor Holmes was found dead in his office day before yesterday. It appeared that he'd slashed his wrist and bled out. Suicide. Or so the first detective there chose to believe."

"And you?"

"I think it was made to look like suicide by whoever killed him. There was a short note found with the body. It was addressed to me. It mentioned a 'Maroon file.' It said 'Tell Monks.' His wife found a file labeled 'Maroon' in his home office. The only thing in it was a list of four names. She said they were the other members of the so-called 'Monkey's Paw Society.' She showed me a letter he'd just received. It just said, 'Come fast. It's happening.' No signature, but the postmark was Bayou Ste. Germaine. Your grandfather was the only one of the four on the list from Bayou Ste. Germaine. So, I'm here."

He was rubbing his forehead and seemed back into his own thoughts. I gave him a minute, but I had to get into his thinking. "Maurice. Talk to me. Can you connect some of this?"

He took a deep breath. He seemed more settled when he looked back at me. "Perhaps we do need to help each other."

"Good. I'm wide open here."

"I told you about the Maroons. I told you they held off the British for over eighty years with guerilla ambush tactics. That part was believable. The Maroons had another explanation. Mystical. Spiritual. It's a strong belief they hold to this day."

"Tell me."

He rubbed his forehead, looking for a place to start. "You have to understand. These Ashanti Africans who became the Maroons, I said they were not like other slaves. They never surrendered their deep African spiritual beliefs. They still believe strongly that their ancestors are living spiritual beings who influence their lives. It gives them an identity. A strength. Even under the brutal hardships of slavery, the Ashanti Maroons had a longer life span than the five years or so of other slaves on the sugar plantations in Jamaica. You understand?"

"So far."

"All right, now add this. The Ashanti always had a reverence, a high respect for their women. Frequently their leaders in Africa were women."

"That old man in the bayou last night. He talked about a woman."

"I'm sure. Some of the Maroons came here to the bayou country south of New Orleans years ago. They have a village out where you were last night. That old man is their spiritual leader."

"What about the woman?"

"When the runaway Ashanti slaves formed the Maroon community in Jamaica, they needed a leader. There was a particular woman. They called her 'Nanny.' The name was from two of their words.

Nana, meaning 'spiritual woman leader'; and *Ni*, meaning 'first mother.' She was real. She left her tribe in Ghana in Africa around 1700. She came over to Jamaica on a slave ship, but they say she was never a slave. They say she came to rescue her people.

"She became the leader of the Maroons. She taught them to camouflage themselves like trees and bushes along the steep path that led up to the village. She organized the guerilla strikes that killed thousands of British soldiers, while they lost less than a hundred. Some say she was the most brilliant military strategist the British ever encountered."

"That's impressive. And believable."

"Yes, well, it goes on from there. The Maroons believed then, and they still believe, that she was an *Obeah* woman."

"Which means?"

"According to African spirituality, she was a very powerful religious being. She had supernatural powers that were given to her by her ancestors. She never had children, but the Maroons call her the mother of all of the eastern Jamaican Maroons. They believe that it was Nanny's magical powers that gave them victory over the British, and still protect their freedom today."

"I see."

"No, you really don't. You have no sense of how deep these beliefs run. Let me tell you a story that you could hear from any four-year-old Maroon. Early in the war with the British, the Maroons went through some defeats. In that isolated mountaintop village, they were cut off from food supplies. They suffered terribly. At one point, they were on the brink of starvation. Their leader, Nanny, was about to surrender. They say in a dream she heard the voices of ancestor spirits. They told her not to give up. Struggle on a bit longer.

"When she woke up, she found three pumpkin seeds in her pocket. She planted the seeds on a hillside. It's still called Pumpkin

Hill. Overnight, the seeds grew into vines with enormous pump-kins. They saved the Maroons from starvation. In fact, they fed the Maroons for many years. They gave them the strength and spirit to keep on fighting the British. I might add, with incredible success."

"Interesting. What do you think about it?"

"It doesn't matter. The Maroons believe it to the core of their souls. In fact, some of the other Black Jamaicans still fear the Maroons. They say they have superhuman spiritual powers. In 1976, the Jamaican government named six people as national historic heroes of Jamaica. Queen Nanny was one of the six. The only Maroon—and the only woman."

"Did she die? Nanny?"

"Of course. Sometime in the 1750s. And yet not."

"How so?"

"The Maroons believe her spirit is still alive and living in the Maroon communities today. She is still to them 'the Mother of us all.'"

"And how does all this relate to your grandfather and Professor Holmes?"

He reached for his cellphone that had burst into a jingly tune. "Hold on."

There was a brief exchange in Cajun French. He hit a button on the phone and tapped the driver on the shoulder. He gave an order in French before he turned back to me. The car took a turn onto an intersecting road and gained speed.

"My grandfather's conscious. He's in the hospital. They say we can see him for a few minutes."

"Perhaps just you should see him."

"No. He specifically asked to see you. We're heading directly to the hospital."

"Whatever you say."

"Whatever *he* says. He was apparently insistent."

I nodded. "Then maybe I should know first. What's the connection with this Nanny?"

"That town the Maroons defended for eighty years at the top of Blue Mountain, it's called Nanny Town. In 1734, a British general brought in heavy new artillery and completely destroyed the town. The Maroons set up a new Maroon village a few miles from the original Nanny Town. It's still there. It's called Moore Town."

"So?"

"I'm getting to it. The Maroons feel deeply that the ground of the ruins of the original Nanny Town is the most sacred place on earth. It carries a curse. It was put on that ground by Queen Nanny herself. No person who is not a Maroon is permitted by Queen Nanny to go near that ground. If they do without permission, the belief is that they'll suffer death in some way. And soon. That particularly applies to any *bakra*—white person."

"I remember the old man kept saying it didn't matter how Professor Holmes died. It only mattered that he did die after violating the curse."

"Yes. They believe in their souls that Queen Nanny is actually alive today, and in some way, she enforces the curse."

"But you don't believe in this curse. Do you?"

"No. But I believe in facts. About ten days ago, this little group that call themselves 'The Monkey's Paw Society,' they got together for an excursion. To Jamaica."

"Where in Jamaica?"

"I'm not sure. I know it started in Port Royal. It might have led them from there to the top of that mountain. The old Nanny Town."

"That's what that old man said last night. What did your grandfather tell you about the trip?"

"Nothing. We always talked about everything, but not this. He seemed almost afraid to get me involved."

"He must have sent that note to Professor Holmes. 'Come fast. It's started.' Why would he say that?"

"Two days ago, I came into his study. He was making a phone call. Before he saw me, he asked for Claude DuCette. He's one of the Monkey's Paw group. He's from Montreal."

"Did he talk to him?"

"No. Whatever was said over the phone must have been a shock to my grandfather. He seemed deeply affected. He noticed me there and just hung up."

"So you don't know."

"Not in detail, but that night I was worried about him. I went into his study. I hit the REDIAL button on his phone. A woman answered in French. I asked to speak to Claude DuCette. She asked what I wanted. I said I was calling for my grandfather. She became very upset. She said it was all my grandfather's fault."

"What was?"

"She just hung up. I'm sure something bad had happened to Claude DuCette."

"That might have been when your grandfather sent that note to Professor Holmes saying 'It's started.'"

"And now you tell me that Professor Holmes was murdered two days ago."

"You're not putting all of this on that curse, are you?"

"No. I'm looking at facts. Claude DuCette and Professor Holmes. Something happens to them within a week of going to Jamaica. And now my grandfather. Three of the five. That's a hell of a lot of coincidence, Matthew."

"What actually happened to your grandfather?"

He took a moment to check our surroundings. "We should be at the hospital in about ten minutes. Here's what I know. My grandfather is a . . . complex man. He's very wealthy. His home is the largest plantation in the bayou. He has unusual interests—which he can afford to indulge. He keeps large enclosures of exotic wild animals."

"How does he take care of them?"

"He doesn't. He hired some Africans to do most of it. About a year ago, he started importing monkeys—baboons, actually—from Africa. He has a small colony of them in a large enclosure behind the main house. He does some of the caretaking of them himself."

"Like what?"

"He goes to the enclosure every morning. He feeds them through an opening in the fence. He seems more attached to them than the other animals. One of the older ones died last week. He took it hard. He had it buried close to the house."

"Are they tamed?"

"No. Never. They're completely wild. Well, one exception. A baby was born about six months ago. The mother died in the birth. My grandfather had the baby taken out of the enclosure. He hand-fed it. Raised it like a pet. He became very attached."

"Did he keep it in the house?"

"Yes. Until it was able to feed on its own. Then he tried putting it back in the cage with the others. He didn't know if they'd accept the baby. It was risky, but it seemed to be working out. When my grandfather'd go to feed the others in the morning, this little one would come to him like it wanted to be held. The strong attachment seemed to continue."

"Would your grandfather take him out of the cage?"

"No. It was too dangerous with the others there. He'd just hand him special food treats through the cage. Until this morning."

"What happened?"

"The caretaker of the baboons called me. That was the call at breakfast. When my grandfather went to do the feeding, he saw the baby on the ground by itself. It was closer to the gate, away from the others. It seemed nearly dead. My grandfather went into the cage to try to take it out."

He stopped for a breath. "The other baboons came at him. He couldn't get out in time. The caretaker saw it from wherever he was. He came running. Somehow he managed to scare the baboons off and get him out."

"Was he badly hurt?"

"I don't know. The real problem is his heart." He looked out the window as we pulled into the hospital emergency entrance.

"We'll know soon."

CHAPTER SEVEN

MAURICE PERREAULT'S NAME apparently carried serious weight with the hospital staff. We breezed through the stations of the emergency room like an ambassador through red lights. I was too close on his heels to let any of the guardians in green stop me. The only pause was to catch the hand signal of one solidly built head nurse aiming us toward a large room at the end of the corridor.

A doctor in scrubs fell in step with Maurice. He spoke softly in rapid French, but there was no mistaking the urgency of his tone.

We stopped at the door. Maurice took my elbow. He spoke close to my ear. "It's what I said. The baboons were on him before he could get out of the cage. He was injured, a lot of bruising, but the real problem is his heart."

"How bad?"

"I don't know."

The doctor gave us a low grunt and a lift of the shoulders that said in silent French, *This is no time for a chat.*

Maurice pulled me closer. "The attack triggered a heart attack." He chin-pointed to the doctor. "They need to get him to the O.R."

"We can wait."

"Apparently not. He won't let them move him 'til he talks."

"Go ahead. I'll wait here."

"Not to me. He wants you. Go on in. But keep it brief."

I pressed past the glaring doctor who hissed a repetition of the word, "Brief!"

My eyes were drawn instantly to the serene face of the man in the bed. In a way that can be sensed but not expressed, the aura of that face held my attention. He actually reminded me of Professor Holmes.

I stood briefly at the foot of the bed. A Black man of sizable proportions at his bedside saw me. It took me a second, but I recognized him as the man who had pulled off my rescue at the cabin of the old man the night before.

He bent down to whisper something that slowly opened the old man's eyes. They managed to focus on me. I thought I saw the start of a weak smile. I could see the fingers of his hand above the sheet move in what I took to be a summoning to his side.

The Black man stood back. I took his place close enough to hear the soft words. "You're Matthew. Yes . . . You came. Thank God."

"Mr. Perreault. I'm sorry—"

His hand rose slightly and waved off more words. He looked directly into my eyes. His hand reached slowly and found my hand. The gentle smile grew. "Much to say, Matthew . . . No time . . . Your Professor Holmes . . ."

I gave him a moment to gather a bit of strength. His eyes bored more deeply into mine. He seemed to be searching for something there. I thought at one point he seemed to find it. His voice was a bit stronger. "I see it in your eyes . . . He loved you . . . like his son, you know."

I knew what he meant. I nodded. "It went both ways."

The burst of slight energy waned. He closed his eyes, but the smile remained. "I had to see it . . . Now I do."

I let him rest with our hands locked together. I saw the doctor in the frame of the door giving every silent signal he could to hasten me out of the way. I didn't move. The hold on my hand said there was more.

The doctor began to walk in my direction, but the Black man moved to keep him at a distance.

I could feel a slight resurgence of energy in Mr. Perreault's hand. He was trying to pull me closer. I bent to put my ear next to his mouth. I feel sure that what I heard in a whispered tone was, "Matthew, I'm sorry . . . A heavy burden . . . Listen . . . Tell them . . . Monkey's Paws . . . no one else . . . Follow the *abeng* . . . Can you hear?"

I whispered, "Yes. I'll write down the word."

His grip tightened slightly. His eyes opened wider. "No . . . No writing . . . Just remember . . ."

"Yes. I hear you."

He closed his eyes in what looked like total exhaustion. I thought I lost him. The doctor at the door seemed close to complete panic. Only the Black man held him at bay.

I tried to take my hand out of his, but he held on a few seconds more. He was forcing the words now. "Matthew . . . Tell them . . . No *gris gris* . . . Trust Kwame . . . His way . . . His way."

The last words seemed to consume the last speck of his strength. I heard a gentle sigh. I knew it took him to a different place.

The doctor ran to push me out of the way. He was probing with his stethoscope to learn something that I already knew in my heart.

*   *   *

The pall that hung over us on the ride from the hospital was stifling. There were so many questions left hanging. Maurice asked me to come with him to their home. I took advantage of the time alone in the back of the car with Maurice to clear up something. "That big man by his bed when we went in, is his name 'Kwame'?"

"Yes. What did my grandfather say?"

"First tell me about Kwame. How does he fit in?"

He leaned back and took a breath. "He's probably the one closest to my grandfather."

My look must have said, "including you?"

"Including me. This goes way back. In his twenties, my grandfather was taken with big game hunting, mostly Africa. On his first safari in Mali in the Sahara, he shot his first lion. That night, after the rest of the safari workers turned in, he ignored what he was told about the first rule of lion hunting. You have to wait twenty-four hours after the shooting before approaching the lion."

"Why?"

"As my grandfather found out, the lion might not be dead. When he got close enough, the lion sprang at him. It caught him in its claws. I've heard this many times from my grandfather. He was under the lion about to be mauled, when he saw a large, dark mass fall on the two of them. He saw the glint of a knife at the throat of the lion. Within seconds, the mauling stopped. The lion rolled off of him. This time it was dead. My grandfather found himself lying on his back at the feet of a tall Black man in tattered clothes with a dripping knife in his hand."

"That sounds impossible."

"I know. But it happened—or I'd never have gotten to know my grandfather. He took the Black man back to his camp. He fed him. He seemed to be ravenously hungry. One of the bearers at the camp could speak his language. The man said he'd been held in slavery in Mali. He'd escaped. He'd been two jumps ahead of the slavers who were after him to take him back. He'd been running for days."

"And that was when?"

"Mid-sixties. Not finished. There's more to the story. That night, the slavers, about six of them, came storming into the camp. Guns in their hands. My grandfather had heard them coming. He had had one of his safari workers take the Black man back in the bush out of sight before they saw him. The slavers said they'd tracked him to the camp. They demanded that my grandfather turn him over."

"I assume—"

"Don't assume anything. There's more to the story. My grandfather was a businessman—first, last, and always. He told them, in his gentle but persuasive way, how it stacked up. He had something they wanted. They had something he wanted—money. That would be the basis for a deal. They flashed their guns and said, basically, 'No deal.' My grandfather could argue with a rock. He said, 'There are six of you and fourteen of us. Are you going to shoot us all before we can kill at least some of you? Maybe you first.' He was pointing at the leader. He had their attention. 'And if you did kill us, you'd never find him. He'd be long gone. On the other hand, we could do business. He's young, tall, healthy. He's well muscled. He'll bring a good price on the auction block. More than enough for all of us.'

"He had them thinking. He figured they'd been on the trail of the slave for days, probably with little time for food. He made them an offer they couldn't refuse. 'Gentlemen, there's much to consider, including a price for this valuable specimen. You look hungry. Our chef was about to serve us his gazelle stew. Much better to do business on a full stomach.'

"He told me his safari chef took the cue. He lifted the cover on his cooking pot. The aroma was more than they could withstand. They came to the *boma,* the fire circle, and sat with my grandfather and some of the safari crew. My grandfather gave the order. Bowls of stew were served. Bottles of scotch were opened. Cups were filled, consumed, and filled again. My grandfather began discussing the price for surrendering the slave to them. Their rifles were set on the ground to free hands for eating and drinking. Except for the locale, it began to resemble negotiations in a boardroom.

"About the time the slavers were lulled into fixing a price, my grandfather stood up. That was the signal. Six of his safari workers had slipped away from the fire and taken rifles from the wagons. They came up behind the slavers with rifle barrels aimed at the backs of their necks."

"And then?"

"That's it. It was over. They tied up the slavers, took their guns, and left them there."

"What happened to them?"

"One can only guess. By morning in that wild country, there were perhaps six less slavers in the world."

"And the escaped slave?"

"My grandfather took him in one of the safari trucks. They drove north 'til they reached the American embassy in Algeria. My grandfather had some serious family political clout even in those days. He helped the man apply for asylum in the United States. The man came back here to Louisiana with my grandfather. That's the whole story, except to say that he and my grandfather have been closer than brothers since then. They're like each other's shadows."

"And his name is 'Kwame'?"

"Yes. Now your turn. What did my grandfather tell you about him?"

I remembered his grandfather's insistence on secrecy. I wasn't sure if the grandfather's words, "No one else," included his grandson. I decided to split the difference. "Your grandfather just said 'Trust him.'"

"That's all?"

"Yeah."

* * *

Our driver finally left the main road through the tepid marshes of Bayou Sainte Germaine. He turned onto what seemed like a mile-long driveway through a plantation of impressive proportions. Interspersed among wide expanses of sugarcane stalks were occasional enclosures of about an acre penning in clusters of exotic wild animals I had never seen outside of the reserves of South Africa, Namibia, or Botswana.

The car let us off at the top of a circular drive before a manor house that met the expectations raised by the approach. Maurice took my arm as we walked up steps between white columns that called back scenes from *Gone with the Wind*.

"Matthew, it's getting late. You'll stay for dinner. Could I impose further? I'd like you to stay the night. I know you were an investigator. Air Force?"

"That's right. But—"

"The local gendarmes will be stomping all over the grounds here to make a show. You might have gathered by now that my grandfather was a major figure around here. I need someone who can put the pieces together before every lead gets trampled."

"Lead to what?"

"To what really happened to my grandfather. He was no stranger to the dangers of those baboons."

I could understand Maurice's suspicions based on my doubts about Professor Holmes' death. "I'll do what I can, Maurice. Speaking of which, can we take a look at the baboon cage right now? Before the stomping starts."

We stopped halfway up the stairs. "Good idea. Come on. It's behind the house."

*   *   *

The baboon cage was a total enclosure of about a half-acre. The inside terrain was sculpted to resemble my recollection of the natural baboon habitat at the southwest tip of South Africa. The ground inside the single gate to the cage was loose, dusty soil. I'm no Daniel Boone, but I looked for the story told by the scuffed dirt inside the cage.

The condition of the ground showed that we were the first new eyes on the site—and more importantly, the first new feet. I took pictures of one set of clear shoe-prints running from the gate to a spot ten feet inside of the cage and back again. There were clear prints of the same shoes running back and forth, four or five feet along the fence to either side inside the gate, and partial prints of the same type of shoe, mixed with an amalgam of what looked like animal prints, in a cluster just inside the gate. I did it from outside the cage under the constant eyes of eight adult baboons that seemed agitated into perpetual motion. They hovered a cautious thirty feet back of the gate.

I noticed the African friend of Rene Perreault, Kwame, scanning the same scene from outside a different section of the cage.

Maurice's eyes seemed transfixed on the baboons. I could only guess at what was running through his mind. Our trains of thought were all interrupted by a convoy of three police cars approaching at full tilt a distance down the main drive.

I could read the reaction in Maurice's eyes. "Right on cue. Our new police chief."

"Must be most of the force."

"More likely the entire force. No one wants to miss a headline on this case. You'll see why I wanted you here."

CHAPTER EIGHT

MAURICE AND I met the convoy at the front entrance of the manor house. The first uniformed legs out of the lead squad car took a direct path to Maurice. The officer pulled off the flat-brimmed hat with his left hand and extended a sweaty palm to Maurice. "*Quelle domage, Monsieur Perreault. J'ai venu que vite que j'ai—*"

Maurice took his hand, but cut in. "Thank you for coming, Chief Bouchard. This is my guest, Professor Shane."

Maurice's primary point beyond the introduction was to shift the conversation to English. The chief picked it up. He transferred the courtesy of the sweaty palm to me, along with condolences in locally accented English. By the time Maurice graciously accepted, the three cars had emptied. Nine uniforms began to circle around Maurice and me with no apparent sense of what to do next.

The chief said something to Maurice in muffled Cajun French. I took it to be a request to see the scene of whatever they were calling the incident. Maurice led the chief with the posse in tow to the gate of the baboon cage. The sight of the approaching cluster sent the baboons another twenty feet farther from the gate in a burst of agitated chatter.

I heard Maurice relating, in English for my benefit, what he had heard of the events that morning. "My grandfather came out to feed the baboons as he usually did in the morning. He saw a baby baboon a short way inside of the cage. It looked nearly dead. The other baboons must have been far enough back in the cage so he thought he could get in, pick up the baby, and run out. Apparently, he was wrong. The adult baboons caught up with him. He suffered a heart attack."

The chief took on the role of interrogator. "And how did Monsieur Perreault get out of the cage?"

"The keeper who tends the baboons came when he heard my grandfather's screams. He must have fired some shots in the air to scare off the baboons. They got my grandfather to the hospital as fast as possible."

The chief took it all in with judicious "um-hmms" and "ahas" interspersed. "Regrettable. Yes. Obviously just an unfortunate miscalculation. An accident, so to speak. But I should like to speak with the keeper of the baboons. You understand. My report."

"Certainly, Chief. But not out here. Let's go into the house. Perhaps a cold drink."

"Ah. Yes. Excellent."

"Good. I'll have the keeper sent for. Shall we?"

At the risk of alienating the chief, I caught Maurice's attention. "Before we leave the scene, and I'm sure this occurred to the chief, might fingerprints be taken on the latch and handles on the outside on the gate? I notice that there is no handle on the inside. No way to open the gate from within."

The chief picked it up. "Precisely my thinking. No stone unturned." He called over one of the uniforms who were trampling of any signs remaining on the ground around the gate. He assigned him the fingerprinting task.

Maurice led the way up the front steps to the house. When it became obvious that the entire troop was in trail, Maurice quietly suggested that perhaps just the chief might follow. Drinks would be sent out for his retinue.

I followed into the main house, after one last check.

*　*　*

Like a scene out of an Agatha Christie novel, Maurice and I and the chief gathered in the drawing room. I noticed Kwame sitting off to the side. Mint iced tea was served by one of the household staff.

The keeper for the baboons was ushered in to a seat at center stage. His weathered, gray-black skin and flecked white hair spoke of an age between sixty and heaven-knows-how-many years. His calloused hands said they were not years of leisure.

The chief assumed the role of master of ceremonies. "*Monsieur*, your name."

In an accent that rang a faint bell, the keeper cleared his throat and said in a dry whisper, "Keku. I was born on a Wednesday."

The chief pondered that last bit of seemingly extraneous information until the witness said in a whisper, "My name means 'born on Wednesday.' It is how we call."

"Ah! Well, fine. And you tend the baboons, yes?"

"I do, Sir."

"And what happened this morning? With the baboons?"

Keku looked to each of the faces before a rather pleading look to Maurice. Maurice spoke gently. "It's all right, Keku. Just tell us what you know about this morning. My grandfather. What you saw happen with the baboons."

He seemed about to answer Maurice when the chief jumped in. "Come, man. Speak up. Were you there to feed the monkeys? What were you doing there?"

That sent him back into a shell. Maurice walked over to him. "You're not in trouble, Keku. It's all right. When did you first see my grandfather this morning?"

"He always feed baboons in the morning. I feed at night."

"Where were you then? This morning."

"I tending other cage. The leopards."

"From where you were, could you see my grandfather come to feed the baboons?"

"Yes, Sir. Like he do every day."

"Did you watch him?"

"Yes, Sir."

"Why?"

"They dangerous. Could be accident."

"Just tell us about this morning, Keku. What did you see happen?"

"He go to throw food in like always. Then he see something. Baby he raised—it lie on the ground. Not move."

"How far inside the cage?"

Keku looked around the room. He pointed to the fireplace. "To there."

"About ten, twelve feet. And where were the other baboons?"

"They take food. Go back in different part."

"How far away?"

This time he pointed to a door at the far end of the room.

Maurice scanned the distance. "Maybe some forty, fifty feet. What did my grandfather do then?"

"Baby his pet. He open gate. He run in. Pick up baby. Run back to gate."

"Did the gate stay open?"

He stopped to think and scan the eyes that were on him.

Maurice said quietly, "Just what you remember, Keku."

"Yes. Gate open. But he not get back. Baboons run. They catch him."

"And what did you do?"

"I run. I run into cage. I fire shots. Scare baboons away. I carry him out of cage. Set him down. People come. They hear shots."

"Who came?"

"People work in house. And Kwame. He first. He carry him to car. Drove off fast."

Maurice stood back. "Thank you, Keku. Thank you for what you did for my grandfather. Chief, any other questions?"

The chief used a few seconds with a thoughtful "Mmmm." Then, "No. No. I think that completes it. An unfortunate mishap. Dangerous beasts, these monkeys. I'll have it in my report."

Maurice and I walked the chief out. I managed a quiet question with the deputy assigned to check for fingerprints. "What did you find for prints?"

He looked to the chief who was repeating his condolences privately to Maurice. I whispered to the deputy, "It's all right. I have investigative clearance."

I have no idea what that meant, but neither did he. It gained me a shake of the deputy's head—negative.

"Meaning what?"

"There were no fingerprints on the gate or the latch."

"None?"

"No, Sir."

I had no answer for that one.

*   *   *

Maurice and I watched the assembled caravan disappear down the driveway. Before we started up the stairs, Maurice called to Kwame. He was back standing by the baboon pen. He walked over to join us.

"I don't think you two have really met. Heaven knows I need you both on my team. Matthew Shane, this is my grandfather's closest friend, Kwame."

It was refreshing to shake an unsweating hand and look into eyes that looked back directly. "Mr. Shane."

"Just Matthew is fine. I'm so sorry for the pain you must be feeling. I know how close you were. Actually, Kwame, yours was the last name he spoke before he passed."

I could see the reaction in his eyes. "Thank you for telling me that, Matthew. You never got to know him, but his greatest final wish was to talk to you." He turned to look directly at Maurice while he spoke. "His grandson was actually the closest to his heart—that's true. He said it to me many times. But this business of the Monkey's Paws was weighing heavily on him. He knew how terribly limited his time was."

Maurice started to speak, but it caught in his throat. He smiled and just patted Kwame on the shoulder. The three of us climbed the steps. This time Maurice led us into a small book-lined study. We sat in a close cluster of three leather chairs. Maurice was the first to speak.

"Gentlemen, any thoughts?"

Kwame looked at me with an expression that said, "After you."

I took the lead. "I don't know for certain what happened in that baboon pen this morning. Just one thing I'd stake my life on—it didn't happen the way the keeper told it."

That drew the full attention of both. Maurice was first. "What did you see?"

"Apparently the keeper was the only one there. No one else saw it. He said, roughly, Mr. Perreault opened the gate. He ran directly to the baby baboon, picked it up, and ran directly back to the gate. Before he could get through the gate, which was still open, the other baboons were on top of him."

"And you don't believe it, Matthew. Why not?"

"There was one set of footprints from the gate directly to where the imprint of the baby was on the ground. Those same prints led back in the direction of the gate. That was your grandfather. That much was true."

"And?"

"Two things. There were footprints back and forth along the fence, four or five feet on both sides inside the gate. Then a confusion of footprints and paw prints just inside the gate. In that order."

"Which tells you what?"

"If the gate had stayed open as the keeper said, one of two things. Your grandfather would have run directly out of the pen, the baboons after him. Or the baboons would have caught him and attacked him right in front of the gate."

"Then what do you think happened?"

"The footprints say that when your grandfather ran back to the gate with the baby, the gate was closed. You know there's no way to open it from the inside. As I read it, your grandfather picked up the baby. He saw the baboons coming after him. He ran back to the gate. It was shut, probably to his surprise. He ran from side to side to get away from the coming baboons. Inevitably they caught him. That was the scuffle of paw prints and footprints right inside the closed gate."

I looked at Kwame. His nod said that he came to the same conclusion. The deep lines in his face said he was wrestling with deep emotions.

Maurice said, "Maybe the gate swung shut on its own."

"That's why I checked the gate before we left the area. It works stiffly. It couldn't have closed without someone closing it. With your grandfather inside."

"And the only one there at the time was the keeper, Keku, who said he saw the whole thing. I can't believe it. I know my grandfather trusted him."

Maurice looked at Kwame. "Did you see anything?"

He shook his head. "I was at the leopard pen. I ran when I heard two shots fired. I only saw Keku pulling your grandfather out of the pen. He was unconscious. I carried him to my jeep and drove to the hospital."

Maurice took a few seconds. "I think we need to talk with Keku again."

Kwame was on his feet. "I'll get him. He's still out by the baboon pen."

While we waited, Maurice offered something stronger than iced tea. I was fully ready to accept when my cellphone buzzed. I excused myself and walked out into the vestibule.

"Hey, Matt, where are you? This is Mac McLane."

"Mac, I'm in New Orleans."

"What the hell, is it Mardi Gras?"

"Not where I am. What's up?"

"Autopsy report came back on Professor Holmes. You might be interested to know you were right. The cause of death was not his cut wrist."

"Then what?"

"There was a heavy presence of venom."

That took a few seconds to digest. "That's out of left field. Have they identified it?"

"Yeah. Also out of left field. It's from a snake. A cottonmouth. It caused him to hemorrhage. He was dead before his wrist was cut. That scene in his office was all staged. You called it."

"I didn't call the snake venom. Do we have cottonmouths up there?"

"I checked. Nowhere near. They're also called water moccasins. They swim in swamps and marshes from Florida to Texas."

"And that would include the Louisiana bayous."

"So it would seem. What are you doing down there?"

"It's complicated. I'll give you a full briefing when I get home."

"Which will be?"

"I wish I knew. That's complicated too. Hey, Mac, a favor for us both. Can you have the lab check out the blood that was under Professor Holmes wrist? If it wasn't his, it might be useful to know whose it was."

"It's being tested as we speak. I got a preliminary. You ready for another jolt?"

"Shoot."

"It's not human."

That caught my breath. While I was thinking of an answer, I heard Kwame yelling for Maurice and me in the direction of the pen.

"Gotta go, Mac. A thought. Ask the lab to check for baboon blood."

"Out of what source did you pull that one?"

"A hunch. I'll put ten dollars on it. Later."

I clicked off and ran out the front door and down the front steps. I caught up with Maurice who was a few paces ahead of me. We both saw Kwame standing outside the baboon cage at a section that was engulfed in a typhoon of dust. We were within twenty feet before we could make out a cluster of baboons, shrieking like banshees and fighting each other to get at whatever was at the center of the melee. We were ten feet from the cage when we recognized the body of the keeper, Keku.

CHAPTER NINE

ANOTHER KEEPER CAME scrambling to the tumult of baboon shrieks and human yells. He fired six shots in the air before he could drive the last baboon skulking away from the still body of Keku.

Kwame was the first into the pen. When I saw him lift Keku's limp body, I felt certain that Keku was beyond adding any more pieces of the puzzle.

Kwame lay Keku's body on the ground outside the cage. I saw him check for a pulse. The expression on his face conveyed the final answer.

Two other keepers came to carry the body away. Before they came close, I watched Kwame pull something from around Keku's neck. He slipped it into his pocket.

*　*　*

Dinner that night was served by the house staff to Maurice, Kwame, and me in the main dining room. The pall that hung over us flavored what would otherwise have been Cajun cuisine fit for Louisiana royalty.

Daylight had been nearly spent by the time we took brandy into what was formerly Rene's study. I was glad to accept Maurice's invitation to spend the night. We needed some semblance of a plan. What was shaping up as my next move was nothing I wanted to tackle after sundown.

The three of us agreed that if there was any doubt about the death of Maurice's grandfather being a homicide, there was no doubt that Keku's demise was deliberate. No one could have been more aware of the threat posed by the cluster of baboons. Yet his mauled body was found inside the closed pen with no way to open the gate.

I asked Maurice about Keku's background. Maurice was only aware that he had come from somewhere in Africa. Kwame picked it up.

"Three years ago, your grandfather began importing baboons. He needed a keeper who knew something about how to take care of them. He called a friend who ran Brec's Zoo up in Baton Rouge. They recommended the man he hired. His name was Andrew. You must have known him, Maurice."

"I did. Slightly. But didn't he leave for some reason? I was away at the time."

"So was your grandfather. He was off with that Monkey's Paw group in Jamaica. This man, Andrew, he came to me about a week ago. He just said he was going back to Brec's Zoo. I offered him more money. In fact, I'd double his salary. People who can tend baboons are not around every corner."

"But he left?"

"That same day. He wouldn't give a reason."

"Odd."

"Odder still. The next day, Keku came to the door. He said he knew about baboons. He needed work. We needed a keeper. I hired him to start that day."

Maurice asked the question. "Where did he come from? How did he know about the job?"

"The fact is, I didn't ask a lot of questions. He said he was from western Africa. He worked with baboons there. Given the sudden need, that was all I had to know. I wish now I'd asked him more."

"Are you thinking he had anything to do with . . . ? I can't believe it. Why would he want to hurt my grandfather?"

"I don't know. But I will. I have a drive to make tomorrow morning. Matthew, this may not be your cup of tea. But you're welcome to join me if you wish."

"Where to?"

He was right about the "cup of tea." But at this point, in for a penny was in for a pound.

*　　*　　*

The rap on the bedroom door came close on the heels of sunrise. Breakfast was short and silent before I was beside Kwame in a jeep. The roadway through the swampy bayous east of Bayou Ste. Germaine was becoming more familiar than I had ever expected, or wanted.

There was little exchange of conversation, but I knew in my gut that we were headed to a spot I could live a lifetime without seeing again. When Kwame turned into the dirt drive that led over the log bridge I'd fled at a dead run two nights before, my stomach was clenching like a fist.

There was no human life in sight. The sounds that might have masked our approach were strictly insect. Kwame drove to the foot of the steps that led to the rickety porch around the front door. He swung the jeep in a circle to be headed out and hit the brakes.

"You can wait here if you want, Matthew. I have business inside."

I was out the door and keeping pace with him up the steps. "It became my business two nights ago."

Kwame stopped at the door. He gave three knocks that could have wakened the comatose. It took about half a minute before we could hear shuffling footsteps coming toward the door.

Whether for drama or impatience, Kwame rapped the heel of his fist against the door hard enough to send screws and bolts flying inside and set the door swinging open. The eyes of the old man standing inside were screaming something between shock and fury.

Kwame was inside the door and a foot from the now teetering old man in three steps. The old man raised his cane like an extension of his fist. Before he could wield it, Kwame slapped it out of his hands. The old man tottered sideways. Kwame caught him by the shoulder and carried him, more than walked him, back to the chair by the table. The old man started to speak. Kwame's mouth was three inches from his face.

"Sit, old man. By damn, you'll speak in a minute."

The old man dropped into the chair. His eyes still radiated fire, but he kept his silence.

Kwame straightened up. He reached into his shirt pocket and pulled out something that he threw onto the table. The old man gasped when he saw it.

The slim rays of sunlight that penetrated the window were just enough to make out a small pouch of rough cloth, stitched together with twine and painted with symbols like hieroglyphs.

"What the hell have you been up to, old man?"

The old man's eyes rose from the object to shoot darts of hate into Kwame's eyes. The old man kept his silence.

"That's a question, old man. Rene Perreault is dead."

The old man spat it out. "I know."

"He was murdered."

The old man shrugged. "No matter."

Kwame leaned closer. "It matters to me. Was this your work?"

The old man leaned back and just shook his head.

"Did you order it?"

I thought I saw the beginning of a grin on the old man's lips. "I didn't need to. It would happen anyway. He was warned."

"That man, Keku. He's one of your Maroons. I know his accent. I come from Ghana too. Did you send him to do this?"

The grin of the old man was now out in full. The rage that had poured out of his eyes had subsided. He seemed to have gained control in spite of the ominous hovering of Kwame.

The old man's tone was low and steady. "She is in control. If Keku was her instrument, or not, so be it. She did not need me to intercede."

"That's enough of that voodoo rambling. I don't believe any of it."

"Then you'll never understand why this man died."

"I believe this, old man. I believe you mumble this curse nonsense. This threat of death. Then you make it come true at the hands of your assassin."

The old man slowly shook his head and raised his hands. "I took no part. I was not needed to work her power." He looked up at Kwame. "That's why you'll never prove that I did. I only knew in my soul it would happen."

Kwame snatched the cloth bag from the table and held it under the old man's eyes. "And this. What superstitious power do you think is in this?"

The old man's eyes were now riveted on the markings on the bag. "How did you . . . ?"

"I took it from the neck of your man, Keku. I took it from his dead body."

For the first time, I saw a flash of shock cross the old man's face.

"He's dead, old man. There was no power in this bag of dust to save him."

The grin was gone. The old man looked up at Kwame with an expression I couldn't read.

"Say it, old man. Did you have Keku killed too? So there would be no link to you?"

The old man shook his head and dropped his eyes. This time I could swear that his expression held the deepest feeling.

The old man mumbled something like, "She'll take him to her. She'll—"

Kwame threw the cloth bag across the room into the fire. "There is no 'she,' old man. Your Queen Nanny died over two hundred years ago. There's just you, and your fear of losing power over these people out here. I believe Keku was your murdering hand."

"No, no. He was . . ."

"What, old man? Say it! He was what?"

His voice dropped to a whisper.

"He was my son."

*   *   *

The drive back was spent in thought for both of us. I finally broke the silence. "What are you thinking, Kwame?"

I could see he was mulling an answer. I threw in a thought. "I think you really gave him a shock when you mentioned Keku's death. His reaction was . . . sincere, unguarded."

Kwame looked over. "Perhaps."

"You don't believe it."

"I believe the facts, not the superstition. I knew the Ashanti tribe in west Africa. I grew up in Ghana. I know their beliefs. I know what they came to believe about this Queen Nanny, these escaped slaves in Jamaica, these Maroons. They still need this cult doctrine to hold themselves together as a people."

"And the facts?"

His eyes were on the road ahead, but his mind was piecing together a puzzle. "Rene Perreault was murdered, we agree?"

"Yes."

"And why? He had no enemies, no one who would want to do him harm."

"Go on."

"He's penned in with attacking baboons that might well have killed him if he didn't have a heart attack. The only one in the area is his keeper, Keku, who conveniently shows up for the job the day the previous keeper of three years suddenly leaves. I knew Keku was from this bayou Maroon community by his accent. Now we hear he was the son of the old man, the leader of the Maroons."

"Yes."

He glanced at me. "The only one with a reason to harm Rene was that old man. Rene's death was necessary to reinforce this cult nonsense about Queen Nanny and her curse for touching their sacred land. The old man had to make it happen. I think he did."

"Through Keku."

"Yes."

"His son."

"I believe it now more than ever."

I was trying to match the logic of Kwame's belief with the depth of stunned sincerity on the face of the old man during everything the old man said—including the denial of Kwame's accusation. Kwame gave me a minute before looking for an answer.

"Do you disagree? Is there another explanation?"

I was still mentally factoring in elements of Professor Holmes' death that connected with what had happened to Rene Perreault— the professor's likely violation of the Maroon Nanny curse together

with Rene Perreault, the venom of the cottonmouth snake indige-
nous to the Louisiana bayous that killed him, the awareness of the
professor's death by that old man thousands of miles away in some
backwater Louisiana bayou.

"What, Matthew? Do you agree or not?"

"I don't disagree."

"Is there a distinction?"

I wasn't sure. "What was that little bag you showed the old man?"

"Ah, one more link. I remember them from growing up in Ghana.
It's all part of their beliefs. It's called a 'gris-gris.' They say it like
'gree-gree.' They're little sewn cloth bags. The symbols on the outside
refer to what they believe are the living spirits of their ancestors.
They put different small objects in the bag for whatever power they
want it to give them. When they wear the bag around their necks,
it's supposed to protect them from evil. They're still used in parts of
Africa."

"Hmm."

"The Ashanti brought *gris-gris* over from Africa when they came
as slaves. The Maroons still use them here today."

"Sounds at least harmless."

"Well, when the slaves were brought to America, they began using
gris-gris to bring injuries to their masters on the plantations. To
bring harm they always used the color red. It's like bringing evil on
an enemy."

"How did you find it on Keku?"

"It was a hunch from his accent. If he had one, it'd be around his
neck. One more tie to the Maroon cult. I looked. Sure enough."

He finally broke another silence on my part. "So where am I
wrong?"

"I'm not saying you are."

"But?"

"I saw the stunned look on the old man's face when you told him about Keku's death. You still think he could have Keku killed just to cut the connection?"

"Why not?"

"Do you have a son, Kwame?"

His silence said "No."

CHAPTER TEN

WE WERE BACK in time to join Maurice for an exchange of updates over lunch. Kwame raised one loose end that hadn't occurred to any of us.

"Maurice, the body of the baby baboon. Your grandfather's pet. Where is it now?"

"I don't know. My mind's been on everything else."

"Your grandfather put a small shed, like a little doghouse, in the baboon pen. The baby used to go in there to sleep at night. You remember?"

"Yes. Why?"

Kwame gave no answer. He stood and walked out the front door. I'd have followed, but my cellphone began playing its jingle. I stepped into the hall to answer.

"Matthew. It's Mac. Where are you now?"

"Still Louisiana. What's up?"

"Score another one for your side. The test came back. The pool of blood under Professor Holmes' wrist was from a baboon. How the hell did you figure that?"

"It was actually more than a guess."

I took a few minutes to fill him in on the events of the previous two days.

"That's one hell of a story. Now you're telling me it's some kind of voodoo? You've got to be—"

"Hold the line, Mac. Don't hang up."

I saw Kwame come through the front door with what looked like a rope hanging from his hand. When he came closer, the rope became a limp snake about four feet long with the head freshly severed from the body. Maurice came out of the dining room.

"What is it, Kwame?"

"Cottonmouth."

The wet machete in Kwame's other hand explained the missing head.

"Where was it?"

"Curled up in the corner of the little shed where the baby baboon used to sleep."

I came for a closer look. "Would it have crawled in there by itself?"

Kwame shrugged. "Possible. I doubt it. The other baboons would have scared it away."

"Which means . . ."

"It was put there for a purpose. I think it did what it was supposed to do to the baby. Someone knew your grandfather would find him dead in the morning."

Maurice asked, "Put there by whom?"

Kwame looked at me. I knew what he was thinking. "Those Maroons in the bayou, they catch these snakes alive. But you still don't agree about the old man?"

"I still don't disagree."

Kwame just shook his head. I was still trying to square his theory of the old man's guilt with the genuine shock I saw on his face when he heard of his son Keku's death.

I recalled something else no one had mentioned. I was about to mention it, but a muted voice reminded me that Mac was still on the line. I took the phone back into the dining room.

"Mac, did you hear any of that."

"Yeah. More voodoo babble. Remember how this thing started as a simple suicide?"

"Such are the vicissitudes of life. I have to go, Mac, but . . ."

"But what?"

"Can you do something else?"

"Like what?"

"Just reserve judgment on this next one, all right?"

"Oh crap. Here it comes. What do you want?"

"Go through the clothes Professor Holmes was wearing when he was found that night. They may be still at the funeral home or the station evidence room."

"Looking for what?"

"A small pouch, like a bag sewn together from rough cloth. Probably symbols on the outside."

"And what'll be in it?"

"I don't know. Whatever it is might tell us why he was killed. Maybe by whom. Just take that part on faith."

"I'll have a sweet time explaining that one to the lieutenant."

"Don't even try 'til I get back. I'll be in touch."

*   *   *

In a way, it felt good to board the two forty-five p.m. plane for Montreal. It was the first time I'd ever felt pleasure in leaving New Orleans.

Our little detective team had split in three separate directions. Since the local police squad had rested comfortably on the decision that Rene Perreault's death was "an unfortunate accident," the body was simply taken to a funeral home. Maurice agreed to follow the trail of Rene's last worn clothing to check the pockets. Kwame told him what we were looking for.

Kwame dropped me at the Louis Armstrong Airport and went on to run down another lead. He would drive the eighty or so miles directly to Brec's Zoo in Baton Rouge. We wanted to find out why the first keeper of Rene's baboons, Andrew, had suddenly quit the job to return to Brec's Zoo with less than a day's notice.

*   *   *

My eight thirty-five p.m. arrival at the Trudeau Airport in Montreal left little time for anything but checking into the hotel Maurice recommended, *L'Auberge de la Place Royale* on *de la Commune Street* in Old Montreal. His taste remained consistently reliable. One reason behind his recommendation was the proximity of the hotel to the Montreal Museum of Archeology. The third member of the Monkey's Paw Society, Claude DuCette, was, according to Maurice, an archeologist with connections to that museum. That much was available on Google. Beyond that, and Claude DuCette's address and phone number in his grandfather's contact book, Maurice was as much in the dark as I was.

It was past nine when I checked into the hotel. I recalled Maurice's description of his phone call to the DuCette home shortly before the death of his grandfather. It began and ended with a steamy blaming of his grandfather for whatever was happening to Claude DuCette and an angry hang-up. Given the hostility of the DuCette home toward the Monkey's Paws and the late hour, it seemed the better part of discretion to simply settle in 'til morning.

Settling in did have its attraction. The second part of Maurice's advice was, in spite of all the distractions, not to miss the culinary artistry of Chef Jean Paul Riopelle at a *Quebecois* restaurant called simply "*Toque.*" As predicted, his *carpaccio de veau* began untwisting knots the length of my back and shoulders. The entrée, *carre d'agneau*, drove every thought of Maroons and baboons to an obscure corner of my consciousness. Whatever dread was left of what Montreal might hold in store was banished by the *gateau au chocolat blanc*. A half-bottle each of the sommelier's recommendation of both white and red wine sent me floating on air back to the hotel for the best night's sleep since news of my old friend's passing.

The rising sun brought with it reality—the need to crack whatever resistance was waiting for me with the DuCettes.

It was a short walk to the DuCette home on *Rue de la Capitale*. A knock on the door brought . . . nothing. A second, stronger knock . . . more of the same. On the unfounded theory that the third try never fails, I was about to give it one more shot, when I noticed the curtain at the window to my right open slightly and re-close. I waited. Still nothing.

I tried another approach. I wrote a brief note on a sheet from a pad I'd taken from the hotel. "Monsieur DuCette. My name is Matthew Shane. I was a close friend of Professor Holmes. My only interest in meeting with you is finding an explanation for his death. Nothing else. Maybe we can help each other. I can be reached at this hotel."

I slipped the note into the mail slot in the door and walked back to the hotel. When I got to my room, the phone light indicated a message. The voice was that of an older woman with a heavy French-Canadian accent. Probably because of my note, the message was in English. It began with a pause and only the sound of tense breathing. When she spoke, the words were simply, "My husband is dead. Isn't that enough? I have nothing to say to you . . . For God's sake, leave me alone . . ." Another pause, and the finality of a click.

I called the number Maurice had given me for the DuCette home. When the answering machine gave me a beep, my message was brief.

"Mrs. DuCette, it's Matthew Shane. I'm so sorry to hear about your husband's death. Please hear this before you hang up. We've both suffered a loss. Losing Professor Holmes was like losing my father a second time. I just need answers. Perhaps you have the same need. I think we can give each other pieces of this heartbreaking puzzle. I'll stay in Montreal one more day. If I don't hear from you, I won't bother you further. I mean you no harm whatsoever."

I stayed in the room until five in the afternoon. Total frustration finally doused any hope I had left for any contact.

By then I needed fresh air. A walk along the west bank of the St. Lawrence River helped clear the cobwebs.

It wasn't totally aimless. In six or seven blocks, I dropped into a branch of the Montreal Public Library. An accommodating bilingual librarian brought up on a computer the obituary of one Claude DuCette, who had passed away two days previously of "natural causes."

My two years of high school French were enough to give me a reason to connect the lives of Claude DuCette and Professor Holmes. According to the obituary, Claude DuCette's life was also deeply steeped in archeology. His focus was the early Aztec civilizations of Mexico prior to the arrival of the unwelcome Spaniards. He had been on frequent digs in southern Mexico, and founded an institute of Aztec studies in the Archeological Museum of Montreal just a few blocks from his home. Semi-interesting, but still—so what?

Then my eye caught the mention of his speaking at a conference of archeologists some months previously in Cairo, Egypt. Professor Holmes came back from that same meeting with a tone of secretive tension, according to Mary. She asked him about it, but got little by way of any specific reason.

That called for another crack at the unreachable Mme DuCette. Another five rapid knocks on the DuCette door that this time could be heard two houses distant produced no more than the first time.

Before retreating to my hotel in defeat, I crossed the front lawn for a look inside the large window—this time with drapes opened. The reaction burst out of my lips—"Holy crap!"

Every cabinet, table, chair, and chest was not just tossed, but split open, even to the point of slicing open every inch of uphol-stered surface. My first look screamed of the randomness of some manic marauder. When the initial shock subsided, I noticed that the broken remains were not randomly tossed around the room. They seemed to be dropped toward the center of the room by someone with an organized pattern of searching. In a way, it was more frightening.

I put aside my first impulse to notify the Montreal police. Contact with the officialdom of two jurisdictions had so far been more frustrating than useful. It could also result in restraints on my own freedom to dig deeper.

On the walk back to the hotel, I was searching my mind for a next step in what seemed like unyielding darkness, when a tiny spark of light popped into my consciousness. It was actually a jangling discord from my reading of Claude DuCette's obituary.

I hailed a cab and gave the driver the address of the mortician listed in the obituary—a Monsieur LaFleur. I arrived a few minutes after six. I was about to ring the bell, when a tall, lank figure with a face suited to perpetual and indiscriminate mourning came through the door. The look on his face said, for a moment, that my interruption of his closing for the day was as welcome as the gout. In an instant, he got a professional grip and donned a smile, soft enough to say, *I take your grief personally.*

"Monsieur LaFleur, I presume."

The smile broadened, but remained consoling. "Yes, young man. How may I help you?"

"My name's Matthew Shane. I'm sorry for the inconvenient hour. This is very personal."

He raised his hands with a nod that said, *At a time like this, there is no such thing as an inconvenience.* He said out loud, "Please," and gave a sweep of the hand to invite me in.

In ten seconds, we were seated in his office. He had forms at the ready to make notations and was fingering a pen. "How may I be of assistance?"

"As I said, this is quite personal."

"I understand your feelings completely."

"Maybe not completely. This is quite personal for both of us."

"I'm sorry?" It was a question.

"Both of us. As in you and me."

The pen dropped. The smile lost some of its warmth.

"You very recently cremated the body of a Monsieur Claude DuCette. Yes?"

He gave a tentative nod. "And you ask this why?"

"I need something from you. It's important that I speak with Mme DuCette. I need a phone number or an address. Some way I can reach her."

His hands, his eyes, and his shaking head all emphasized his very conclusive, "Oh, Monsieur—Shane, is it?—I couldn't possibly. There is a question of privacy. Professional ethics. No. I'm sorry. Not at all possible." He gave it finality with a nod.

"I see. Quite impossible. You know, Monsieur LaFleur, I've found that what is possible or impossible often depends on how the question is asked. Let me rephrase."

I lowered my voice and picked up the tempo, which drew him a bit closer to catch each word. "You personally cremated the body of a man listed as dying of 'natural causes.' An investigation by the police will quite likely prove that Claude DuCette's death was an act of violent murder."

That was a guess, but given the rate at which Monkey's Paws members were being done away with, not that much of a stretch.

He was shaking his head, but with less conviction. "That . . . could hardly . . ."

"Let me put this in context. You're wondering how this concerns you. Your immediate cremation destroyed the evidence that could well have proven that it was murder. I would not want to think of your being charged as an accessory in a homicide investigation. But then, we both know how the police tend to reason in these matters. Yes?"

He stared at me in obvious shock. He started to speak, but the words never came out.

"But let me go on, Monsieur LaFleur. I said this matter is personal to me too. At the moment, I have no interest in bringing this unfortunate problem home to roost with you. None whatsoever. My greatest wish is to leave you in peace. I do, on the other hand, have an immediate need to reach Mme DuCette as soon as possible. I'm sure she's in great danger. I can assure you that no one else has an interest in her well-being."

He took in every word, but still—silence.

"I've been brief, Monsieur LaFleur. I hope not too brief to convey my full intentions. I need that contact information. Are we on the same page?"

I gave him ten seconds of silence to process what I knew was a shaking decision. His color was turning gray. Tiny beads of sweat over his white eyebrows and his rapid breathing began to play on my conscience. I nearly backed off, but my concern for him was trumped by my thoughts of the shambles of Mme DuCette's home.

I had to shake him off of dead center. I rose with a speed that I hoped would punctuate deliberateness. His eyes followed me. I turned to walk to the door. I was stopped by his voice that was almost too low to make out.

"Where can you be reached?"

CHAPTER ELEVEN

ON THE WALK back to the hotel, I needed a place to do a quick bit of business and refuel at the same time. An inviting pastry shop on *Place Royale* filled both needs. If there is a more definitive example of the elegance of life in Montreal than a freshly made *éclair au chocolate* at *Maison Christian Faure*, it could only be that same delicacy under a blanket of their freshly whipped *Chantilly*. With a *café au lait* to gild the lily, I settled into a far corner table and made two calls.

I reached Maurice Perreault first. After complimenting his selection of hotel and restaurants, I asked if he had been able to check the pockets of his grandfather's clothing.

"I did."

"And I'll bet my next paycheck you found something unusual."

"Right again."

"While I'm on a roll, Maurice, same bet. It was a rough little sewn bag with symbols on it."

"What are you, psychic?"

"If I were, your grandfather and Professor Holmes would still be alive. Did you look inside?"

"Yes. Any guesses?"

"Not this time. You tell me."

"It's just some kind of small cloth doll. Do you know what it means?"

"I'm not sure. Perhaps. Would you send it to me at my office at Hawthorne University Law School in Salem, Mass?"

"I will. How are you doing up there?"

"I'm not sure. Not yet. I'll be in touch. Did Kwame get back?"

"Yes. He's here. I'll put him on."

There was one golden moment of silence for a bite of the *éclair* while they exchanged the phone. The next voice was Kwame's.

"Matthew, I have news."

"I thought you might. Did you find the baboon keeper, Andrew, back at Brec's Zoo?"

"Yes and no."

"Hmmm."

"Yes, I found him. No, he wasn't at Brec's Zoo. He never made it back."

"Can you break that down?"

"The manager at Brec's told me he hadn't seen Andrew since he left months ago. I started checking with the police in the communities between our bayou and the zoo. About halfway there, a body was found three days ago in a swamp just off the road. They found it before whatever lives in that swamp had done too much damage to identify it. I saw the body. It was Andrew."

I could feel the hair on the back of my neck stiffen. Whatever the hell was behind all of this was consuming human life at a chilling pace.

"Were you able to check the pockets of the clothing he had on?"

"That raised some questions with the local police. Good thing Andrew was African. I could say he was my brother. Only way I could see his clothing."

"I have a feeling you found another cloth bag?"

"Yeah. This one held a tiny handmade sort of doll. Straw and cloth. Red cloth. That's significant. I told you. The Maroon slaves in Jamaica used these *gris-gris* to bring injuries to their masters on the plantations. The bag was on a string around his neck."

"I see."

"Do you, Matthew? Do you finally agree with me? That old man in the bayou has his hand in every bit of this."

Tempting as it was to just say "yes," I couldn't. "Let me give you just two reasons why I'm not fully on board, Kwame. First, how could that old man in a little shack in a Louisiana swamp cause the murder of Professor Holmes three thousand miles away? Or of Claude DuCette up here in in Montreal?"

"Dear God, is Claude DuCette dead?"

"Yes. The obituary has it listed as 'natural causes.' Highly unlikely, given everything else that's gone on. I might know more later tonight. Anyway, my point is that this is a hell of a long way from that old man in his little shack down there."

"Maybe not as far as you think. A couple of hundred years ago, the French were urging the Maroon slaves in Jamaica to attack their British masters. It was part of the French plan to capture Jamaica from the British. The Black slaves outnumbered the British whites ten to one. So the British put hundreds of their Maroon slaves on three ships and sent them to Halifax, Nova Scotia. That's true. Most of them left the cold climate in a couple of years, but there are still pockets of Maroon settlements in eastern Canada. It's not so impossible that that old man has long arms."

"You may have a point."

"So what's your second reason?"

I felt a buzz on my cellphone. "I have another call, Kwame. I have to take this. You two be careful down there. Call you later."

The call was from Mac McLane. I could have put the words in his mouth. He checked the clothes Professor Holmes was wearing when his body was discovered. In one of the pockets, he found one of those bags. This one held a tiny makeshift cloth doll. It sounded like the one Kwame found on Andrew. I was beginning to cave in to Kwame's suspicion of the old man in the bayou.

I asked Mac the color of the doll.

"Red."

* * *

I finished the call, and the *éclair*, and walked back to my hotel. As I headed for the staircase across the lobby, my name, preceded by "*Monsieur*," broke through my mental cloud. I saw the elderly concierge across the lobby hobbling in my direction and repeating "Monsieur Shane."

I met him halfway. I noticed he gave a cautious glance around before speaking. "A message for you, Monsieur Shane."

I held my hand out, but he lowered his voice and spoke close to my ear. "No writing, *Monsieur*. Just these words. '*La Musee d'Archeologie*.' You know it?"

"I know it's close by. I can find it. Go on."

"Tonight. Midnight. Rear entrance."

"It'll probably be closed."

"The rest of the message is this: 'A door in the back will be unlocked. Follow signs to the Aztec/Mayan Room. Second floor.' That's all of it."

I checked his badge. "Thank you, Henri. Who delivered the message?" I needed to know what I'd be walking into.

He smiled. "Ah, *Monsieur*. There was a request for discretion. You understand."

I smiled back. "I assume that request was accompanied by some transfer of currency?"

The smile broadened. "Mmm, Monsieur, you are a man of the world."

"And I would never ask you to betray a confidence, Henri."

As I spoke, I slipped into his hand several folded Canadian bills that I was sure would be at least double the amount he had received. His slight glance down and fanning of the bills with two fingers was enough for his trained eye to recognize the sum. He didn't speak, but neither did he walk away.

"On the other hand, Henri, a small shake of the head, a mere nod, without a word of course. These might not offend your delicate sense of discretion."

"You have my attention, Monsieur."

"Was it perhaps a woman?"

A slight raising of the shoulders and sideward glance I took for a "No."

If it was not Mme DuCette, there was only one other person I knew in Montreal. "Perhaps a tall, gray-haired gentleman in the black suit of a mortician."

He simply smiled. His code of ethics was intact, and I had what I needed. Monsieur LaFleur had apparently held up his end of our understanding.

*   *   *

A cab dropped me at the front entrance to the Museum of Archeology a minute before midnight. I began walking around the outside of the building. Toward the back, I noticed a door slightly ajar. I took it as an invitation. Once inside, I followed the corridor to a sign that pointed up a flight of stairs to an exhibition room labeled "Aztec/Mayan."

The room was weakly lit in a blue light. The shadowy outline of carved, life-size figures stood like frozen guardians. My footsteps echoed off the stone walls as I walked to the center. There were no signs of life. I tried a whispered "Hello." Nothing. I followed that with a more robust, "Anyone here?" The only sound back was the echo of my own voice.

I gave it another fifteen seconds. My confidence level was dropping with each second. One louder "Hello" met with another twenty seconds of silence. I turned back with the disheartening decision to call the whole Montreal fiasco a dead end.

Before I could take two steps, I heard a whisper from the far corner of the room. "Are you alone?"

All I could see was an open door. I spoke to the darkness behind the door. "Yes. I came alone. Madame DuCette?"

Another few seconds and I saw the silhouette of a tall woman in the doorway. I tried again. "Madame DuCette? I'm alone. Can we talk?"

Another pause before "I told you once. I have nothing for you. What do you want from me?"

"Just to talk. I'm so sorry about your husband. I lost someone too. Can we just talk? I'll leave any time you say."

I started to walk toward the shadow. The voice stopped me. "Stay there. I can hear you from there. Who sent you?"

I stood where I was. The connection felt delicate and easily breakable. I spoke slowly, with forced calmness. "My name is Matthew Shane. My best friend was Professor Holmes until his death a week ago. The police want to call it suicide. I know in my heart it was murder. I promised his wife, his widow, that I'd find the person responsible. And I will. If it takes the rest of my life."

There was a hanging silence.

"Can you hear me? Are you listening?"

The shadow figure in the doorway seemed to split into two. Another tall shadow was beside her. It seemed to be holding her by the elbow. This time the voice came from the second shadow. It was a man's voice. "Answer the question. Who sent you?"

"No one sent me. Who the hell are you?"

"The real question is who the hell are you?"

"I'll say it just once more. I'm a friend of Professor Holmes."

There was a slight pause. The man's voice again. "What was Holmes' first name?"

"Barry."

"Real name?"

"Barrington."

"Middle name?"

"I haven't a damn clue. In ten years, I never heard it. If we're through playing twenty questions, I need to speak with Madame DuCette. Five minutes. Then I'll be out of her life."

I could see the two shadowy heads come together. There were echoings of whispers that I couldn't make out. When it stopped, I heard the man's voice. "You don't need to speak with Madame DuCette, Mr. Shane."

"Yes I do, whoever you are. I've come a hell of a long way."

The male voice again. "You need to speak with me."

The male figure stepped forward into the dim light. I could make out a man who looked to be Professor Holmes' age.

"I'm sorry. Who are you?"

He came forward with his hand extended. "I'm Claude DuCette."

CHAPTER TWELVE

I was barely into the adjustment of having Claude DuCette back among the living. The voice came again. "I'm putting both of our lives in your hands, Monsieur Shane. God help us if I'm wrong."

"If it's any comfort, I can say the same thing, Monsieur DuCette."

I followed them back into his small office. We sat huddled in a tight circle. We kept the room in darkness since it had a window to the outside.

"For a man who's just been cremated, Monsieur DuCette, you seem to have come through it in good form. How did you pull it off?"

"You met our mortician, Paul LaFleur. We've known him long enough to ask a serious favor."

"So he faked the cremation, the obituary, the whole show. Which leaves one question. Why?"

Claude DuCette reached into his pocket. He put something in my hand. I could tell by the feel that it was another of those small *gris-gris* bags. I could feel a lump inside. "What's in it?"

"One of their straw dolls. It's neck was snapped."

"And you knew what that meant?"

"Better than anyone who's not a Maroon. I've been on many digs in Jamaica. I know enough to take the message personally. I have no place to hide that they wouldn't find me. My wife, Elaine, she had the idea. If I couldn't hide, I had to get them to stop searching. What better way than to be dead and buried?"

"My compliments. It seems to have worked."

"Until you, Monsieur Shane. The weak link was apparently our mortician."

"Your secret's safe with him. I made him an offer he couldn't refuse."

"That's good to know. So now you have us here. What do you want from me?"

I gave him a quick briefing on the deaths of Professor Holmes and Rene Perreault, and my encounter with the old man in the bayou. "It's an easy bet that these are all tied together. A man with more experience with the Maroons than either of us keeps trying to convince me that the old man who controls the Maroons in a Louisiana bayou is behind it all. He says it's the religious belief in their Queen Nanny that's driving it."

"And you?"

"I'd like to believe it. It'd be a simple answer. I could get my life back."

"Then why not accept it."

"There are a couple of things that don't jibe. I'm hoping you can help. For a starter, I need to know more about this group called 'The Monkey's Paw Society.' Why that name?"

In the faint light I could see him turn to his wife. She whispered to him, "Why not? What more can we lose? He might even help."

He leaned closer, but took a few seconds, probably searching for a starting point.

"You have an instinct for the heart of the matter, Monsieur Shane."

"Please, make it 'Matthew.' For one thing, it'll save time."

"Agreed. We're Claude and Elaine. So, the name, The Monkey's Paw. It goes back to a moment in time I wish to God I could erase. The five of us, your friend Barry Holmes, Rene Perreault in New Orleans, Wayne Barnes in Barbados, Roger Van Allen in Jamaica, and me. Two things brought us together. We all have a madness for archeology—or at least obscure treasures—and a love for a good poker game, especially with each other. We played once a year wherever an archeological convention brought us together. Some months ago, that was in a room in the basement of the Giza Museum in Cairo.

"It was about midnight. We were all exhausted. The long day, the hour, a few drinks through the game. There was a rap on the door, which was unusual. Roger Van Allen opened it. There was a man. How do I say this? Do you know the poem 'The Rhyme of the Ancient Mariner'?"

"Yes."

"Well, if you were casting the part, that weathered old man of the sea would be typecasting for the title character. I think we all just stared at him. He smiled from one to the next of us, but the tortured look in his eyes said he'd been to hell and back.

"He walked into the room. There was a sixth chair against the wall. He pulled it up to the table and sat down. He looked deep into the eyes of each of us when he asked, 'Could you deny an old salt one hand of poker, no more?'

"He looked around for a nod from each one of us in turn. It was as if we were committing to something more than a hand of poker. When he had our permission, he gave a sigh like some burden had been lifted off of his shoulders. I remember his exact words. 'Then deal, and God help all of us.'

"We anted up for a hand of five-card draw. The old sailor reached into the bag he had on the floor beside him. He tossed into the pot a gold coin that could cover the ante for a hundred hands.

"I forget who said it. 'It's too much. This is just—'

"'Let it ride!' He said it with a force that silenced us all. He reached into the bag again and pulled out what looked like folded pages of parchment tied with a red ribbon. He tossed those into the pot too. He smiled again and said, 'Let the games begin.'

"I dealt us each five cards. I don't know what the others got, but I gave myself two jacks. There was a round of betting. Rene and your friend Barry folded. Roger and Wayne Barnes drew three cards. I drew three too, including a third jack. The old sailor stood pat. Roger and Wayne and I bet against each other until they each dropped out. The old sailor just stayed in at each round. Finally, it was just the old sailor and me for the call."

Claude stopped for a moment. He seemed to be reliving the last moment when he could have changed the course of what was to follow. He looked years older when he looked up at me and began again.

"I laid down my three jacks. The old sailor looked at them, I swear, as if they were the key to his prison. He tossed in his cards, face-down. He stood up and looked at the five of us. 'It's your pot. All of you. I suggest you share it among you. And God help you all.'

"He walked to the door. Before he left, he turned around for one last look. I'll never forget his last words. 'Beware of the Monkey's Paw.'

"We just looked at each other in silence. Roger was the first to move. 'Shall we do as he said? Share the pot?'"

"I looked at the gold coin and the sheaf of parchments. I was the first to nod. We all nodded. Roger divided the cash in the pot among us. He held the gold coin up for a suggestion. I said, 'Leave it there for now.'

"Roger reached into the pot for the parchments. When he untied the red ribbon, we could see that it was five folded pieces of parchment paper. Each one of them was sealed shut with red sealing wax. When Roger spread them out, we could see that each one had one of our names on it. Roger handed them out to each of us. Mine said, 'For Claude DuCette. Show no one.' I assume the others had the same order."

"Did you open it?"

"No. Not then. None of us did. Roger said there was a note addressed to us all. He read it aloud. 'Gentlemen. You have five instructions, one apiece, to locate a treasure beyond any archeologist's dream. Keep your silence. Show your instruction to none of the others. Six weeks from today, you will meet at Morgan's Harbour Hotel in Port Royal, Jamaica. You'll know what to do then.'"

"So what did you do?"

"Nothing. Then. We were between disbelief and being stunned senseless. There was little or no discussion. We each went back to our rooms with our own parchment."

"So did you . . . ?"

"But wait. Hear this. I was the last to leave. Before I left the poker table, I turned over the hand of cards the old sailor had thrown in facedown. He had a full house, kings and tens. He actually had my three jacks beaten."

Claude fell silent. I finally said, "Did you go to Jamaica in six weeks?"

"Yes. We all did." He smiled. "We used the gold coin the old sailor threw in the pot to pay part of the expenses for all five of us. I think he had that in mind to be sure we'd go."

"What happened in Jamaica?"

"We met at Morgan's Harbour Hotel. By then, we'd each read the particular parchment he'd addressed to us. Together they'd lead us to whatever the pot of gold was supposed to be."

"Your parchment didn't say what it was?"

"No."

"And none of the others?"

"I don't know. We were to disclose the messages to each other, one at a time, in the order mentioned in the parchments. We were to follow the first clue to the end before opening the second, and so on. Mine was to be disclosed first."

"And what was the clue?"

Claude looked at his wife as if he were about to open some fearsome Pandora's box. Her expression said, *You've gone this far. Why not?*

"The order on my parchment was for us to meet in the hotel lobby the morning after we arrived. We were to be prepared for a hard trek. There'd be someone to guide us."

"And was there?"

"Yes. Three Black Jamaican natives met us in the lobby after a quick breakfast. Believe me, we were ready."

"Did they speak English?"

"Yes. With a heavy accent."

"I'm sorry. Go ahead, Claude."

"Port Royal is at the end of a peninsula that curves around to make a bay at the south side of Jamaica. The three guides first took us by boat across the water to the mainland. There was a van waiting. We drove for, I don't know, maybe half an hour or an hour. We kept going deeper into the jungle to a place in the middle of nowhere. We stopped at the base of what looked like a high hill or a mountain. There was a pathway leading up. Our three guides told us to get out of the van and follow them, which, of course, we did.

"The climb got steeper and narrower late in the morning. It got down to a width where only one person could occupy the pass at a time."

"Did you have to rest?"

"Of course. Several times. I mean, look at our ages. The heat was oppressive. By noon, we were at a point where we could see the top of the climb about two hundred yards ahead. Our guides gave us water. They told us to wait there. They said their orders were to go on ahead. We were to rest, and follow when we were ready. When we reached the top, the clue in the second parchment was to be read to the five of us."

"Who had that one?"

"That was Rene Perreault, the one from New Orleans."

That was jarring. I remembered the last words of Rene Perreault in the hospital. He whispered to me to tell the Monkey's Paws—*and no one else*—"Follow the abeng." Whatever that meant, it must have been the clue from his parchment.

Claude had stopped. He looked at Elaine again as if he were at a fork in the road. She took his hand and nodded. When he looked back at me, I swear I could see terror in his eyes.

His voice was hesitant. "We were tired, but we were all anxious. After about ten minutes' rest, Roger got us on our feet. We made that last part of the climb single-file to the top of the mountain ridge.

"From there, the path led straight ahead, but it was wider. Still trees thick on both sides. I had my eyes on the ground because of the rocks and roots. I just followed the man ahead of me. I think it was Wayne. Rene was beside me. Then . . ."

"What?"

"A scream, a curse came out of Rene that stopped my blood cold. I've never heard a sound like that from a human being. I turned. He was looking straight up at a tree branch overhead. I saw it. My legs nearly fell out from under me. One of our guides was hanging from a branch by a red cloth rope. He was hanging upside down. I was sure he was dead."

"What did you do?"

"At first, I froze. I couldn't move. Then I ran like hell. We all did. Like a stampeding herd. Back down the path. We'd stumble, pick ourselves up, and run faster. We ran down the path about a hundred yards. Then we saw it. A second guide was laced with vines to a tree at the side of the path. His mouth and his eyes were open, but one look. Damn, we knew he was dead too.

"We stopped and banded together before going on. No one spoke. We had no words. Roger started on ahead. He waived us on down the path at a slower, saner pace. We were all right until we reached the bottom of the climb. That's where we saw the third guide. He was just lying there beside the path. He was dead. He was holding something in his arms. It was a large straw doll in a red cloth dress. It's neck was broken, just like the man on the ground holding it." Claude looked at his wife. "Just like the small doll I later received in that little bag."

"Dear God. You must have been petrified."

"That's a good word for it. We made our way back to the hotel and made arrangements to leave as soon as possible. That was about nine days ago."

"Have you heard anything from the others since then?"

"Rene Perreault called me a few days ago. It was after I'd received that cloth bag with the doll. I couldn't talk to him. Elaine took the call. She blamed Rene and the rest of the group for getting us into this. I haven't heard from any of the others."

I started to speak, but he interrupted. "I'm sorry, Matthew. I haven't said this, and I meant to. I'm so sorry to hear about the death of your friend Barry. He was my favorite of the group. A good man."

"Thank you. He was that, and more. Did you ever find out what the thing was you were all looking for?"

I thought he would look to Elaine again, but he didn't. He just said quietly, "No. Is there anything else?"

"Yes. Where we started. Why the name 'Monkey's Paw Society'?"

He was in thought for a second. "It was those last words that old sailor said when he left the poker game. 'Beware of the Monkey's Paw.'"

"Do you know what it means?"

"I didn't then. I think I do now. Did you ever read a short story by that name, 'The Monkey's Paw'?"

"It's not familiar."

"You should read it. It's a classic. Written by W. W. Jacobs around 1902. It involves an old mariner. A family takes him in on a stormy night. He gives them a gift, a shriveled monkey's paw that he claims has the power to grant three wishes. The catch was that every wish granted came with an unspeakable tragedy."

I thought back over the number of deaths that occurred since that old mariner threw this quest into the poker pot. Claude put it into words.

"Be careful what you wish for. Every wish granted has consequences."

CHAPTER THIRTEEN

I WAS ABOUT to leave when Claude took my arm. He whispered, "Before he died, did Professor Holmes tell you the clue in his parchment?"

I recalled that the first clue to be opened was in Claude's parchment. It had brought the five Monkey's Paws to guides who led them up the narrow path to the crest of the mountain in Jamaica, but took them no farther. The death of the three guides had short-circuited their trek. None of the other four parchments were disclosed to the group.

I said truthfully that I'd heard nothing about a clue from Professor Holmes.

He held me closer. "You saw Rene Perreault before he died. Did he tell you anything?"

Perreault's dying words rushed through my mind—"Follow the *abeng*"—whatever that meant—and "Tell the Monkey's Paws. No one else." Another voice in my head was warning, Rene said tell the "Paws"—not any one individual Paw. A hair-splitting distinction, but I followed the voice. I just shook my head rather than put the denial into words.

"What are you going to do now, Matthew?"

I was wishing I had an answer. "Touch base at home. God only knows what from there. There's just one thing I can't do." I had the attention of both of them. "Give up."

Claude just shook his head. "For some reason, I trust you. We're leaving now. If you need to reach me, I'll be in Quebec City at—"

I stopped him. "I don't want to know. You'd do well to trust no one. I mean *no one.*"

"Probably best. No location. I'll just give you my email address. Just in case."

I took it, without the faintest inkling of what "just in case" might involve.

*   *   *

I took stock of the fact that my mental machinery was now running on dwindling fumes. In the sweet words of Curly Putman, I had an impelling desire "to touch the green, green grass of home." It also seemed a good time to reset my compass by face-to-face contact with the only two I could trust with my life—Mary Holmes and Mac McLane.

Mary was first. An hour after my plane landed at Logan Airport in Boston, we were looking at each other over a steaming bowl of Mary's truly New England clam chowder.

"You look worn, Matthew. Tell me the truth. Are you in danger? Personally?"

I did a rough count of the bodies that had mounted up since I first heard that kid on campus shout to a classmate, "No class today. The old man died." And yet, with the exception of my first encounter with the old man in the bayou, somehow I had not been touched personally by the rampant violence. I said, "I don't think so. I seem to have an immunity." But I had to wonder *why*. And, for that matter, *if*.

When I sensed the right moment to dive back into what neither of us wanted to revisit, I brought it up. "Mary, there's a piece missing. I think it's critical—did the professor ever show you an old folded parchment paper with his name on it?"

"No. Nothing like that."

"Could I look through Professor Holmes' papers? It was something he could have kept hidden."

The two of us scanned everything in his home office—desk, file cabinets, closets. Nothing.

After a goodbye hug, I was halfway to the door. My next intended move was to search his university office. Suddenly a thought. "Mary, his suitcase, any luggage he used for the trip to Jamaica. Where is it?"

She took me up to a storage space inside their attic. I searched the pockets of a small carry-on bag. No luck. Mary went to the far corner of the room for his full-size suitcase. I noticed a strange look on her face when she found it on the floor.

"What, Mary? What is it?"

She just shook her head. "Senior moment. My memory. I have more of these lately since Barry . . . Ah well."

"Tell me."

"It's nothing. I could have sworn I last saw that suitcase up on the shelf here, not down on the floor. It's just my memory."

I went to the suitcase and lifted it onto a table. I took one uncomfortable breath before opening it.

The first look in that dim light showed another empty space. I was about to close it, when I noticed the zippered lining of the inside top. The zipper was sealed with a tiny padlock. In the dull light, I noticed a slit, large enough for me to slip my hand inside the lining and feel around. Empty. But what first seemed like another dead end began to trigger a chain of deductions that had me on full alert.

"Mary, have you noticed anything missing around the house? I mean since Professor Holmes got back from Jamaica?"

"No. I can't think of anything. What do you make of this slit? Why would Barry do that?"

"I'm not sure." That was actually a lie, but Mary had no need for more edgy thoughts at the moment. It seemed to me unlikely that the organized mind of the professor would misplace the key. The slit seemed more like a shortcut by someone making a hasty search. I ducked the question. "Maybe Barry couldn't get the lock or the zipper to work. Tell me. Just curious. Do you keep the doors locked when you go out?"

She gave me a quizzical look. "Why would I? We're in a university community. Salem was a bit edgy back in the witch trial days. But now? I know almost everyone in this neighborhood. I suppose it's naïve, but no one locks doors. What are you thinking?"

I saw no point in disturbing her with either the news of Rene Perreault's death or the ransacking search of the DuCettes' home. The fact that a slashed suitcase lid was the extent of any search of the professor's home said to me that whoever did it found what they were looking for on the first try. That part was disturbing, but it also suggested that any danger to Mary had quite likely passed.

"Nothing, Mary."

"Do you think I'm in danger?"

I gave an honest answer. "Truthfully, no. I don't."

I was about to add that it wouldn't be the worst idea to begin locking the house any time she left it. On the other hand, sometimes well-intentioned advice can do more psychological harm than good. I also figured that the DuCettes probably locked their doors, for all the good it did.

* * *

Mac McLane was at the table first. When I called him that after-noon and said we could flip a coin for the bill for dinner at the Hawthorne-By-The-Sea, his only words were, "What time?"

We let business slide until we had each gone through three of their signature popovers and were well into a double Jack Daniels on the rocks.

There was much to discuss, but out of respect for the boiled lob-sters that had just given their lives, we first gave full attention to their careful dissection—a New England art we had both practiced since childhood.

Coffee came. It was time to get down to business. I filled Mac in on what I'd learned from the DuCettes. That, plus his bizarre report of cottonmouth venom and baboon blood relative to the death of Professor Holmes, had pulled him out of the suicide theory. He was open to alternatives, but my explanations of Maroon beliefs in the powers of long-dead ancestors and self-executing curses from Nanny Town led to a look that asked without words how far I'd drifted into voodoo beliefs.

I returned the look with one that said I was still on his plane.

"On the other hand, Mac, someone who knows the Maroons bet-ter than you or I ever will has been selling me on a halfway theory." I was thinking of Kwame. "There are clusters of Maroons in places outside of Jamaica. They range from Louisiana to Montreal, that I know of. This Nanny curse is deep in their blood. More than you can imagine. There's an old man in a New Orleans bayou who calls the shots down there, and heaven knows how far away."

"You telling me he has voodoo power?"

"No. Just human power. He believes these Monkey's Paws invaded their sacred land in Nanny Town. Maybe he's been nudging the curse along with a little human enforcement of his own. It could explain what happened to Professor Holmes, Rene Perreault, and the DuCettes. So far."

"Do you buy it?"

"I'd like to. It'd give me a rational explanation I could live with."

"But . . . ?"

My turn for a headshake. "Couple of loose ends."

"So what's next, Matt?"

"I can go places your jurisdiction doesn't reach. There were five members of the Monkey's Paws. I've touched base with three of them. I think I'll check out a fourth."

"Which one?"

"Good question. One's in Jamaica, and one's in Barbados."

"How will you decide?"

"I've been thinking about that." A sudden thought occurred. I reached for my cellphone. "I may have an answer. Sit tight."

Mac had lost the coin-toss for dinner. He waived to the waitress for the check while I hit the speed dial on my cellphone. Mary Holmes was surprised to hear my voice so soon. The trick was to sound conversational.

"Mary, I know the professor didn't say much about that trip to Jamaica. They stayed at a hotel in Port Royal. I'm just curious. Did the professor mention if he had a roommate?"

"As a matter of fact, he did. Barry called me when his plane got into the Jamaican airport to let me know he'd arrived. He always did that."

"I'm not surprised."

"While we were on the phone, the one from Barbados, Wayne Barnes, asked him if he could share his hotel room. I'm sure Barry would have said yes. Why do you ask?"

"No big deal. Just filling in details. I'll be home for a while if you need anything at all."

I was getting used to telling half-truths to people I thought I'd never lie to, no matter what. I could give a rational excuse for every half-lie, but it never erased the discomfort.

Mac was tuned in before I hung up. "I couldn't help hearing. Why the roommate question?"

I told Mac about the slit lining in the professor's suitcase and no other signs of a search of his house.

"It's a guess, Mac. If someone, say one of the Monkey's Paws, wanted to get to the clue in the professor's parchment, they could have searched his whole house when Mary was out. She never locks the doors. Someone certainly tossed the DuCettes' house. But Mary said there were no other signs of a search. I'm thinking maybe whoever it was knew exactly where to look. Maybe he saw the professor stash his parchment in the lining of his suitcase and put on the little padlock. Who better to know that than whichever of them was sharing a hotel room with the professor when he packed?"

"Matt, you should have been an investigator."

"Thank you. I was. Air Force intelligence. Turns out the professor's roommate was the one from Barbados. I'll get to him after the one in Jamaica. One other thing, Mac. Just to be safe, could you be sure to put some protection on Mary Holmes. Especially at the house. I don't think she's in danger, but this is no time to be wrong."

"She'll have it. Where to from here?"

"Home. A night's sleep in my own bed."

"Ah. The green, green grass of home."

Mac and I have always shared a weakness for the real country music.

*   *   *

By seven p.m., I'd had a fifteen-minute shower, a mail and phone check, and a catch-up on local Salem TV news. My gyro-compass was beginning to feel reset. It needed just one last retuning.

I walked at a slow, recuperative pace a few nostalgic blocks down Washington Street. I always feel I'm home in Salem when I pass the old courthouse where the witch trials were in full swing in 1692. It was just a few blocks more to my always oasis-of-choice, O'Neill's Irish Pub and Restaurant.

They say it's the sense of smell that most powerfully evokes mental images. I could have been blindfolded and earplugged, and just two steps inside the door, the slightly pungent scent of Dublin-brewed Guinness stout, mingled with just a whiff of Jameson's fine blended Irish whiskey, would have told me that I was in O'Neill's. I also knew on instinct that just fifteen feet away, Mick O'Flynn, my favorite barkeep, was about to place a pint of the former and a shot of the latter on the bar—for me. It was a ritual.

And if the aroma didn't give it away, the lilting promise of Marty Day, the house band's tenor, assisted vocally by every lad and lass in the house, to "I'll Take You Home Again Kathleen" would most convincingly bespeak O'Neill's.

The house was full and the bar was two deep, but Mick, all six foot six of him, and not long off the boat from County Kilkenny, cleared wedging room for me to edge up to the brass rail.

"You're a sight, Matthew Shane. And when was the last time you got a night's sleep?"

"I think around last Saint Patrick's Day. Thank you for asking, Mick. And how's yourself?" I always find Mick's brogue contagious.

"Fit as an Irish fiddle. We've missed ya."

Three calls for immediate service down the bar met with one wave of Mick's gargantuan palm.

"Go ahead, Mick. You're in demand."

"To hell with them. What else are you havin' tonight, Matthew?"

I started to ask if I could just have a couple of Irish bangers and a boiled potato there at the bar, but Mick slapped his forehead.

"Damn! I'd be forgettin' me name if it weren't sewn in me underwear. There's a man askin' for ya. He sounds like he's in from the islands. He's at the far table in the corner in the back."

I thanked Mick, took a glass in each hand, and wove my way through clusters of tenors and an occasional baritone. By now they were singing a little treason with "The Harp That Once Through Tara's Halls."

I broke through the crowd toward the back of the room. Seated alone at the corner table, and looking as comfortable as an Eskimo at a luau, an older gentleman with skin like midnight, in a three-piece suit and tie, sat rigidly erect with his hands folded on the table.

I walked to the table and nodded. "My name's Matthew Shane. Were you looking for me?"

He bolted straight up. He squinted a bit until he recognized me, which brought a pleasant smile and a gesture to sit across from him. I accepted.

"Mr. Shane. A pleasure."

Mick, the bartender, was right. His East Indian Island accent was as pronounced as Mick's brogue.

"Have we met?"

"Actually, no. But I work for a gentleman who is very desirous of meeting with you."

"Really. And your name is?"

"Inconsequential to our business. What is consequential is that I convey a very personal invitation."

Given the previous week, I decided that a healthy sip from each of the glasses I was holding might blunt the shock of whatever was coming. It didn't.

He continued, "My gentleman wishes you to accompany him in the exploration of the Spanish galleon, the *Nuestra Regina*."

"Uh-huh . . . You catch me a bit off guard. Where is this ship?

"It was sunk in approximately 1671 by a Spanish warship. It's at the bottom of the Caribbean Sea."

CHAPTER FOURTEEN

THAT OUT-OF-LEFT-FIELD invitation brought a smile to my lips and more questions to mind than I could get out at the moment. He filled the silence.

"My gentleman assures you that he will provide everything you could possibly need. You need only . . . accept."

I was treading water while my mind organized what to ask first. "Well, that is one of the more unusual offers I've had today. I guess the first of many questions is . . . why me?"

"That would be for my gentleman to say. May I simply note that he is sufficiently serious to defray the entire cost. Again, you need only accept."

"Exactly when did your gentleman have in mind?"

"This minute. His private plane is waiting on the airport runway."

Beyond a smile, that brought a laugh. "Even if I were to say yes— which is a leap—I have no clothes with me, nothing for a trip. I wasn't quite expecting . . ."

"As I say, Mr. Shane, there is nothing you might need that will not be provided by my gentleman."

"That is . . . most generous." I said it slowly while I took inventory of anything else I couldn't do without—just in case I lost my mind and accepted.

"Ah! One thing your gentleman can't supply. My passport."

To my shock more than surprise, he reached into his suitcoat pocket and handed me an American passport. The shock became mind-blocking when I opened it to find that it was mine.

"Where the hell did you . . . ?"

"Please forgive any discourtesy you're feeling. You just returned from Canada. I took the slight liberty of retrieving it from the top of your bureau where you left it before coming to this establishment."

The shock was not wearing off. "You broke into my apartment? That was the 'slight liberty'?"

"I say 'slight' because I assure you, nothing in your apartment has been disturbed. Nothing else. And by way of explanation, you must understand, time is very much of the essence. If we can just begin, my gentleman will explain fully."

I admit to being totally flummoxed. The answer I was formulating was in the distinct and unmistakable negative, but just out of curiosity I asked, "How long does this gentleman expect me to . . . ?"

"My guess is two to three days. Perhaps four. But, Mr. Shane, you are asking the wrong questions. All of these answers will come soon enough. I believe there is only one question that matters. I also believe that when you hear the answer, you will accompany me to the airport immediately."

I had been so stunned that I had overlooked a possible connection to the rest of the week's fantasy. I caught his drift and asked the question. "Exactly who is this 'gentleman'?"

"He is the Monkey's Paw who resides in Barbados. His name is Wayne Barnes."

*   *   *

Within forty-five minutes, we were in a privately owned jet at thirty thousand feet, cruising southeastward toward the island of Barbados. The plane could accommodate twenty people. My guide and I were the only passengers.

Once we reached cruising altitude, he suggested that I step into the chamber at the rear of the plane to change clothing. "The apparel you'll find there will be most suitable for you when we arrive. Time, as I say is . . ."

"Of the essence. Right."

In five minutes, I emerged from the back chamber in an outfit from shoes to cap that I probably would have chosen, but for the price, to wear on the deck of a yacht in the south Caribbean Sea. I was beyond being surprised that everything was a perfect fit.

*   *   *

We landed in approximately two and a half hours and taxied to the east end of the Grantley Adams Airport in Barbados. Before the jet engines had fully wound down, my guide had me in the back seat of a black Lexus with discreetly tinted windows.

We drove southeastward along the shoreline of the most richly colored expanse of open sea I had ever experienced. The contrast with recent excursions through the swampy backwaters of the Louisiana bayous was stark. The tension, however, was distinctly familiar.

We arrived at an area of private docks in a town called Oistins. The driver stopped at the base of a wharf that anchored power boats of every size, speed, and description. One power yacht stood out as the choice of the fleet. *The Sun Catcher*. My guide hustled us both directly to the carpeted gangplank that led on board a vessel that could pass for a floating Ritz-Carlton.

The engines were already revving. I was escorted to a padded deck-lounge with maximum view on the foredeck. I had scarcely settled in, when we were slicing through late-afternoon sea-swells that barely caused a rise and fall.

My guide, still in suit and tie, brought me, without either of us asking, a tall, cool, planter's punch with an ample kick of Mount Gay Rum. For the first moment since Mick O'Flynn told me that someone was asking for me, I made a fully considered decision. This entire fantasy could easily turn into a disaster that could outstrip New Orleans and Montreal together, but to hell with it. It was just too elating not to accept it at face value—at least for the moment.

My mind was just settling into a comfortable neutral when I heard footsteps from behind with more heft than I imagined my guide could produce. I made a move to swing out of the padded deck-chair when I felt a hand with authoritative strength on my shoulder. The accompanying voice had the same commanding undertone.

"Stay where you are, Matthew. I'll join you."

A matching deck-chair was set beside me. I found myself looking up at a shadow against the setting sun that appeared double my bulk and yet compact as an Olympic hammer-thrower. The voice came again.

"You're an interesting study, Matthew. I may call you 'Matthew,' right? I should. I probably know more about you than anyone you know. You might have guessed that by now."

An open hand reached down out of the shadow. I took it. The handshake fit the shaker. It took some seconds for the feeling to come back into mine.

Before I could answer, the voice was coming from the deck-lounge beside me. "No need for coy name games. You know that I'm Wayne

Barnes. And you know that I'm one of the, shall we say, associates in that little clique we call the Monkey's Paws. In fact, your escort here, Emile, tells me it was the mention of my name that swung your decision to get on that plane."

He nodded to my nearly empty planter's punch. "Another?"

Before I could answer, he gave a slight nod to someone behind us. Before I could say "Yes," or possibly, but less likely, "No," a native Bajan in a server's uniform was at my left taking my empty glass and handing me a full one.

I was three good sips into the second glass before I said my first word since coming aboard. I looked over at Wayne. I seemed to have his full focus. His engaging smile carried a message of relaxed hospitality, and none of the threatening undercurrents I was scanning for. "You have an engaging way of delivering an invitation, Mr. Barnes."

He raised a hand. "Wayne."

"'Wayne' it is. You must have an interesting social life."

"I do. Do you find it offensive?"

I looked over the bow, past the deepening blue crystal water to the reddening horizon. I felt the soothing caress of the slightly salted ocean breeze. I took one more sip of the most perfectly balanced planter's punch I'd ever tasted and looked back at Wayne. "Not in the slightest. Yet."

"Ah yes, 'yet.'"

"Right. I'm sure this won't impress you, Wayne, and it's not a complaint, but I've had a week full of enough tragedy to fill a lifetime. Hence the 'yet.'"

His smile and focused attention remained. "I know more about your week, perhaps, than even you do. But go on."

The second planter's punch definitely was having a mollifying effect. "I have no idea what you mean by that last statement, so I'll just pass on. Given that week, and the abrupt transport from hell on earth to . . . paradise on earth, I'd have to be Mrs. Shane's backward child not to listen for a second shoe to drop."

The smile expanded. Still no alarms. "Or perhaps you've come into a sea change of good luck. Why not go with that?"

"Why not indeed? For the moment. Just one question."

"All right. One question. For now. Make it a good one."

"Oh, it is. It's a beaut. Ecstatic as I am with all this, why the hell am I here?"

That brought a bursting laugh. "I think I'm going to enjoy having you around for a couple of days, Matthew. You have an instinct for the jugular. No chipping around the edges. We won't waste each other's time."

"Thank you. But that's not an answer."

"No, it isn't." He looked out to the diminishing sunset. "The only answer I can give you at the moment that would do justice to the question is this. And you'll just have to live with it for now. You're here for a quick but depthful education. I think you'll find it well worth two days of your life. Are you in?"

"Do I have a choice?"

We both looked back at the rapidly diminishing shoreline behind us. "None that comes to mind. Now are you in?"

That brought a smile from me, another healthy sip of the planter's punch, and a deep breath of the ocean-fresh breeze. "I'm in."

We chatted through the sunset on far-ranging subjects that had no association whatsoever with Monkey's Paws, Maroons, murder-suicides—in fact, nothing that gave a clue as to why my gracious host had chosen my company over the vast range of his acquaintances. By then, the moon had risen.

At some point, I was aware that the engines had stopped. The splash of two anchors could be heard on either side. The sun had set.

The shift from twilight to a darkness, penetrated only by a quarter moon, went unnoticed.

I was slowly sipping away at my third or possibly fourth planter's punch when I became aware of a bobbing light approaching from the port side. Without interrupting the flow of conversation, I noticed that Wayne was following its approach as it reached the side of the yacht.

Within a few minutes, my original guide, still in suit and tie, approached Wayne's side with an inaudible whisper. I sensed that a bit of steel crept into Wayne's otherwise conversational tone. "I'll see him."

I began to get up to provide privacy. Wayne held my arm in position. "Stay, Matthew. Let your education begin." My guide nodded to someone behind us and lit his path with a small flashlight.

I settled back as a fiftyish man with narrow, cautious eyes and thinning gray hair that might have last been combed by his mother came up along Wayne's right side. The loose wrinkles in his ageless cotton suit indicated that he might have been close to six feet, but for a constant stoop as if to pass under an unseen beam. The stoop caused his head to bob and gave him the look of one asking for royal permission to approach.

Wayne's eyes turned to him. I noticed the stoop of the back became more noticeable. Wayne's voice was calm and soft, but it commanded his visitor's full attention. "Do you have it? I assume you wouldn't be here without it, yes, Yusuf?"

The thin mouth cracked into a smile that conveyed no humor. "Of course. Of course. But perhaps our business . . ."

Wayne nodded toward me. "No fear. Mr. Shane is here for an education. We shouldn't deprive him of that, should we?"

The smile on the man's lips did not match the apprehension in the tiny eyes, but he nodded. "As you say."

"Then what are you waiting for?"

The man gave a slight glance to either side as if it were the habit of a lifetime. He reached into a deep pocket inside his suitcoat. I noticed a slight but telltale hesitation before he slipped out what appeared to be a hard, flat, roundish object, about seven inches across. It was wrapped in several layers of ragged cloth.

He held it until Wayne extended a hand and took it onto his lap. He laid it on the small tray on his stomach. He looked back at the man, who simply forced a smile.

"I assume it all went well?"

"Oh yes, Mr. Barnes. No problems."

Wayne smiled back. "How I do love to hear those words."

My eyes were glued to Wayne's hands as he carefully peeled back one layer of cloth after another. When he turned over the last layer, the object in the shape of a disc sent out instant glints of reflections of the rising moonlight.

I could see Wayne running the tips of his fingers over the entire jagged surface of the disc. He took a flip cigarette lighter out of his pocket, opened it, and lit the flame. When he held it close to the object, I could make out the resemblance of a human face, coarsely pieced together from chips of green stone.

Wayne held it up toward me and ran the flame in front of it.

"Do you recognize it, Matthew?"

"I'm afraid not."

He nodded. "Most wouldn't. Your friend Professor Holmes would spot it immediately. The Mayans made death masks to protect their important rulers in their journey to the afterlife. They go back to around 700 A.D."

"What stones are these? They look like jade."

"Good spotting. The eyes were made of rare seashells."

"And I assume valuable?"

He laughed again. "Right to the crux of the issue. Right, Matthew."

He turned the object over and ran his fingers over the back side of it. "One that apparently goes back as far as this and belonged to the ruler we have in mind, the right collector will pay half a million. Isn't that right, Yusuf?"

Yusuf's grin became genuine. "Oh yes. Oh yes. And more, as you would know, Mr. Barnes."

Wayne swung his legs over the deck-lounge toward me. He sat up and very carefully replaced the wrapping that had covered the mask. He stood up and walked toward the man. "And the key to its value is that it is absolutely authentic."

Wayne looked down at the grinning eyes of Yusuf for several seconds. I think I let out a yell that came from the pit of my stomach when Wayne hurled the wrapped object over the side of the yacht, into the pitch blackness that absorbed it with barely a splash.

I thought that the man would crumble to the deck. He barely held his balance. In the blackness of the night, I couldn't make out his features, but I know to a certainty that every drop of blood left his face.

Wayne called a uniformed attendant.

Before the man moved, Wayne took hold of his arm. I was almost as frozen to the spot as the man. I think we were both certain that he would be following the object into the blackness below.

Wayne held him close enough to speak directly into his ear, but spoke loudly enough, I'm sure, so that I could hear.

"It's a fake, Yusuf. I'm sure you know that. But you'll live to do me a service. You're a delivery boy. Nothing more. I want you to take a message back to Istanbul. I want you to say just this. 'You had my trust. I give it sparingly, and not twice. Rest assured, we'll speak of this again.' Do you have that, Yusuf?"

The man nodded.

Wayne signaled his attendant. "Take him back."

The man was escorted, practically carried toward the back of the vessel. In a few minutes, I could see running lights heading away from the yacht.

Wayne sat back down. "What do you think, Matthew? One more planter's punch before dinner?"

I could only smile at the abrupt change of tone and subject.

"No? Then shall we go in to dinner? The chef should be prepared by now."

When he stood up, I saw that he took something from under his deck-lounge. My mouth sprung open when a glint of light from an opening door of the yacht cabin lit up the death mask. I could see amusement in the smile of my host.

"What on earth did you throw overboard?"

"Oh, that. I substituted my lap tray in the wrapping for the death mask. I'll keep the mask."

"But if it's a fake . . ."

"It is, but a fake by a well-respected forger of these antiquities. It has enough value for that reason alone to pay the expenses I've already incurred in acquiring it. Shall we go to dinner?"

CHAPTER FIFTEEN

DINNER WITH WAYNE was much like the poetic chat of Lewis Carroll's walrus and the carpenter. The time had indeed come to talk of many things. And we did, still none of them touching on the quest of the Monkey's Paws, or, more to the point, why I was there. That did not, however, detract from the charm of my host or the sublime quality of his Bajan chef.

Immediately after the ritual of brandy and cigars, most likely of Cuban origin, the evening came to an abrupt halt. The hour was ten. Wayne rose from his chair with a distinct air of finality.

"Tomorrow we begin early. You'll be awakened before dawn. Dress in the clothes laid out for you. We have a mission that will likely be life-changing for both of us. 'Til then, sleep well."

Before I could respond, my guide, Emile, still in suit and tie, was beside me leading the way to my cabin for the night. As Emile led me slowly up an outside flight of stairs, I glanced back at the foredeck. I could just make out the moonlit silhouette of my host standing on the prow. For no reason I can put my finger on after an evening of charm and grace, I had a fleeting image of Captain Ahab on the bridge of the *Pequod*.

* * *

Given the quantity of planter's punch, wine, and brandy consumed, not to mention the consummate feast of Bajan delicacies, my mind and body were ready to drift into the first unbroken sleep I could recall. It ended abruptly seven hours later with the appearance of Emile at my bedside whispering, "It's time, Mr. Shane. Come. He's waiting. Your clothes are there."

I hustled through a quick shave with the implements provided and slipped into the bathing suit and tank top set out on a chair. A fine cotton robe was provided to complete the ensemble.

My host, Wayne, was at breakfast when I arrived. His "Good morning, Matthew" had enough steam behind it to suggest that I serve myself from the sideboard breakfast buffet with dispatch. The time for relaxed luxuriating over food or drink had apparently passed.

I served myself and took a seat at the table with Wayne. A uniformed attendant kept our cups brimming with coffee strong enough to chase away any mental cobwebs and the spiders that spun them. Conversation was clipped and minimal.

At some point, Wayne leaned over and spoke quietly. "We have a mission. I know you've had enough experience with diving to help me pull this off. That's why you're here."

"Is there time to tell me what 'this' is?"

"Yes. Briefly. I know you've been told of that midnight poker game in Cairo six months ago. That was the night the Monkey's Paw Society came into being. Just five of us—your Professor Holmes included. The old seaman who joined us that night for one hand of poker threw more than an ante into the pot. Losing the poker hand was his way of giving us each a folded parchment with a clue. We were each to keep our clues secret from the others until we were instructed to disclose them one by one. I don't know why the regimen. He might have been keeping us honest with each other. Apparently, the combination of clues would lead to something an archeologist would die for. Anticipating your next question— whatever it is apparently has an extraordinary dollar value as well. All this you already know."

How he knew that I had no idea. He seemed open to no other response than a simple "Yes."

"Good. You also know that, so far, only one of the parchment clues has been opened to the rest of us. That first expedition to Jamaica was cut short by the murder of our three Jamaican guides. You're aware of that too."

"Yes."

"I followed the old seaman's rules. In fact, I didn't even open my parchment until I returned from Jamaica. That old sailor seems to have tailored the clues to each of our capabilities. My clue is what brought us here. It told me that—"

"Wait a minute, Wayne. Given all the secrecy, why are you telling it to me?"

"Two reasons. First, I need your help to follow up on the clue. Second, I feel secure. Is there any doubt in your mind about what I could, and most certainly would, do to you, and possibly others, if you ever betray my trust? Any doubt whatsoever?"

Now I knew the cards were on the table. "No doubt at all."

"Then shall we proceed? There's reason for action without delay here."

"Yes."

"Good. I was saying, my parchment disclosed the exact location of a sunken Spanish ship. The *Nuestra Regina*. In spite of the Christian name, it was a slaving ship. It brought slaves from the west coast of Africa to Barbados."

"I didn't realize slavery ever reached Barbados."

"It began here in the British-held Caribbean. Around 1636, British investors formed the first Black Slave Society to squeeze their profits out of the most inhumane brutality to slaves that occurred in the islands. Black Africans were imported as disposable labor to make a money machine out of the sugar plantations.

"That same ship, the *Nuestra Regina*, would then sail from Barbados to Panama City, Panama, to pick up a cargo of gold, silver, and gems to carry back to the Spanish throne, feeding the empire. On one of those legs, just off the coast of Panama on the way back to Spain, it was captured at sea by the pirate Henry Morgan. He added it to his fleet. What happened to it from there, no one knew."

"You say, 'knew.' Past tense."

"The writing in my parchment gives the exact location where the *Nuestra Regina* is lying at the bottom of the Caribbean Sea."

"Off Panama?"

"No. Apparently Henry Morgan or one of the pirate lieutenants in his fleet sailed it to a position just south of Jamaica. It was sunk in a battle. Right here. We cruised here last night. We should be right above it."

"Did anyone dive down to it before this?"

"According to my parchment, no. You and I'll be the first."

"Why hasn't someone done it before? Are we looking for gold doubloons, silver, treasure?"

"No. The parchment suggested that before it was sunk, nothing of value was left aboard. That may be why no one's looked for it. There are plenty of old wrecks on these sunken sandbars."

"Then why are we here?"

"According to the clue in my parchment, there's a box somewhere in the ship that holds a writing that ties in with the other four clues to find the real pot of gold—whatever that is."

"Wouldn't anything written be dissolved by seawater after these centuries?"

Wayne was out of his chair and heading for the door. "Let's find out, Matthew."

I followed him to the aft deck where I saw two sets of scuba gear that were so far out of my price range, I'd have made the trip just to try it on.

In fifteen minutes, we were at the break in the rail of the bottom deck. We were suited up in full scuba gear. Wayne was about to slip in his mouthpiece. Just before he covered his mouth, I tapped him on the shoulder. He glanced around with a "What now?" look.

"One last question. Why the big hustle? We couldn't be more alone out here."

"I got a message yesterday morning from a man I do business with. He lives in Marseille. He'd been contacted by a man who claimed to be the old seaman who started all of this at a poker game in Cairo. The old seaman was not quite as far out of this game as he'd like to be. He sent me a warning. It includes you. Ours may not be the only oars in the water here. That was when I sent Emile for you."

"Did the old sailor say who else was after it?"

"No. My man in Marseille is reliable. When he says, 'Get in there and get out, and do it *now*,' I do it. It's how I stay . . . afloat, you might say. Now. Let's go. Stay close."

That was his last word. He was over the side and into the water. Anything more I had to say would be said to bubbles. I followed him through that particular moment that only those who dive can comprehend—an instantaneous passing, as through Alice's looking glass, into a world as alien as outer space, the submerged realm of the sea.

Wayne was ten feet ahead, clearly visible through the most crystalline water I'd ever entered. We dove straight down in tandem through ten feet, twenty feet, thirty feet. The more filtered the sun, the less light that penetrated until we entered a depth of moving outlines and shadows.

I followed his lead. My eyes were on any of the moving forms picked up below by the bath of light from our lanterns. Then, a moment came over me like an enlightenment. As we dove closer, the vast shadow of merely suggested outlines below us took on a single massive form.

Great lengths of poles and crossbars jutted at slanting angles affixed to a mammoth ark. The closer we came, the more my imagination could fashion a galleon of three masts, stripped and abandoned, recumbent and still, sleeping on its side.

We swam together from the mainmast to the prow. Gaping holes eaten into the sides of the hold gave a chilling view inside of a long rotting slave dungeon, cleared of everything but long rows of chains with ankle locks. Nearly four hundred years later, the immense weight of human agony that still clung to the walls like an invisible shroud was numbing.

We circled the prow back around the hull, peppered with large, circular holes, to the mainmast. I felt Wayne's fingers lock onto my arm. I followed the language of his free arm. He would scour the starboard side of the cabins on the third deck astern. He waved me to cover the port side. He mimed a reminder that our quest was some sort of box that could be holding a book. We were to meet back at the same spot amidships in no more than fifteen minutes. I tapped his hand twice for agreement.

The aft half of the galleon was like the torso of a sleeping giant, moss covered and streaming with swaying strands of greenish-brown growth. It seemed solid as a rock from a distance, but centuries of rot were evident in every surface picked up by my light. I could sense that one crumbling beam could bring it down like a house of cards.

I skirted the port side, rising with the third deck directly to the stern. The captain's cabin was always the farthest aft on the top deck. If the book we were after had significant value, it made sense to start with the captain's quarters and move down the chain of command.

I finally spotted the entry I was hoping for. A row of four heavily leaded stained-glass windows astern lined the back wall of what I assumed to be the captain's cabin. Three were intact. One had succumbed to the forces of time. It lay gaping open like an invitation from the former master of that ill-starred hulk.

I prayed to God that my girth with the tank on my back would not wedge solidly in the opening. I suddenly realized the impossibility of one of Wayne's size passing through any of the openings I'd seen. Perhaps that was why he needed an ally of my dimensions.

I tucked every appendage in as tightly as I could and swam straight through the window into the still blackness of the cabin inside.

Time was fleeting, which coincided perfectly with my desire to get the hell out of there. My light beam picked up the decayed trappings of what small luxuries were enjoyed by the captain of a Spanish galleon. Cabinets and shelves that once held books and personal items lined the walls. A bed against the wall and the remains of what might have been a dining table and two chairs were still secured to the floor.

I could scan the space quickly, since even the cabinets had lost the doors that would have concealed the insides. My focus was Wayne's description of some kind of box, hopefully still intact. The most prominent and well-preserved feature in the cabin was a solid block of wood the size of a small desk in the center of the room. I could only guess that it was the chart stand used by the captain to plot the galleon's course.

I scanned it with the beam from every side and angle. There was no seam, no openable crevice to be found. Just before accepting total failure, I ran the beam across the floorboards around the chest. One slight line of shadow a foot long, running under the massive block, gave me hope. I used a knife attached to my dive belt to dig and pry at the crevice until one of the boards came loose. I managed to pry it just high enough to get my fingers under it and lift. The rot in the board caused it to break free.

Now the beam picked out a small enclosure under the floorboards. That was it. I could just make out a small box-like shape, blackened with age, large enough to hold the shape of a book.

I managed to pull it free of the hedging floorboards. I just knelt there holding it for the seconds necessary to get back my breath—and to thank God for what felt like the first minor, perhaps major, victory since the entire odyssey had begun.

My mind took a few more seconds to wonder whose hands must have touched that box last over four hundred years ago.

I relished the moment, knowing it might not last.

It didn't.

CHAPTER SIXTEEN

I WAS JOLTED out of the moment when a bolt of panic ran through me like an electric shock. I felt, or sensed, a thud that seemed to reverberate through the whole cabin.

I flashed my light on the back windows. Nothing was moving, but I could swear that the middle two panes, about four feet across, had been bowed inward.

Ten seconds of pregnant silence. My consuming fear was of being trapped by the collapse of the entire rotting cabin around me.

Before I could plan, let alone make a move, a second shock wave struck. This one felt like twice the power of the first. My light was still on the windows. I could see the bulge bursting toward me. The glass shattered. Only the metal framework held. Something grayish-black and alive was battering inward. It backed off, only to drive again. And again. And again.

The framework bowed more with each thrust. It barely held under the last charge. My mind went from frozen fear to grasping at any possible action. The only way out was being battered to pieces.

I scanned the walls and ceiling with the light beam. My mind was groping for something I thought I'd seen before the attack. Just before the next strike, I saw it. It was hung from the ceiling.

I checked back at the windows. The thing was gathering steam for the next thrust. Its ice-cold eyes were now fixed on mine. I knew its next drive would carry it straight to its quarry.

I reached up and pulled the ten-foot metal-braced harpoon down free of its mounting. I thanked God it was the real thing, not some mock decoration.

Without a fraction of a second to spare, I braced the butt end against the most solid thing in the room—the anchored chart table. I swung the cold steel of the barbed point around to face into the attacker's path.

And I waited. Somehow, I don't know how, my fear morphed into the coldest calm I have ever felt in my life. My eyes were now lasers piercing into his. I could see fire building into his glare at probably the first thing that had ever faced him head-on.

The wait was eternal—or maybe four seconds. One phrase echoed repeatedly but quietly through my consciousness—"God be with me."

Then it came—the pent-up power of a solid ton of muscle and sinew driven to kill. It smashed through what was left of the windows and wall like straw. There was nothing left between us.

It came faster than I thought possible. In the last twenty feet of the attack, the great jaws flew open. Two gaping rows of teeth came for my head and chest. Its aim was dead on. But so was mine.

At the last instant, I pointed the business end of the ten-foot harpoon at the dead center of that gaping jaw. I forced the butt end as hard as I could against the chart block. I let the lunge of the beast do the rest.

It happened in a flash. Those gaping teeth drove for my face. The steel blade of the harpoon disappeared into its mouth. I could feel it pierce deeper and deeper into whatever organs lay behind its throat.

I closed my eyes and ramped up the praying. The first contact quivered the shaft of the harpoon. But it held. I could sense the blade penetrating until it must have struck something vital. The forward thrust of the beast gave way to a sharp vibration through its entire body. And then it stopped cold.

I could now see most of the twenty, maybe thirty-foot length of the creature. The part of its body that made it through the window sank slowly to the floor, skewered on the nearly swallowed harpoon.

It was over. There was nothing I wanted more than to drop down myself, just breathe, and get my heart back inside my chest. A rumbling somewhere in the ship reminded me that those rotting timbers had been shaken to the core by the assault. How long they'd hold was not another gamble I was up for.

I grabbed the box we came for under my arm like a fullback hitting the defensive line. There was barely enough room to squeeze between the mangled frame of the window and the back end of the beast's body.

I was nearly out when I caught sight of Wayne coming around the starboard side. I could see his eyes growing wider as he watched my final squeeze through the wedge.

I signaled him that I had the box. I also made clear an urgent desire to get to the surface and back on the deck of his yacht. He nodded, but his eyes were still like a couple of half-dollars.

*   *   *

Within twenty minutes, we were stripped of the scuba gear, wrapped in a cotton robe, lying on lounges on the foredeck, and ingesting a well-laced planter's punch. Wayne afforded me that much time before the question burst out of him. "Matthew, do you know what the hell that thing was?"

The best I could do was, "A fish."

"That was a fully grown tiger shark. The three deadliest sharks in the world are the great white, the bull shark, and your recent acquaintance, the tiger shark. How in hell did you . . . ?"

"Hell had nothing to do with it." I pointed to heaven and the one who had pulled it off for me, as I'd prayed.

He gave me time to piece together my recounting of the episode. Wayne listened, just shaking his head. When I finished, he raised his glass. "Son, here's to you. A bit more than I had in mind when I sent you the invitation. A bit more than you expected?"

We clicked glasses in agreement.

For the first time since we came back on deck, I noticed that the anchors were up and we were picking up speed. I looked at Wayne. "We're off?"

He pointed with his glass to something port and astern. I elbowed up to look around. I could see in the distance a power boat, about a quarter the size of Wayne's, aimed in our direction and skimming the water at a rapid clip. Wayne gave it a long scan with binoculars.

One of the officers in Wayne's crew came up beside us. He whispered something in Wayne's ear. Wayne just shook his head. "Not yet. Let's see their intentions."

We continued at the same speed for another two minutes. Wayne kept the binoculars focused. The chase ship continued to gain on us until I could read the lettering on the side. *The Sea Hunter.*

The officer beside us was getting more antsy the closer it came. He whispered another question that sounded more like an urging. Wayne held on. "No. Hold it steady. I want to see—"

From the direction of the boat, I heard several rapid cracks. Even through the roar of the wind, they could only be gunfire. An instant later, spits of water shot up in the wake behind us. Wayne yelled, "That's it. We know their intentions. Full speed."

The officer shot a hand signal to the man on the bridge. The response was instant. The yacht thrust forward with a force that pressed me back against the lounge. The prow rose out of the water and planed back down.

We were coursing over wave-tops at a speed beyond anything I could imagine from a yacht that size. The boat to our rear began dropping farther and farther behind until it was a dot on the horizon, and then nothing.

By this time, Wayne and I had gone back inside the lounge. The box I had brought up from the *Nuestra Señora* was sitting on the table between us.

Wayne seemed hesitant. "Matthew, you have no idea how much has gone into this moment. You know some of the lives that have been lost so far."

I was stung again by the memory of Professor Holmes. "I know."

"Actually, you don't. What you've seen is the tip of the iceberg. No matter. We're here now. This next moment may change our lives in ways you can't imagine, or . . ."

"Then let's do it."

He nodded. He lifted the box, about the size of a jewelry case, now cleaned down to its coating in silver. Two latches held the lid tight.

Wayne slipped his finger under one of the latches. It snapped open with an ease that surprised both of us. The second was just as easy. Wayne placed the box on the table between us and looked up.

I said, "Go for it."

He needed the edge of a blade to pry the lid open the first inch. After that, it slid fully open.

Amazingly, after four centuries under seawater, the inside was dry. Wayne lifted what appeared to be a leather-covered logbook out of the case as if it were a Fabergé egg. He laid it on the table.

"Go ahead, Matthew. You've earned the honor."

I delicately lifted the cover, expecting the inside pages to crumble to dust. They didn't. In fact, the book was as well preserved as any volume in Hawthorne University's rare book collection.

Wayne leaned in with a magnifying glass. He scanned, word by word, the handwriting the length of the first inside page. I gave him a minute to look up. "Is it what you were hoping for?"

He took a deep breath before a tentative, "I think so."

He scanned two more pages before he leaned back with a smile. "Yes. I'm sure of it."

"Is it the clue your parchment mentioned?"

"Yes. This is it."

Now the grin was on my face. "So what now?"

"We reap the reward."

"Meaning?"

"First, we read a tale written in the hand of one who lived a life you and I can't even imagine. That's for starters. And then we put the pieces together for the quest of a lifetime."

"You mean whatever the Monkey's Paws were after."

"Of course."

He stood and picked up the book. I stopped him with the question I'd put off as long as I could. "Wayne, I need an answer to this."

He looked down. "I know."

"I'll ask it anyway. Why am I here? You could have handled that dive. The fish part was unexpected. Why me?"

He took a breath. "I'll tell you anything you want to know. But this comes first. I'll have a photocopy made of it right now. It should be ready by this evening when we reach shore. I want the both of us to read every word. Then we'll talk."

"Do I take a copy back to Salem with me?"

"I don't think you should go back just yet. Stay in Barbados a couple of days, at least until we read this. And talk."

"There are things I need to—"

"Matthew, the men in that boat out there. They want the information in this book. Your life would be a minor price to pay. You've seen enough death to understand that."

"And if I stay?"

"I can keep you out of harm's way."

*   *   *

The moon was well up when the yacht's engines stopped several hundred yards from a dark shore. A craft small enough to be used for water-skiing pulled alongside.

Wayne walked me out to where a ladder ran off the side of the yacht. He handed me a wrapped package. I assumed it held a copy of the book. "Go now, Matthew. I'll be in touch tomorrow."

The ride to the shore was slow, quiet, and without lights. The Bajan man who drove docked on the shore. With few words, he led me up the dark beach to the seaside entrance of what looked like an island resort of unquestioned luxury.

Given the stealth, I asked in a whisper, "Where do I check in?"

His voice was low as well. "You don't. Everything's been arranged. Follow me, please."

The suite he led me to faced the ocean on the top floor. It was at least three steps above the price range I would have booked for myself. I again found everything I could need, from clothing down to toothpaste. Within ten minutes of my arrival, a knock on the door announced delivery of an exquisite dinner.

I ate by candle on the patio, listening to the rhythms of the sea. When I finished, I felt the day catching up with me. I could easily have slipped between the sheets and been out cold in the next breath. Only the tug of intense curiosity trumped the urge to sleep.

I unwrapped the sheaf of pages and settled in.

The words began: *My name is Dylan. I was seventeen, yet large for my age, when I was called from the Welsh farm of my raising to a life at sea. Had I resisted that call, my life could be told in a single page.*

CHAPTER SEVENTEEN

From the Memoir of Dylan Llewellyn
Anno Domini 1672

My name is Dylan. I was seventeen, yet large for my age, when I was called from the Welsh farm of my raising to a life at sea. Had I resisted that call, my life could be told in a single page. As it is, there is more to tell than time to tell it.

From the age I could first read, a wealthy man of our village fed my ravenous curiosity with every scrap of writing he brought back from his far-flung travels. It could be said that I went to sea well before my teen years. My young mind inhaled every volume that reached our town, but it was the tales of those who lived and died by the cutlass on the decks of pirate galleons that captured my dreams.

It was through those writings that I realized that I would not be the first lad of Llanrumney to heed the lure of the sea. For eight years, I savored every written word that came to us from the West Indies of the gallant doings of another lad of our town. He rose from ship-hand to chosen captain of a sea-going band of brigands—more feared by the Spanish crown than any other that sailed under the black flag. I put pen to this memoir to attest to his gallantry. His name is Captain Henry Morgan.

It was a cold October morning. I left home and all that I knew for the port city of Bristol with one goal—to be at sea. The dock area of Bristol was lined with ale-houses trafficked by men who smelled of the sea. For no good reason, I chose the Crow's Nest.

It was nine in the evening. The din of a crowd, already raucous with rum, was my first awakening. I was jostling my way to the barman and an ear that I might catch for a question. I felt a hand under my arm and a tug toward the far end of the bar. I clung tighter to the roll of shirts and spare shoes in a bundle under my arm. I looked around at a face that was more hair than skin with a grin that was sparse on teeth.

"A bit out of your element, laddie? You look in need of a friend. Come over here with old Flint. Let's see if we can sort you out."

We were at the bar before I could answer. The old man at my arm was calling the barman and ordering two rums. When they came, the old man pushed one in front of me and slugged down the other in a gulp. I didn't move. He looked up at me. "Not to your taste, laddie? Well, we mustn't waste it." He slugged down the second.

The barman was standing with a hand out for the price. The grin on the wrinkled old face broadened. He said to the barman, "This round's on the lad here—in repayment for the good direction I'll be givin' him."

He nudged me with an elbow. "Pay the man, laddie. I'll be makin' it up to ya in good advice."

I could think of nothing to do but to give the man at the bar some of the change I'd kept deep in my pocket.

"There's a good lad. Now let's find a table." He winked at the barman. "We'll take the bottle for good measure."

Another nudge with the elbow and he walked off to a corner table. The barman caught me by the arm with one hand and held out the other. I pulled out more of my diminishing coins to buy release from his grip.

I followed old Flint to the table. I sat across from him while he continued to take draughts direct from the bottle. He finally wiped his beard with his sleeve and looked up at me.

"Now, laddie. How do they call you?"

"Dylan."

"Ah. A fine Welsh name. You look fresh from the fields. Never set foot on a deck tossed by the sea. Never clung to riggin' that's whip't by the wind. Am I right?"

I just nodded.

"You'll be needin' a ship under a worthy captain. One to teach ya the ropes, as we say. Let's see now."

His tiny eyes went scanning face to face around the room. I could see his ragged eyebrows lift when he spied a heavy-set block of a man with skin creased like leather around eyes that looked cold as shucked oysters.

Old Flint tapped my arm. "Sit here, laddie. I'll do ya a good turn for the rum."

He scuttled across the room. I saw him whisper into the ear of the man at the table. The man turned those cold eyes on me. Old Flint looked back and gave me a sign to stand. I did. The man looked at me like my father would look at a heifer before making a bid.

The man gave a slight nod. I saw something pass between the hand of the man and Flint. Flint came back to me. He took me by the elbow and led me toward the door.

"You're a lucky lad this day. You can thank old Flint. I've got you signed onto the crew of the best merchant ship in the port. Come quick. We'll get ya aboard before he changes his mind."

I knew no better than to go with Flint. I could only think to ask, "Where does it sail to?"

"Ah, you're in luck there too. She sails with the morning tide. Jamaica. It's in the West Indies."

And well I knew it was. My heart was dancing. From all I'd heard, Port Royal on the island of Jamaica was home port to the man I wanted more to see than anyone on earth—my fellow Welshman, Captain Henry Morgan.

We walked double-time to the end of a wharf. A swaying plank with ropes on the side led up to the deck of a ship twice the size of any building I'd ever seen. I could see little of the ship's features in the dark, but I counted two large masts with a smaller one in the rear against the half-moon. The creaking sounds of wood scraping in rhythm with the waves gave my blood a boost just to know that at dawn I'd be at sea.

Old Flint led me up the plank. He exchanged a few whispered words with a gruff-spoken figure at the top. The only thing I understood was what I took to be my first order as a seaman. "Stand here."

The man barked another order and a second man I assumed to be a crewman appeared. I heard the order, "Take him below."

Old Flint gave me one last grin. "Now, laddie. You go with him. Do as you're told. You'll make a fine seaman."

I followed the lantern held by the man leading me to what I assumed would be my bunk for the voyage. He led down steps to what must have been the lowest region of the ship. There was a door that he opened with a key. The chamber was dark, but by the lantern's light, I could see five or six others, my age or older at a guess, asleep on bunks.

The man held the lantern high enough to point out an empty bunk. No words passed his lips, but I took it as an order. The door closed behind me. I found the bunk in the dark. I'd been walking for days with little food in my stomach. I was asleep as soon as I hit the bunk.

Some hours later, a jab to my ribs brought me around. There was daylight coming through high slits of openings to the outside. I was aware of a hand thrusting a metal plate of gray gruel in front of me.

"Take it. Eat it before those others come for it. It's the last food you'll see for this day."

The words sank in slowly. I rose up on my elbow and took the plate. The lad in front of me, my size but no older than me at a guess, made a sign that I was to eat with my fingers and do it quickly.

Beyond sleep, food was my most immediate need after the trek. I finished it in short order before looking up.

I heard a whispered "What's your name?"

"Dylan."

"A word, Dylan. Tomorrow, be up and ready when they push the plates through the hole. They'll not let me pull this off twice."

"Who?"

"Them. Those five. They've been here longer than me. It's every lad for himself down here."

For the first time, I was aware of the tossing and rolling of the ship. I looked in his face. "We're at sea. Are you part of the crew too?"

"Are you that simple, lad? You don't get it. You've been tricked. We all have."

"Meaning what?"

"We've been shanghaied. When they get us to Jamaica, they'll sell the lot of us to the sugar plantations. They call it indentured servitude. It's slavery for white lads like us. The only difference from the black blokes is we can work it off with seven years' labor."

"Seven years?"

"Forget it. They'll have worked us to death before we ever see a day of freedom. Gimme the plate."

"Wait. Who are you? Why did you help me?"

"Name's Angwyn. I heard you talk in your sleep. You're from around Cardiff. Your accent. So am I. We have to stick together, for the little good it'll do us."

*   *   *

For the next week, two weeks, heaven knows how long, the days were marked only by the light or dark I could see in the slit openings at the top of the chamber that held us, and the pushing of metal plates of the same thick gruel through the opening in the door after every sunrise.

Angwyn and I were the only ones to exchange words. We mostly talked of our lives on the farms in Wales to keep our sanity. As the days wore on, we heard voices and sounds from the deck above that caused us to wonder if the lives of the crewmen were much better than our wretched existence. The grumblings of the crew made it clear that their number had been cut to the bone to make room for more cargo, so that each man was being worked almost beyond his tolerance.

The first port of call we gathered from the chatter above was off the coast of northwest Africa to take on a large number of black slaves to be crammed into the chamber forward of ours. From the voices we heard, many of the crew had not been aware of the cargo they'd be carrying. Some openly objected. When we were at sea again, we heard a gruff voice, slurred with drink. We came to know it as the captain's. He called all the crew to the deck. He ordered those he had heard grumbling to be tied to the mast. The sounds of the whippings and cries that followed gave us a view of life at sea that neither of us had counted on.

The grumbling of the men from that day on were in hushed tones. They took on what Angwyn and I judged to be the sounds of an approaching rebellion. The whippings had caused there to be even fewer able men on deck to obey the demands of the captain. When the work of any exhausted crewman failed to meet the captains demands, the sounds of the lash in the hands of the officers were sure to follow. The climax came the day the captain drove the men beyond their endurance. He tried to push them a step faster by ordering their rations and rum cut by half.

It was that same day that a voice we judged to come from aloft in the crows-nest called out the approach of a ship from the starboard side. She flew the black flag of piracy.

The captain barked orders to turn to starboard and hoist all sail to outrun her for the shelter of an island just beyond the horizon. There came a garble of rough voices of the crewmen that sounded like the outbreak of an open rebellion. We heard a rush of footsteps toward the voice of the captain. There were shots and screams and sounds of hand-to-hand scuffles. At last, the cheers of the crewmen said the captain and his officers had been overcome.

One of the crewmen seemed to be taking command. He ordered the man at the wheel to turn toward the approaching pirate ship. He ordered another to run up a makeshift white flag.

It was an hour or more before Angwyn and I heard the hard rubbing of wood. We both guessed it was another ship tying up to the side of ours. New voices were heard clambering aboard. One voice in particular—we assumed it was the captain of the pirate ship—was ordering his men to bind the captain and his officers and to call the crew of our ship to line up on the deck.

There was some shuffling about, and then silence. We heard the voice of the pirate captain. "Crewmen! Men of the Sea! I'll make you an offer. The choice is yours as free men with no harm either way. I've need of able seamen to man ships of my fleet. Make no mistake. We fly the black flag. The sea is our kingdom. We live as we choose. We take what we choose. No man is our master. If you come to join the Brethren of the Sea, you'll get an equal vote on who captains your ship, and where to plunder the richest treasure. The covenant you'll sign will grant you an equal share of the bootie taken with every man of the crew.

"But know it well. At the height of combat, you'll be expected to earn every Spanish peso with grit and valor. If need be, for loss of a

leg, you'll get 600 added pesos, a hand, 600 pesos, an eye, 500 pesos. That's a month of good rum in Port Royal for the loss."

While the captain spoke, we could hear footsteps coursing about the ship. Suddenly, the door to our chamber was thrown open. After weeks in that hole, the light was blinding, then welcome, as was the rush of fresh salt air.

We heard a voice yell to the pirate captain, "There's men locked below. White men. And a hold of black slaves." The captain gave orders to bring both up from below. The black slaves were brought out to the deck first. We could hear the captain tell his men to remove their chains. The sight of them must have caused him to order that food and water be given immediately.

We heard the captain address the slaves, now freed men. "Do any of you understand my words?"

One stepped forward. "I was owned for a year by a white Englishman in North Africa."

"Then tell these men they'll be fed and cared for. We'll take you to an island inhabited by Maroons, escaped slaves. You can make your way from there."

By this time, Angwyn and I and the other boys had been brought on deck. The sun was still all but blinding. When I looked in the direction of the pirate captain's voice, I could only make out a tall figure against the glare.

He looked down on the seven of us. "Do you understand my language?"

One of the boys yelled, "We do. We're all Englishmen."

I yelled, out of a quick impulse. "Not all! My friend and I are Welshmen."

The captain looked down at Angwyn and me with a keen eye. "From where, lads?"

Angwyn yelled, "Cardiff City."

I yelled, "Llangwyn."

The captain looked at the seven of us. "Did you hear the offer I made the crew?" There were nods. "Then I make you the same offer. If you'll take the oath of the Brethren, step forward."

Angwyn and I took the first step. Then all followed with a whole-hearted commitment.

"Then join you shall." He turned to look directly at Angwyn and me. "You two. Up here. Stand by my side."

I heard the coarse voice of the merchant ship's captain from the mast where he was tied. "And what of us? You'll not be joining us with that scurvy lot of scum. I'm twenty years a captain. I'll be treated as a captain."

The pirate captain beside us gave a nod and said, "And so you shall." He ordered the lowering of the flimsy life-boat to the water. When it was afloat, he ordered the merchant captain and his four officers to be dropped into it.

He yelled down to them, "This is your new vessel to command, Captain. It's better treatment than you've given these men. Hear me. There's an island due west. It's the only one in reach. If you put your backs to the oars, you can be ashore by first light tomorrow."

I heard the bellowing voice of the merchant captain from below. "I'll see you hung from the highest gallows in London."

"You'll have to reach London yourself first. A word of advice. Be cautious of the natives on that island. The last captain we dropped there was served up for their dinner."

The small boat was cut loose from the ship. The pirate captain beside me yelled down to them one last word. "If you ever do see London again, give my regards to the king. Tell him I appreciate the use of his ship. He has the thanks of Captain Henry Morgan."

CHAPTER EIGHTEEN

Memoir of Dylan Llewellyn (continued)

From that moment, the orders came fast. The man I now knew to be my fellow Welshman, Captain Henry Morgan, spoke first to his own crew. "Time's not on our side, lads. Look sharp." As fast as he spat out an order, it was seen to by the men of his band.

The black slaves were given food and clean water. Those who were able pitched in with the chores going on around them.

That done, the captain gathered the crew of the merchant ship on the deck before him once more. He laid out the quarry he sought—the Spanish treasure galleon, Nuestra Andora.

"She carries Mexican gold and Peruvian silver to feed the thirst of the Spanish king for the conquest of Europe. We have other plans for it."

I heard rumblings of disquiet among the merchant crew until one lad had the courage to yell out, "She'll be heavily armed with cannon. Can she be taken?"

Captain Morgan yelled back, "No! It's impossible."

He jumped down and spoke directly to the lad who asked, but he was addressing the whole merchant crew. "Impossible. For anyone else. But not for me. Follow my orders to the letter, lads, and by this time tomorrow, you'll have wealth to spend in Port Royal to last you for months."

His words were few, but I could see them sinking in. I could see the merchant crewmen scanning the resolute faces of Captain Morgan's crew.

He gave them a minute to think before a final word. "Decide now, lads. There's likely close combat ahead with the best Spanish fighters afloat. I'll not hold it against a man with no stomach for this life of the Brethren. But know this well. If you commit, by damn, you'll live up to it with the gallantry I expect of my own Brethren. Courage to the death, if that be your lot. Is that understood?"

There were a few whispered words among the crew.

Once more, at double the force. "Is that understood? I'll have an 'aye' or 'nay' from every one of you. I'll know the true heart of every man who fights beside me."

I was swept up in the passion of a moment I'd dreamed of from the age of ten. From his side, I yelled in a voice to be heard back in Llanrumney, "Aye, Captain."

Angwyn's lusty "Aye, Captain" followed mine. I saw a faint smile creep across the captain's mouth.

The merchant crew's voices began coming, first from a few, then more in rapid succession, until the "Aye, Captain" of every merchant crewman had been heard.

The captain leaped back up on the deck above. "Then that's how it is, lads. My officers know the plan. Put your hearts and your backs into their orders."

The orders came, and every able crewman was set in motion. The decks of the merchant ship were stripped of everything that occupied space. Most of it was thrown overboard. The crews of both ships and any slaves who were able set their backs to hoisting cannon over the rails from Captain Morgan's flagship, the Satisfaction, *to the deck of* the merchant ship. Twelve cannon were set in a row on the prow of the merchant ship facing forward. Spare sails were draped over them to give them the look of normal cargo.

All hands were then turned to hauling goods from below deck to be jettisoned overboard in the interest of speed.

That done, Captain Morgan placed command of the merchant ship in his own trusted officer, Captain Greene, with orders to hoist sail and set a course due east.

Captain Morgan beckoned Angwyn and me to follow him. We crossed with the rest of his own crew to his flagship.

The two ships were unbound from each other. Once the merchant ship was under sail, Captain Morgan let it take a running start. When it was a good half a league ahead, he ordered his crew to set just enough sail to keep the faster pirate ship at the same distance behind.

With all the pieces in place, the captain took Angwyn and me to his cabin. He offered us both a drop of rum. "You might as well start now, lads."

This time I accepted. I found the taste to my liking.

He spoke to us of the farm and the family he had left some eight years previous, and asked about ours. While I told him of our sheep and sows, and what crops we grew each year, I could see his mind drifting back over those Welsh fields, perhaps with a bit of longing.

We talked until the afternoon sun was three-quarters to setting. A sharp knock on the door pulled us all out of our visions of home. The captain yelled, "Open. Come."

A seaman with one sleeve hanging empty, straight scars the length of his sun-scorched face, and an accent I'd never heard opened the door. He called in, "She's there, Captain. The Nuestra Andora. Like you said. Fat and sleek and mean. I count twelve cannon on each deck. Two leagues ahead."

"Then let's have her. Signal Captain Greene to raise the white flag and head straight for her. Full sail."

Captain Morgan went to a large sea-chest and pulled up the lid. "This is your first bit of action, lads. Learn quickly. Stay aboard the Satisfaction and watch this time. But take these in case the fighting spills over to this ship."

He tossed us each a short, two-edge sheathed cutlass like we'd seen at the side of each of the pirate crew. "Carry this in your right hand. There'll be time enough to learn to use it for future battles. But this . . ."

He handed us each a flintlock pistol. "Care for it well. This has saved the life of many of the Brethren. It might someday save yours. Now come."

He led us up to the highest deck of the Satisfaction. We could see the merchant ship ahead, cutting through the waves toward a ship larger by half and flying the Spanish flag.

Captain Morgan pointed to the galleon. "She's the Nuestra Andora. See the captain's deck. He spots us."

There was a glint of light off of a glass that said the Spanish captain had spotted our merchant ship and the Satisfaction under the black flag giving chase behind her.

"Now let's give them a show."

With a signal from Captain Morgan to the men at the cannon below, a firing began that seemed to shake the very deck we stood on. Cannon balls set off explosions of water where they hit beside and behind the merchant ship ahead of us.

Another hand signal to the watchful eye of Captain Greene ahead of us and the merchant ship raised a large, billowing white flag as if begging help from the Spanish galleon. The course of the merchant ship was now directly toward the galleon under full sail.

Another reflection of light from the captain's spy-glass on the deck of the galleon and she came to starboard to sit broadside to the *oncoming merchant vessel. At Captain Morgan's order, more sail was hoisted on the* Satisfaction *to increase our speed in pursuit. I knew then that the plan was to make it look as if we were attacking the unarmed merchant ship and that Captain Greene was desperately fleeing to the protection of the heavily armed Spanish galleon.*

Captain Morgan said a quiet word for our hearing. "Now, lads. The trap's set. Will the Spanish captain take the bait? Will he let the merchant ship come within the protection of his cannon?"

He signaled another round of cannon fire to come close to the merchant ship. Again, the waters exploded, this time a bit closer. The Spanish galleon held fast. There was no response. Another five minutes and the merchant ship was clearly within the galleon's range.

I summoned the courage to ask it. "Why will a Spanish captain protect an English cargo ship?"

"That's the gamble, Dylan. I'm betting the Spanish captain has less love for a pirate ship that's sunk many of her sister ships than for a harmless cargo ship. Besides, my guess is the captain of the galleon thinks he's less rescuing than capturing an English cargo ship for whatever she's carrying."

The air was tense with the waiting. The merchant ship drew closer to the Spanish galleon every second, with our Satisfaction *in full pursuit. I could see movement around the cannon on the deck of the galleon, but she held her silence.*

Then the moment came. The merchant ship was close enough to be enfolded in the protective cannon range of the Spanish galleon. Our Satisfaction *was now also within range. The deck of the Spanish galleon erupted in clouds of black smoke. Twelve cannon on her side facing us thundered a report. Eruptions of sea-water beside us told us their cannon-fire was aimed, as hoped, at us and not the merchant ship. Their aim was good, but not perfect.*

In the next instant, Captain Greene ordered the uncovering of the cannon we'd anchored to the deck of the merchant ship. A moment later, the cannoneers fired full charges at close range. I could see splintered wood fly from the hull of the Spanish galleon. Her main mast was cracked in half.

Bare seconds later, before the galleon crew could re-aim, the merchant vessel cannoneers fired a second volley that drove smoking holes into the side of the galleon at the water-line. Within minutes, she began to list to the side towards us.

A third volley from the merchant ship's cannon, echoed by a volley of the cannon on the Satisfaction, flew true to the mark. I saw sailors and fighters on the deck of the Spanish galleon blasted from their positions at their cannon.

"Full sail! To the attack, lads!" Captain Morgan leaped down to the main deck and ran forward. Before the smoke of cannon-fire cleared, the Satisfaction was alongside the Galleon. Hooks on ropes were thrown to lash the galleon to the Satisfaction.

Angwyn and I, cutlasses in hand, ran to follow Captain Morgan to the front of the line of the pirate crew. Captain Morgan took a moment to turn to us. "Not this time, lads. You're not ready. You'll have your day. Stay here."

Before we could answer, Captain Morgan leaped on the high rail, cutlass and pistol in hand. With one yell to his Brethren, he made a bound to the deck of the Galleon. He was met with an onslaught of Spanish troops. I thought he'd be slashed to pieces by the flailing swords, but in an instant, his Brethren, swords flashing and pistols firing, were at his side.

The shrieks of pain and fear that accompanied the spilling of Spanish blood were burned in my memory forever. Curses and prayers, mostly in Spanish, rose above the clashes of steel on steel. Many a time since, I've lived through a like scene and worse, drawing blood myself in the thick of battle. But the pulse-pounding sight of that first life-or-death clash will never leave me.

From where Angwyn and I stood on the deck of the Satisfaction, I could see what Captain Morgan, in the heat of one slashing victory after another, could not. The captain of the Spanish galleon was watching the action from a secure position on the top deck. When the battle seemed all but lost to the Spanish, with most of their number lying on the deck in pools of their own blood, I could see him making his way down to the main deck. He was out of the view of Captain Morgan. I could see the sun glint off of what I now knew to be a flintlock in the Spanish captain's hand.

I knew instinctively where he was headed. Without time to think, I scrambled over the rail onto the deck of the galleon. I made my way through the fallen bodies of Spanish soldiers until I stood three paces behind Captain Morgan.

His focus was on the Spanish soldier whose every slash with a cutlass he repelled and followed with a slash of his own. Just as he drove the blade home for the kill, I could see that he was in the sights of the raised flintlock in the hand of the Spanish captain.

With no time to load my pistol, I broke forward past the dead Spanish soldier to the deck just under the Spanish captain. I think I closed my eyes before driving the cutlass in my right hand straight upward. I could feel it penetrate and heard the shriek of the captain. I heard the crash of his flintlock as it fell harmless beside me.

I turned around. Captain Morgan's eyes were on me. He understood in a glance what had happened. For one moment, frozen in my lifetime of recollections, I saw him smile and give me a salute with his flowing cutlass. That moment is with me to this very hour.

CHAPTER NINETEEN

Memoir of Dylan Llewellyn (continued)

I was shaken out of that golden moment by lusty cries of victory from the throats of every member of the pirate crew. They were picked up and echoed by the newest recruits to the Brethren band. It seemed that the death of the Spanish captain signaled with finality the conquest of the Nuestra Andora.

By now, cannon holes blasted in the hull of the galleon were below the water-line. The galleon had taken an ominous list to the port side.

Captain Morgan cut short the victory cries to set his band to the business of hauling chests of silver and gold out of the hold of the galleon before she capsized. All hands lent their backs to the task.

Mere minutes after the last chest of treasure was loaded onto the Satisfaction *and the last member of our pirate band had scrambled back over the rail, what sounded like a mighty groan rose from deep in the galleon's hull. The once unconquerable* Nuestra Andora *surrendered to the pull of the sea. She slipped slowly beneath the churning waves. And with her, the bodies of the gallant Spanish fighters went to a liquid grave.*

That night, barrels of rum were brought up onto the deck of the Satisfaction. There were sea songs lifted to the skies until the last man on deck had passed into a blurred victorious unconsciousness.

At first light, a course was set for Port Royal on the British island of Jamaica, the home port to most of the pirate Brethren of the Sea. The day before we caught sight of Jamaica's shore on the horizon, the chests of Spanish treasure were brought on deck. Before all eyes, the coins and bars, hammered out of the gold and silver mined by the Aztec and Inca slaves of their Spanish conquerors, were distributed in the agreed portions to the pirate brethren who had accomplished the impossible victory over the Nuestra Andora.

To the apparent displeasure of some of the seasoned brethren who had stormed the deck in the first assault on the Nuestra Andora, *Captain Morgan ordered that Angwyn and I were to receive a partial share. Their displeasure remained unexpressed in the presence of Captain Morgan. Regardless, the share I received was as welcome as it was unexpected, since what few coins I had left after my earlier encounter with Mr. Flint in Bristol had disappeared during my confinement with my fellow indentured servants.*

*   *   *

The docks of Port Royal became crowded with a mélange of men of the sea, bar owners, and the women who gave expensive pleasure when the sails of Captain Henry Morgan's ship were first sighted. The mob swelled to get first word of the extent of the flood of gold and silver coins our arrival would soon pour into their pockets. It was scarce sundown after our docking that word spread through the town that riotous prosperity beyond anyone's expectation had arrived at Port Royal.

For a lad from a farm in the Welsh backland, the first walk down Lime Street was like being dropped into the center of our minister's description of Sodom or Gomorrah. Saloons and houses of prostitution were crowded one upon the other in every direction. It was a kingdom ruled by the free and open practitioners of the trade of piracy. Its coffers were glutted regularly by the Brethren of the Sea, returning from the plundering of Spanish towns and treasure ships with gold and silver that needed profligate and immediate spending.

Some legitimacy, if it mattered, was lent to what could be called the conscienceless trade of piracy by English Royalty. Being at war with Spain, and lacking the funds to build a warrior fleet, the English king converted the disparate bands of pirates into his private navy by giving letters of marque, i.e., royal permission to pirate captains to plunder Spanish ships and towns at will. Under that guise of patriotism, everyone from the royal governor to the lowliest barmaid gave open welcome to those who returned to Port Royal with their plunder.

Captain Morgan kept a secluded mansion at the far side of the island. He distanced himself from the din of Port Royal, and invited Angwyn and me to board with him. He said it was for our physical safety. I suspect he had the moral survival of two callow lads from Cardiff in mind as well.

*   *   *

Not one to rest on past conquests, and true to his oft-repeated mantra, "Time is not on our side," Captain Morgan set himself in quick order to the task of laying plans for his next conquest. In the three weeks that followed his triumphant return to Port Royal, he rode the crest of fame that resulted from the one measure that mattered to other captains of the pirate trade—the value in spendable booty of his last plundering.

Angwyn and I saw little of him for those next three weeks. His full attention was taken in inducing captains of other pirate vessels, from Jamaica to the British-held island of Barbados, to join a fleet under his command, dominant enough to attempt another impossible assault. His stock in trade was his conquest of the Nuestra Andora. *Word had spread. By the time he returned to us in Port Royal, ten captains of the Brethren were considering committing their vessels to his fleet before he had yet disclosed his next quarry.*

On one evening during those three weeks, Angwyn and I gave in to our Welsh farm boy's curiosity. Contrary to the parting order of Captain Morgan, we wandered through the pulsing, riotous streets of Port Royal.

Our heads were on swivels, dodging drunken, stumbling seamen and taking in sights never dreamed of in Cardiff. We had coursed our way down half of Lime Street when we felt the soft warmth of a girl press between us. She slipped a hand under the elbow of each of us. At a glance, she looked to be in her late twenties, but some sense inside me said that she was barely older than we were.

She whispered an invitation to join her inside the saloon that stood behind her. Tempted though we were, the last words of Captain Morgan put steel in our resolution to keep walking.

When we started to pull away, her tug on our arms became more resolute. The vacuous grin on her face redoubled, but there was something more than the solicitation of a prostitute in her voice.

"I saw you when you docked. You boys are the ones with Captain Morgan. Please, listen."

The tone caught Angwyn as well. We both stopped in our tracks. She went on. "This is not for me. It's important. There's a room inside. We can talk."

Angwyn and I looked to each other for a decision. She pulled us closer with a forced laugh that had nothing to do with her tense words. "My word to God, I have a message. You have to carry it to Captain Morgan. It could mean his life. And yours."

Perhaps it was her pleading tone or the desperation in her eyes. Angwyn and I both nodded. She gave another burst of mock laughter for any ears close by. She whispered to each of us. "Give me some money. Doesn't matter how much. Do it now. Let it be seen."

We each passed her a few coins. She dropped them into a pocket in her dress. "Come with me. Quick. It wouldn't hurt to smile."

She clung to our arms as we passed through the swinging doors of a saloon that reeked of sweat and cheap rum. With a smile on her face that looked frozen in place, she led us upstairs to a room that was adorned with nothing but a bed with a well-worn bare mattress.

Once inside, she closed the door. Our first surprise was that she handed us back the coins we gave her. She pulled us close and spoke in a low, almost trembling tone.

"Can you get a message to Captain Morgan?"

I answered. "When he gets back. Yes. He's at sea . . ."

"I know what he's doing. He's getting other captains to join him for his next battle. He was here talking to some of them last week. One of them was a man named Captain Trace. Can you hear me?"

We both nodded.

"Then listen carefully. Later that night, Captain Trace was drunk. He took me. I'm one of his favorites. I heard him whispering to one of his officers. He plans to set a trap for Captain Morgan."

"How?"

"When Captain Morgan gathers the other captains together for a meeting, he'll propose the Spanish town or ship he plans for his next attack. The other captains will probably vote for it because of his last victory. When Captain Trace hears where it is, he'll send a ship to

*warn the Spanish leader there. The Spanish can build up their
fortifications. They'll be ready to crush Captain Morgan and his fleet.
The Spanish will pay Captain Trace heavily for the betrayal."*

*Angwyn and I looked at each other for a sign of belief or disbelief. I
asked her, "Why are you telling us this? What does it matter to you?"*

"That's not important."

"It is important. Why should we believe you?"

She hesitated, but then spoke in words that rang true to both of us.

*"Captain Morgan doesn't come to these places. But one night, a
drunk, a seaman who'd spent his last coin, wanted me. He couldn't
pay. There's someone who watches us to see that we collect first. I
refused to go with the seaman, but he forced me into the street and
back behind the building. He had a knife. He slashed me once, but
before he could do it again, he was hit from behind. The man who did
it picked me up. He took me to where my arm could be tended. It was
Captain Morgan."*

*She could still see hesitation in our eyes. She pulled up the sleeve of
her blouse. She showed us her arm, and we believed her.*

* * *

*It was three days later that Captain Morgan's ship docked in the
harbor. That night at dinner, we asked him if he recalled the incident
with the girl. He was first displeased that we had gone against his
wishes, but that passed when we gave him word-for-word the message
she had for him.*

*He sat silent for a minute. I broke the silence with the question we
both had. "What will you do about Captain Trace?"*

*He smiled. "Learn this, lads. In a fight at sea or on land, we all
have the same weapons, the same measure of courage. To win or lose is
a matter of chance. But hear me. What gives you the edge is this—if*

you use it." He tapped the side of his head. *"So I'll ask you. What would most men of our breed do about a traitor?"*

Angwyn and I both answered almost in unison. *"Kill him."*

He sat back and took a draught of wine. *"Hmm. I suppose."*

I asked it. *"What will you do?"*

He tapped his head again with his finger. *"Right now? Absolutely nothing."*

We looked at each other. *"And later?"*

"More of the same."

"You mean you'll let him get away with it?"

"I didn't say that. This will be your second lesson. Learn it well."

*   *   *

Two nights later, we three were back aboard Captain Morgan's ship, the Satisfaction. *One by one, ten diverse figures came aboard. Some lacked an arm or a leg. Two had a patch that covered an empty eye socket. Their garb ranged from blazing red sea-coats to no coat at all. The scars that showed bespoke vicious battles and the handiwork of crude ships' surgeons.*

The one feature in common to all of them, that both Angwyn and I noted and spoke of later, was a silent statement of carriage that said it clearly—this man is subject to no man's will but his own.

Captain Morgan took command of the meeting. "Captains! Each of you is here at my invitation, accepted as a matter of your own choice. I'm ready to go into battle with each of you at my side. We're here to agree on a prey that most of our Brethren would say can't be conquered. Well, lads, they said that of the Nuestra Andora.*"*

I noticed interested grins on some of the captains, undoubtedly remembering the flood of treasure that had kept Captain Morgan's entire crew in a state of unbridled drunken profligacy for three weeks.

Captain Morgan fed their lust for a rich harvest. "This next plundering of Spanish gold will make the Nuestra Andora *look like a lost venture. Who's up for it? Who hasn't lost his nerve for a good fight in the soft pleasures of Port Royal?"*

One of the captains shouted out. "I'll scuttle the man that calls me soft. But I'm not drunk or stupid either. I'll know first before I commit. Where does that ambition of yours take you this time, Captain Morgan?"

Captain Morgan stepped down from his platform. He strode to stand in front of the man who spoke. He said it with the finality of a firm decision. "Maracaibo."

There was first a hush, and then comments I couldn't grasp. One of the captains yelled, "I'll give you this, Morgan. You've a long reach. Perhaps this time you're reaching for your own death. And taking the lot of us with you."

Captain Morgan spoke above the grumbling. "Perhaps! Most certainly it's complete insanity—if the command were in someone else." His voice grew louder. "But not in my command! Join me, lads, and we'll do the impossible. Because you know I can."

One captain yelled from the back. "But how, Morgan? That city's the largest in Venezuela. I've seen it. Two forts have cannon trained on the Gulf. You can't come within cannon range of the city without being blown apart. You're right. It's insane."

"Captains, it was my breed of insanity that put our lads aboard the Nuestra Andora. *I'll say no more of my plan for Maracaibo until I have your names on the Articles of Agreement. But I pledge you this. I can do it. Might some of us lose our lives in the battle? Of course. But those of us who sail home will be the richest men of the Brethren on any of the seas."*

He jumped up on the platform behind him. He spread a parchment out on the table in front of him.

"*The Articles of Agreement are ready. The terms for splitting every ounce of gold we take will be to your liking. I'll have the signature of every one of you who still has the stomach for a fight—and a rich purse.*"

Angwyn and I listened to the curses and profanity-filled words exchanged by the men who had been in past battles and survived for far less reward than Captain Morgan was dangling in front of them. We both knew that it could go either way, with no odds on either side.

I was at the point of sensing defeat, when, by the look of him, the oldest captain in the room strode forward to the edge of the table. He looked Captain Morgan in the eye. "I've been in more battles, come closer to the reaper than any man in this room. If this be my last, then let it be for a prize worth dyin' for. I'll take the pen."

He signed the document and looked back over the men who were silently eyeing him. One other broke ranks and signed, then another. Within ten minutes, the names or "X"s of every captain in the room were on the document.

I glanced down at it. I noticed that the last signature on the sheet was that of the betrayer, "Captain Trace."

CHAPTER TWENTY

Memoir of Dylan Llewellyn (continued)

As the day of departure approached, word was carried quietly through the saloons and houses of Port Royal that Captain Morgan was building a crew and a fighting force. The game was on. Within two days, the best seamen and soldiers willing to follow Captain Morgan to hell and back, in varying states of sobriety, made their way aboard the Satisfaction.

They were mulattos, Italians, French, Portuguese, escaped black slaves, and survivors of indentured servitude. Many had done battle on the side of the Brethren before. Their shares of prior booty had flown freely into the pockets of the salooners and women of Port Royal. They were again penniless and welcomed the call to arms.

The day and hour for sailing finally came. The early tide carried ten vessels, from brigantines and frigates to Captain Morgan's three-masted Satisfaction, *through the sea-gate of Port Royal. I can still feel the fever in my heart at the sight of billows of white sails and black flags against the red sunrise.*

The eleventh vessel, the frigate commanded by Captain Trace, remained alone in the harbor. Captain Trace had sent word to

Captain Morgan at the last minute that necessary repairs would delay his joining the fleet for several days.

Captain Morgan received the word with unruffled calm. He confided to Angwyn and me that the news came as no surprise. "Do ya not see his plan, lads? He sent a ship ahead six days ago to warn the Spanish commander in Maracaibo. The commander there has had time to bring in enough reinforcements from the other Spanish islands to blow our fleet and every man of us to the bottom of the sea. Trace'll set sail a few days behind us. He plans to sail into Maracaibo Harbor to a hero's welcome from the Spanish. He'll expect a bountiful reward for betraying me."

I ventured the question again. "Then what will you do?"

"To Trace? I told you. Nothing."

"Then what . . . ?"

"I also told you that battles are not won by cutlasses and cannon. They're won by use of the brains God gave us. Never forget it."

We asked no more questions. Nor did we need to. When the pirate fleet, with the Satisfaction at the point, cleared the horizon out of sight of Port Royal, Captain Morgan struck all sails and dropped anchor. The other ten ships followed his lead. With all ships of the fleet at rest, he sent a hand-written message by small boat to each of the other captains.

"We change course. We head south by southwest. A different golden goose is waiting to be plucked. Portobelo. If you want out, so be it. I release you from the articles of covenant. But if you want to fill your chests with treasure, set full sails. Follow me."

When the word had reached the last ship in the line, without awaiting a reply, Captain Morgan ordered full sail, and full rudder to port. Angwyn and I scanned the sea behind us to see which, if any, of the captains would follow the new course in spite of Captain Morgan's breach of the Code of the Brethren to give each man a vote on the prey.

I dared to ask Captain Morgan. "Will they follow?"

He never looked behind us. "Aye, lad. They will. Portobelo is at the Panama end of the treasure trail from Potosi, the mountain of silver in Peru. There are enough silver pieces-of-eight in Portobelo waiting shipment to Spain to conquer half of Europe."

"But won't it be protected?"

"More than most any other city on the Spanish Main. The cannon of the two castles of Santiago and San Felipe guard each side of the harbor. Sir Francis Drake tried to take Portobelo by direct assault. He died in the attempt. It's impregnable."

"Then why will the other captains join us?"

He looked at me directly. There was a sharpness in his tone. "Have ya not learned yet, lad? They'll follow me."

I asked no more questions, but I looked back. The sails of all nine ships behind us had caught the gusty wind south for Portobelo.

*   *   *

We cruised south for days. None in the fleet of ten but Captain Morgan was aware of his strategy. To a man, the crews and captains behind us focused on booty enough for a month-long drunk in Port Royal. It helped drive out the sense of impending death by cannon blast or cutlass in an assault on Portobelo.

Finally, in the black heat of a moonless night, at Captain Morgan's order, we anchored off the shore of the bay of Boca de Toros, well south of Portobelo. Nearly five hundred men lowered themselves from the ten ships into the tiny boats that had been stored on the decks. Under cover of darkness, we paddled north, barely in sight of the moonlit shore.

Before the rising of the sun, we beached and hid on the steaming, tree-covered shore. We slept in the dank, mosquito-infested underbrush until in darkness we slipped our boats back into the waves and paddled north silently in the current all night.

Just before our fourth dawn of rowing by night and sleeping by day, our fleet of rowers came upon a tiny fishing boat. Two black men and a zambo, a man of mixed African and Indian ancestry, were taken prisoner and grilled for information on Portobelo. The refusal of the black men to give information led to their early demise at the pleasure of sharks. Seeing this, the zambo became more free with the information. He confided that a dozen English prisoners, taken in the Spanish conquest of Providence, were being held as slaves in a dungeon in Portobelo.

What Captain Morgan learned from the zambo solidified his plan. He led us ashore at a point three miles south of the twin castles of Portobelo. From there, we trekked at an exhausting double-time march through the fetid, steaming forest to within sight of the two castles. Panting for breath and without rest, we silently ran the last hundred yards to the base of the inland wall of the Castle of Santiago. We were now only an open field behind us from the streets of the City of Portobelo.

We hovered there to catch our breath. For the moment, we were still unseen by the castle's watchmen's eyes and out of danger from cannons that were all aimed to defend the city against an assault from the sea.

Scarce minutes were taken for a fresh loading of every pistol. Cutlasses were sharpened and taken in hand. All of the Brethrens' eyes were now on our captain. He scanned the line of us. He first said a quiet word to Angwyn and me: "Stay close to me. Hold your fire. You may need it."

He raised his cutlass above his head and called the order. "Follow me!" Our band of five hundred Brethren stormed across the field into the streets of the city, firing pistols in every direction, driving terror into the heart of every person in hiding. Panic seized those who ran to seek cover for themselves, their women and children, and their fortunes. The Brethren pursued close on their heels.

Within minutes, the city of Portobelo was under the domination of our marauding band of Brethren. Angwyn and I followed the order of Captain Morgan to seek out the city dungeon. A Spanish soldier at the point of our pistols shortened our search. We broke through the chained door and, to our horror, released the English prisoners. They had been reduced to staggering skeletons by the treatment of the Spanish. The pitiful sight of them fired the sense of British loyalties of our captain and every man of us.

Before the sacking, plundering, and burning could get out of hand, Captain Morgan leapt atop the fountain in the center square. He barked orders to the other captains. "We have no victory yet! There are still two castles to take. We need to get our ships in and out of the harbor to carry the treasure. This way, lads! The taking of booty can wait!"

He ordered a hundred of the Brethren to stay and keep control of the city while he led the rest of us back to the city's edge facing the Santiago Castle. He sent a dozen of our best marksmen with French flintlock rifles to a high ground and gave them orders. By then, the guardsmen of the Castle had rushed to position some of the cannon to face back toward the city, toward us.

At the captain's order, our marksmen picked off every Spanish soldier who dared to stand in position to fire their cannon. A dozen Spanish soldiers were dropped before the threat of cannon-fire abated.

This was the moment that would tell all. The vaulted wall of the Santiago Castle ahead of us was impregnable, but the massive door was of wood. I finally knew that Angwyn and I had the captain's trust when he gave us the order.

At the captain's signal, Angwyn and I and three others dashed at full speed across the open plain with a sack of gunpowder, a bundle of kindling, and a torch. We packed the gunpowder against the door and heaped on kindling. I stood to one side and hurled the torch onto the kindling. In seconds, with one deafening blast, the massive wooden door was blown into flaming shards.

Captain Morgan led the band as a screaming rush of cutlass-wielding Brethren charged the opening. The battle was bloody but brief. With no loss to the Brethren, the surviving Spanish troops fell back in total disarray.

The Spanish commander made a vain attempt to reorganize his troops in the center of the Castle yard, firing from any point of cover. Captain Morgan climbed to the highest wall of the castle. He drove the final spike into the Spanish resolve. He hoisted the red flag. Panic and fear displaced any Spanish commitment to fight to the death for their far-distant king. They knew the red flag meant "no quarter." To fight on would mean no surviving Spanish soldier. The first castle was in our hands.

Captain Morgan declared the conquest sufficient for the day. Within an hour, our valiant Brethren were far enough into the stores of rum to make them an easy prey for the Spanish, but a counter-attack never came.

One obstacle remained: the castle of San Felipe. The following day, Captain Morgan sent a demand for surrender to the commander of the castle. As fate would have it, the Spanish had under-manned and under-armed the castle's defenses. The code of valiance of Spanish soldiers in Spain had decayed among soldiers in the far-distant colony after years of neglect by their king.

The commander of the castle of San Felipe had witnessed the fighting fury of our band of Brethren. He had seen the raising of the red flag. Within minutes, he surrendered without terms.

The city was ours for the plunder of every coin and bar of Potosi silver and gems that would have fed the Spanish king's wars in Europe. But our captain had more in mind.

Word of our conquest of Spain's treasure city of Portobello reached the Governor of the city of Panama fifty miles to the south within a day. He conscripted an army of eight hundred. They took to the trail to recapture Portobello, but their progress was delayed by the hasty neglect to provision the force with adequate food and armament.

Captain Morgan got word of the Governor's plan. He immediately dispatched a message to the Governor. He made it clear that unless the immense ransom of 300,000 pesos and all armaments of the castles were delivered to us immediately, he would burn the city of Portobello to the ground and take all within as prisoners. He emphasized to the governor that the Spanish prisoners would be shown "the same kindness" that the English prisoners were shown by their Spanish captors.

There was a vitriolic exchange of negotiating messages. In one, the Spanish governor referred to Captain Morgan as a "pirate." I have never seen him so incensed. He fired back a reply: "I sail under letters of marque in service to King Charles II of England. The ransom is now 350,000 pesos."

It was finally realized on both sides that the diseases rampant in the fetid Portobelo area were claiming more casualties than the fighting. Captain Morgan accepted a ransom of 100,000 silver pesos, paid by the Panama merchants and delivered in ponderous mule-loads of silver bars and coins.

With the next tide, Captain Morgan's fleet of ten ships set sail for Port Royal. They had a rendezvous off the shore of Cuba, where the split of the booty according to the Articles of the Brethren gave each man the equivalent of three years' wages for investment in a business, or, more likely, an unending stretch of drunken carousing in the welcoming dens of Port Royal.

CHAPTER TWENTY-ONE

Memoir of Dylan Llewellyn (continued)

Angwyn and I were content to spend the next week with Captain Morgan at his mansion outside of Port Royal. We were out of the stream of seafarers' tales that coursed like lightning through every saloon and brothel of Port Royal. Yet one bit of news filled a great gap of our curiosity.

Captain Trace had sought to betray what he thought was Captain Morgan's plan to attack Maracaibo. As anticipated by Captain Morgan, Captain Trace had sent a message to the Spanish commander at Maracaibo. It had led the Spanish to speed troops and armaments from other Spanish cities, Portobelo among them, to Maracaibo, leaving those other cities under-manned, under-armed, and vulnerable.

The crew of a merchant slave ship, fresh into Port Royal from the shores of Barbados, brought word of the fate of Captain Trace. After Angwyn and I had warned Captain Morgan of the betrayal, he had secretly shifted his target to the sacking and pillaging of Portobelo instead of Maracaibo. Word of our plundering of Portobelo reached the Spanish commander at Maracaibo just before Captain Trace sailed his frigate into the Maracaibo harbor. He was expecting a warm welcome and hero's reward for the betrayal. The Spanish welcome that greeted him there was warm, but in a steamingly hostile way. The Spanish commander at Maracaibo made it unlikely that Captain Trace, his vessel, or his crew would ever be seen again in the waters of Port Royal.

The report of Captain Trace's misfortune recalled to Angwyn and me the words of Captain Morgan that his forbearance to take action against Captain Trace did not mean that Trace would escape consequences of his betrayal. Again, by example, he proved that battles are won by the mind and not by the sword.

*   *   *

Angwyn and I knew it would be several months before Captain Morgan would mount his next foray. We used the time to ship out with a small fleet under Captain Roderick. For six weeks, we coursed the eastern Spanish treasure route. We plundered, practically at will, Spanish vessels in the unending flow of wealth from the Spanish Main to the war chests of Madrid royalty. Angwyn and I used the ventures to master quickly the arts of seamanship and close combat.

After six weeks at sea, the urge of our crew of Brethren to rid themselves of their shares of booty into the waiting pockets of Port Royal brought us back to what was becoming home.

*   *   *

The Spanish King Carlos II's response to the sacking of Portobelo became clear in the months that had followed. New letters of reprisal issued to Spanish sea captains signaled his resolve to retake from the British the Caribbean islands he considered to be his entitlement. One of those islands was Jamaica, and in particular, the nest of the Brethren, Port Royal.

The growing threat of attack by Spanish privateers stirred Captain Morgan from his lull between ventures sooner than we anticipated. His quarry this time would have to serve a double purpose. It had to promise enough booty to induce an assembled fleet of Brethren captains to return to arms, and it had to signal a shot across the bow of the Spanish king's ambitions in the Caribbean. There was only one city on the Spanish Main that could provide both.

I had never doubted the word of our captain that no quarry was beyond his grasp. I'll state truthfully, however, that his next venture tested the faith of both Angwyn and myself.

From the time of the Spanish conquest of the Aztec empire by Hernan Cortes and of the Inca empire by Francisco Pizzaro, the collection center of Aztec gold and Incan silver for shipment on the treasure route to Spain had been the city of Panama on the Pacific coast of the Isthmus of Panama.

When Captain Morgan offered up to the Brethren captains as our next prize the city of Panama, there was stunned murmuring, but eventual rallying to the quest. Impossible as it seemed, it held out the dream of a captive treasure that would exceed anything the Brethren had ever known. And the message to the Spanish king would be unmistakable.

*   *   *

December 2, 1669. The day is burned in my memory. Angwyn and I watched as thirty-six captains of the Brethren signed Articles that would commit their lives and their vessels to follow our leader into a hell from which no sane warrior could expect survival.

Word spread throughout the Caribbean. Captain Morgan was manning a fleet for a conquest that promised inconceivable treasure

*for every soldier and seaman who could survive the trials ahead.
Blind trust in our captain drew a wave of buccaneers from every
British port within reach.*

*On December 18, 1670, the thirty-seven-ship fleet of the Brethren
hoisted sail to follow in the wake of the flag of Captain Morgan to
once more conquer the unconquerable—Panama.*

*This richest of all cities on the Spanish Main was fortified from
attack from the Pacific Ocean to the point of invulnerability. The
only other choice, and that a seemingly fool's choice, was the fifty-mile
inland stretch of Isthmus to the northeast of the city. Its fortifications
were those of nature—steaming swamplands thick as mist with
disease-carrying mosquitoes, venomous snakes, flesh-eating predators,
and the unseen threats of dysentery, cholera, and yellow fever.
Captain Morgan chose that inland route.*

*The first obstacle was the fort at San Lorenzo. Its cannon guarded
the entry to the Chagres River. Our captain dispatched three groups
of one hundred Brethren—one, I'm proud to say, under my
leadership. We took to the shore and slashed through heavy jungle
vines to a position from which we could mount a charge through open
space to the walls of the fort.*

*At the signal from our Captain Bradley, with no cannon or
sharpshooters for cover, we charged, screaming at the top of our lungs.
We nearly made it to the fort's wall, but the barrage of musket-fire
from above, as thick as hail, forced Captain Bradley to call a retreat.
We could scarcely find ground on which to run back that was not
strewn with the bodies of our Brethren. Many of us made it. Many
more did not.*

*While we awaited darkness, our Brethren agreed that the only
thing more loathsome than the thought of death was the prospect of
accepting defeat. With the glaring sun down, we charged again. This*

time our own musketeers dropped to the knee and picked off their riflemen on the wall. My band charged the wall, hurling fireballs up at the dried leaf rooves over their musketeers.

The fighting raged like a scene out of hell, until one of our buccaneers committed an act of incomparable courage. An arrow from above pierced his back and burst through his chest. He pulled it out of his breast, wound its tip in cotton, and set it ablaze. He loaded the arrow into his musket and fired it over the wall. As only fate could dictate, the fire it spread inside the wall reached a store of power. The explosion rained sheets of fire on every tinderbox within, finally setting off an explosion that blew open a gaping maw in the fort's wall.

With ear-piercing screams and an eruption of sheer will that would not be denied, we stormed through the gap. We engaged them with hand-to-hand victory after victory until the day was won. To their credit, the Spaniards fought to the last man with a valor that could be reported with pride to his Spanish majesty. They sought no quarter, and received none. But the fort was ours.

The watery inlet was open to us. Captain Morgan left a small body of Brethren to control the fort until our return. He transferred the rest of us to a number of small oared craft that could navigate the unpredictable depths of the Chagres River inland. His one miscalculation was that we could leave our provisions at the mouth of the Chagres and live off the land. It was a deadly error.

Within three days, the muted flow of the Chagres forced us to take a painfully slow course on foot, slashing a path through log-sized vines and roots of mangroves for every foot of advance. The stifling heat and constant attack of swarming insects took its toll, but even more so, the complete lack of food. The anticipated replenishing with game proved to be an illusion.

And so it went for days. Rest, even in exhaustion, was tormented by the stinging of disease-bearing insects and the venom of snakes in *the undergrowth. At times we approached Spanish fortifications along the Chagres. A spark of revived hope for something to alleviate the gnawing pain of hunger was each time crushed in the realization that the Spanish had taken everything edible and fled, burning every source of shelter to the ground.*

In desperation, instead of following the curving, meandering path of the Chagres, we began hacking a direct path through the wall of jungle in a straight line toward Panama City. Our suffering was only multiplied by thickening vines with thorns that cut into our flesh with every step.

Our hunger was now in its fourth day. Our depletion was beyond exhaustion, when we came upon another abandoned fort. This time, a few sacks of grain had been left.

The sway of Captain Morgan's command over starving troops was now at a low ebb. It was there put to the test. He ordered the small cache of grain to be given to the weakest and sickest among us. The others were to abide their pain and press on. I was awed at the force of our captain's will to keep these starving, diseased, suffering individuals together as the band of Brethren that we were. Not a man rebelled.

On the fifth day, a small but desperately needed respite came in the discovery of a small barnful of corn. This time, there was enough for a few handfuls to be swallowed raw by each of our troops. It was meager, but it gave a surge that drove us on.

On the seventh day, we reached the headwater Vente de Cruces. We were halfway there. Captain Morgan gave the order that kept us on the march for ten hours a day to arrive before even the strongest of us was too weakened for the battle ahead. At long last—after a test of endurance that made us even more a band of brothers—we reached the crest of a hill and saw the gleaming waters of the Pacific Ocean. And more than that, after five days without food, we saw below us a herd of cattle. Our human stampede fell on, slaughtered, and burned in the flames of gathered brush fires enough beef to feed the hunger that was now at the edge of starvation. The food and a night of sleep restored not our will to fight—because we never lost that—but the strength to let our human bodies do what we were to demand of them. The city of Panama lay before us.

*   *   *

After three days, on January 28, 1671, Don Juan Perez de Guzman, commander of the Spanish force, led his uniformed troops onto the great plain outside of the city. Our two forces of combat took opposing positions. A battle of classic strategies was in the making.

Each of us looked across the divide at the faces of those we must cause to die if we were to survive. By then, I'd been there many times. I said it again before drawing my cutlass. If God willed this to be my last, so be it.

We could see Don Juan aligning his troops for three waves of assault. My heart caught when I saw that the first wave was to be cavalry with lances, mounted on Spanish steeds, pawing the earth, ready to trample our band into the dust. Lines of Spanish musketeers and sabre-wielding troops would follow to extinguish survivors.

We looked to our captain for some reason to hope for survival, if not victory, in the onslaught ahead. As one band of Brethren, we aligned our troops as he ordered. And we awaited the inevitable.

It came. The horsemen wheeled their mounts into a full charge. The earth rang as if with thunder. Our entire front line of musketeers went down on one knee, took aim, and froze in position. The thunder approached. It was close enough to hear the grunted breaths of the horses when Captain Morgan finally shouted the word. "Fire!"

As if in one deafening crack, our line of muskets spit fire and death. The entire front line of horses went down. The second line of charging steeds went tumbling over those that had fallen. The third line desperately reined in their mounts. By then, panic and complete disarray sent the surviving cavalry into a full-gallop retreat.

Our second line of troops ran to engage the now grounded horse-soldiers with an attack more to the style of men of the sea. Again, quarter was neither asked nor given.

The next wave of Spanish foot-soldiers had seen the total dismantling of their legendary cavalry. They rallied to Don Juan's call for an attack, but a volley of firing by our crack musketry took down half of their advancing line. The fever of fear for their lives seized the rest. The second line of Spanish assault was thrown into disarray approaching panic.

Within minutes, before the disbelieving eyes of Don Juan, the entire Spanish army was dissolved in flight. The city of Panama was ours. It had seemed impossible, and it probably was, for any but our Captain Morgan.

Whatever remnants of exhaustion and hunger remained were swallowed up in the unrestrained charge of victory of the Brethren through the streets of the formerly unassailable Panama. To our increasing realization and shock, however, the departing Spanish had left welcoming gifts for us in the form of powder charges in nearly every building of the city. As we advanced down each street, explosions and wind-swept fire showers set the entire city ablaze like a massive funeral pyre.

Worse yet, the expected mountains of gold and silver coins and bars laying bare and open for our taking were nowhere to be found. The city had been left nearly vacant of treasure or human occupancy.

It was not until the interrogation of Spanish stragglers in the days that followed that we felt the full force of what had happened. Don Juan had news of our approach from the time we took the fort at San Lorenzo. His confidence in an army, long ignored and unpaid by the

Spanish crown in Europe, must have suffered realistic doubt. The very name of Captain Morgan had by now the effect of mythological terror. The closer we penetrated the jungle barriers, the more certain his plan became for survival of his people and their fortunes.

Don Juan had ordered every scrap of treasure in the city loaded on ships of the Spanish fleet in the harbor. Barely a day before our assault on the city, most of the citizens of Panama were brought aboard. The fleet had sailed out of the harbor just hours before our two forces had clashed on the plain. Any ship that bore no cargo or fleeing citizens was burned to prevent us from any possibility of pursuit.

* * *

The first night of our victory was spent by the Brethren in rum-soaked revelry amid the flames of our conquest. But in subsequent days, scouring of the charred remains of every building and forced interrogation of every Spaniard and slave left behind opened further our awareness of the numbing truth. The prize of unfathomable treasure that had driven us to inhuman heights of endurance had escaped our grasp.

When the seizure of whatever meager caches of gold and silver left behind by the Spaniards was complete, and divisions of the shares were made to the Brethren, another truth became evident. The one linchpin that held the Brethren together in loyalty to our captain was the prospect of captured wealth. That gone, our band began to fracture irreparably into bitter factions.

CHAPTER TWENTY-TWO

Memoir of Dylan Llewellyn (continued)

In the days that followed, Captain Morgan took residence in a farm building just outside of the city's perimeter. Angwyn and I and a small band of loyal buccaneers remained in his company.

It was the dead of night a week after the fall of the city. Two tall men of a race I had never seen before woke us from sleep. One of them was clearly the leader. The other had enough grasp of English to make known to us what he said.

The leader stood with a bearing that said clearly that his spirit was proud and unconquered, in spite of the marks of chains on his wrists and ankles. He would speak only with the one the Spanish feared as a mythical conqueror, the man with white skin who had brought the Spaniards to their knees.

Captain Morgan came out and stood before him. It was like two spirits who could see in each other's eyes an equal that could be found nowhere else.

As I learned later, the man said that his name was Cualli. He was the leader of a great and ancient civilization called Nahuatl, which I learned later was known to the Spanish as Aztec. His people had ruled a vast realm, spreading their civilization and religious convictions for centuries before the Spanish fleets came with their weapons and even more deadly diseases to enslave his people.

I watched as these two took measure of each other in quiet words beyond my hearing. There was a moment. I could feel it. It seemed a barrier was broken and a trust was born between them.

The man gave a signal to whoever was in the darkness of the forest outside. Two men of the same appearance came out of the trees bearing a covered object of great weight, nearly half the size of a man. At the leader's gesture, they laid it down at the feet of Captain Morgan.

More words were spoken between the two men. I could tell only by the tone that they were of the gravest importance. There were several moments of silence, then another exchange of words between them, and finally what I could sense was a nod of commitment by Captain Morgan. It was their last communication. The strangers walked back into the darkness of the forest. They were gone as quickly as they had appeared.

I had hardly understood a word, but the feeling came over me that what had just happened would change the lives of many to come— whether for good or evil was not yet to be known.

*   *   *

By then, the full awareness that the treasure we had chased, to the death of many Brethren and unspeakable suffering of us all, had slipped from our grasp had fully eroded the ties that had held us as a band. Angwyn and I could feel the intense heat of the Brethrens' growing hostility to Captain Morgan himself for leading them through hell to a vacant dream.

There was another change. Since the passing of words I could not hear between Captain Morgan and the tall figure who appeared the previous night, the captain had become resolute on one course of

*action. It apparently involved only Angwyn, me, and two of the
Brethren whose loyalty he still held.*

*In the dead of night, we mounted five horses the Spanish had left
behind. We led another to carry supplies and a sixth to carry the
still-shrouded object that had been handed over to Captain Morgan
by the night visitor. We retraced the path we had hewn from the
Chagres River to Panama.*

*We used two of the boats we had left on the bank of the Chagres to
make our way to the Gulf. Once there, we boarded two of the smaller,
swifter sailing vessels we had left after conquest of the castle. Captain
Morgan and the two Brethren boarded one. He placed me in
command of the second, the* Nuestra Regina, *with Angwyn as my
mate. We quickly hoisted sail for the voyage back to Port Royal.*

*Before we parted, Captain Morgan sat with Angwyn and me in
the cabin of his ship. He poured a ration of rum for each of us. He
raised a toast to our Welsh ancestry and the bond that had grown
among us. It gave me a somber sense that he was saying a farewell in
the softest way possible—but yet a farewell.*

*He confided that the object he had accepted from the night stranger
had come with an obligation. It had made an abiding change in the
perspective of his life.*

*I asked if he would explain, or at least tell us what the object was.
He declined both, except to say that he committed himself under oath
to secure the object from the grasp of the Spanish. He added only that
he was taking the object back to Port Royal. From there he would see
to carrying it up into the Blue Mountains to a specific place to be
known only to him and the stranger who entrusted it to him. Their
agreement was that the object was to be restored to the leader of the
Aztecs once the yoke of Spanish slavery had been lifted.*

*That was all the captain would say—but for one exception. He
knew I was writing this memoir. He asked specifically that I include*

in its pages what he had just disclosed. I asked him why. He said that since the two of us were to be on separate ships in waters patrolled by Spanish war galleons, the chances would be doubled that at least word of the object's existence and his oath to restore it to the Aztec nation would survive if I recorded it.

With those few words, we set sail for Port Royal.

* * *

Our course was set two points east of due north. It was easy to maintain under the steady prevailing winds of the season. And yet, the most disturbing premonition plagued the hours I spent at the wheel. Though Angwyn and I never spoke of it, we shared the awareness that we were traversing the sea-path of the most heavily armed Spanish treasure galleons. More unsettling was the certainty that the warships sent by the Spanish monarch to destroy his greatest nemesis, Captain Morgan, would be scouring the route we followed.

The fragile peace of the first two days turned to a dread that coursed through my body shortly after dawn on the third day. It was a black dot on the eastern horizon. It continued to grow through the morning. By noon, I could see through the glass an outline of a war galleon, its decks bristling with cannon and the Spanish flag aloft.

By mid-afternoon, two facts were plain. The galleon's captain had our two-ship convoy in his sights. His course would directly engage us in a matter of hours. The second was that we could count on neither flight nor fight for survival. She could run either of us down under full sail, and once close, her cannon would blast our hulls to shreds.

There was little time for decision, but I had foreseen this consequence as a premonition before we left the cabin of Captain Morgan. I had taken what was necessary to carry out a measure that was extreme, but one to which I could commit myself. It was time to see if Angwyn would share my commitment.

With a forced calmness, I laid out my thoughts. It wasn't necessary to recall that each of us had freely chosen the brash seagoing life of the Brethren over a gentle life on a Welsh farm. And the one who brought us through pinnacles of pain and hunger to excesses of victory and wealth in adventures of which we could scarcely have dreamed was Captain Morgan. It was time to repay.

I shortly realized that I was merely putting into words what was in Angwyn's heart as well. With little time for thought, we committed to the plan.

I went below and brought up what I had secretly taken from the ship Captain Morgan now commanded. With Angwyn's help, we raised to the top of our mainmast the unique flag that was known in every corner of the Caribbean as the flag flown only by a ship under the command of Captain Morgan.

That done, we steered hard to starboard. We set a course that would take us as far as possible from our captain's ship. We held our breath to see if the Spanish captain would take the bait and pursue us rather than Captain Morgan's ship.

It was five, then ten minutes of agony until we saw it. The warship wheeled to port. It was clear they had seen the flag. They were coming for their prime quarry in full pursuit.

Once the scene became clear, Angwyn and I took to the top deck. We could see Captain Morgan staring, almost in disbelief, at what he clearly understood to be our grateful recompense for the life only he could have given us. With one last look, we saluted him with all our hearts.

I know he was torn by our decision, but to come after us would have meant the certain death of all three of us. I believe there was another weight in the balance—his oath to the stranger who had come to him in the night. I could see resolution, and pride, and pain in my last look into the face of the one who had become our second father.

He returned our salute. With hearts as heavy as stone, we turned back to our commitment. We set a course that would look like a vain attempt to outrun the warship. She took the bait. They raised every yard of sail she had and coursed to intercept us.

I left the wheel in Angwyn's hands. I went to the captain's cabin on the top rear deck of the last ship we would ever feel under our feet.

I'm now sitting at the captain's desk. For the last time, I'm taking the pen. This will be my final recording of a life that God granted me out of the dreams of an innocent, youthful Welsh lad. When I write my last line, I'll seal this book in a metal case I see here in the cabin. This book is not for the eyes of the Spanish. I'll hide it below the boards under the captain's chart box. Only God knows if it will ever be seen by human eyes.

My last words are to God, who sees my scribbling and will understand my heart. I ask Your forgiveness for all that might have displeased You. And I thank You that You never left me in spite of it all. I can hear the first volley of cannon fire that will soon bring me to You. I go to Your arms.

CHAPTER TWENTY-THREE

THE BAJAN SUN was almost blinding when I opened my eyes. I was still in the clothes I had on when I began reading the young Welshman's memoir. I must have dropped off after finishing the last word. I had to force my mind through a fog to bring back all that happened the previous day, but I could recall every event in Dylan's book as if he were writing it directly to me.

The chime at the door and the Bajan-accented word "breakfast" sounded almost simultaneously with the ring of the room phone. I caught the phone on the way to the door.

"Matthew, did you read it?"

"Wayne?"

"Of course. No one else knows you're in that hotel. At least no one dangerous. So did you read it?"

"Yes."

"Good. Meet me in the coffee shop of your hotel. Ten thirty. Do you have your cellphone?"

I checked my pocket. "I do."

"Don't use it before we talk. Those things can be traced. Ten thirty." *Click*.

The Bajan breakfast delivered on a cart helped settle nerves that were jangled by the tension in Wayne's voice. I reached for my cellphone a couple of times to speed-dial Mac McLane or Mary. Wayne's precaution put both on hold.

* * *

It was ten thirty sharp when I walked into the hotel coffee shop. I caught sight of Wayne across the room at a table with a sea view. By now I was conditioned to check around. I saw two large, athletic-looking Bajan men at a table just inside the door. I was aware of their eyes on me as I walked across to Wayne's table.

"Matthew. Good morning. Sit."

I nodded backwards to the two behind. "Yours?"

"Yes. A precaution. You've had breakfast?"

"I did."

"Good. More coffee?"

"Definitely."

One quick nod from Wayne brought a waiter with a fresh cup and a pot for the table. Then privacy.

Wayne leaned in closer. "Do you understand where that logbook leaves us?"

"As far as it went. That young man, Dylan . . ."

"Young in years. Not so young in experiences."

"Clearly. Drawing that Spanish war galleon away from Morgan's ship must have cost him his life."

"I'm sure it did. You and I saw his ship yesterday. The hull was riddled with cannon holes. We also know it worked. Captain Morgan made it safely back to Port Royal."

"How do we know that?"

"History. Sometime after he reached Port Royal, the governor had him taken into custody. It seems the English and Spanish had signed a peace treaty. Part of the agreement was that English raiders like

Morgan would no longer have the legitimacy of the king's letters of marque to raid Spanish cities. Morgan was probably unaware of the treaty when he sacked Panama City. No matter. By then the treaty made it an act of piracy. In fact, it was an embarrassment to the English king. He sent an order to the Port Royal governor to send Captain Morgan back to London to stand trial."

"And did he?"

"Yes and no. He was sent back to London under arrest. But Morgan was a folk hero to the British people. King Charles was afraid to treat him as a criminal. He actually knighted him. He sent him back to Jamaica as the Deputy Governor."

"The man led a charmed life."

"You might say. After all the times he faced hand-to-hand combat at sea without quarter, he died of pneumonia at the age of fifty-three on his Jamaican plantation."

"Hmm. And young Dylan went down to a watery grave in his early twenties. Maybe the other Dylan was right."

"You mean *Bob Dylan*. 'The good die young.' Ah well. Who's to judge?"

I had to smile when he caught my obscure reference to a Dick Holler song sung by Bob Dylan, "Abraham, Martin, and John."

"The question, Matthew, is where does all this leave us?"

I sipped coffee and waited for him to answer his own question.

He did. "We know now the object at the center of all of this Monkey's Paw business is whatever that Aztec leader entrusted to Captain Morgan in Panama. We have no idea what he said to Morgan. Whatever it was, I take it from Dylan's logbook it caused Morgan to commit himself deeply to keeping the object out of the hands of the Spanish. That may be why he allowed young Dylan to sail off as a decoy. Even at the cost of Dylan's life."

"So it would seem."

"All right. Here's what we know. That first parchment of Rene Perreault told the Monkey's Paws to gather in the lobby of Morgan's Harbour Hotel and wait for a guide. We know from Dylan's logbook that Morgan intended to hide the object somewhere in the Blue Mountains of Jamaica. That would put it someplace within reach of Port Royal. Remember, he was arrested shortly after he got back there. My guess is he hid it either before he was arrested or after he came back as deputy governor. The question is where in the Blue Mountains exactly."

"Again, so it seems."

"That excursion by the five Monkey's Paws to Jamaica a few weeks ago was actually set up by that old sailor the night of the poker game in Cairo. He was the one who told us that night to meet at Morgan's Harbour Hotel in Port Royal in six weeks."

He was telling me what I had already heard from Claude DuCette in Montreal. I just listened. I wanted to hear his version.

"Claude DuCette was the first to open a parchment. It just told us to be in the hotel lobby in the morning. There'd be someone to guide us from there."

He stopped for a minute in thought. I primed the pump. "And was there?"

"Yeah. Three Jamaicans. They took us across the bay to a van. We rode inland for about an hour. Then we started a trek up a mountain path to the ridge of the Blue Mountains."

"And?"

"We got as far as the top of the path. It was a nightmare. We found the body of one of the guides. He'd been killed. It spooked us all. We headed back down the path. Before we got to the bottom, we'd found the other two guides. Both dead. Murdered. It took the steam out of all of us. We split up and went back where we'd each come from."

"So the other parchments were never opened? At least no one ever told the other four what they said. Right?"

"That's right."

"What got you back in the game? Was yours the next parchment to be opened?"

"No. Mine was to be actually the fifth. It told me to find Dylan's sunken ship and look for the logbook. I think the idea was for us to locate the object first in Jamaica by the first four clues. I guess we'd know it when we saw it. Then the logbook of Dylan would tell us how it came to Captain Morgan. Why it was significant over and above the dollar value."

I nodded. I was sure now that the second parchment clue had been given to Rene Perreault. On his deathbed, he passed the message to me. "Follow the abeng." I had an urge to disclose it to Wayne to see if it made sense to him, but I still wasn't sure who was on the side of the angels in that game. I gave him a non-committal "Go on."

"A week after I got back to Barbados from Jamaica, I got a message from that man I've done business with in Marseille. I told you he'd been contacted by someone who said he was that old sailor, the one who passed the five parchments to us in the Cairo poker game."

"What was the message? Tell me all of it."

"He told me to open my parchment now if I hadn't already. He said the trail is still open to us."

"I think I'm deep enough into this thing for you to trust me, Wayne. What did your parchment say? I mean specifically."

"It told me to find the sunken ship. The *Nuestra Regina*. It directed me to recover the logbook from inside the ship."

Another tumbler fell into place in my mind. "Whoever made up those five parchments must have known you five well. Each one seems to call on some skill you have. He obviously knew you were an experienced diver."

"Yeah. That man in Marseille said something else. He mentioned you by name. He said if we wanted to see this thing through, we should bring you into it. Immediately."

Now I was flabbergasted. "How in the world would he know me? Even Professor Holmes never told me about this Monkey's Paw business."

A strange wave of *déjà vu* ran through my mind. I recalled having an unexplainable feeling that the whole staging of Professor Holmes' death to appear as a suicide was a message to me. I mentioned it at the time to Mac McLane. He dismissed it, and I buried it in the back of my mind.

There was a missing piece that was gnawing at my trust of Wayne's story. I thought it best to get it out in the open. "If no one saw that logbook before we found it yesterday, how did you know where to find the ship?"

"My parchment gave the coordinates for locating it."

"How could the writer of the parchment have known the coordinates? There are lots of wrecks out there."

"The sinking of the *Nuestra Regina* was widely publicized. The captain of the Spanish galleon thought he had sunk the flagship of Captain Morgan, and Morgan with it. That was big news. I did some online research in the Spanish archives. The Spanish captain was very detailed in his report to the Spanish crown. He gave the exact location of the sea battle with the *Nuestra Regina* relative to a small island close by. The sunken wreck of the *Nuestra Regina* has been located and recorded by a number of divers since then."

"Then why hasn't it been searched? It looked pretty well intact."

"Remember, a few weeks after it was sunk, word reached Spain that Captain Morgan was still alive. He'd arrived back in Port Royal. He hadn't died on the *Nuestra Regina*. The ship became just one more sunken wreck. As far as the public knew, Morgan brought back little of value from Panama. It was assumed that there was nothing worth searching for aboard the *Nuestra Regina*."

"So who was in that boat firing shots at us yesterday?"

Wayne took a moment for a sip of coffee, which I interpreted as a hesitation to answer. I gave it a nudge. "I need to know, Wayne. I'll be leaving here today. I have just one more of you Monkey's Paws to talk to. Roger Van Allen in Jamaica. If those shots were aimed at me, I need to know whom to avoid."

"They weren't. They were aimed at me."

"How do you know?"

"Because three of the Monkey's Paws are already dead. Probably murdered. Just Roger and me left."

"Any idea who's doing it?"

"Not yet. But . . ."

"But what?"

"I got another message last night from the man in Marseille."

"What was the message?"

He looked up at me. "You may not be up for this. You have to decide for yourself."

He had my full attention. "Decide what?"

"How deeply you want to get involved."

Our eyes were meeting now. "The man in Marseille figured by now we'd recovered the logbook. He said it was important that he meet with you as soon as possible."

I felt like a cork in a whirlpool being sucked in deeper and deeper. "Why me? Why not you?"

"I have no answer for that one. The message is that he won't talk with anyone else. I'm sorry, Matthew. I can't tell you it won't be dangerous."

It was my turn to take a sip of coffee to steady some flaming nerves. My only tie to any of this insanity was my promise to Mary that I'd find an answer. On the other hand, I'd never made a promise that felt more binding.

"Where does he want to meet?"

Much as I hoped for a comfortable location, the answer was, "Marseille. He seldom leaves his compound. Don't let that fool you. He's a major player in the world of smuggling antiquities. He's like an octopus with a thousand tentacles. They reach everywhere."

"And you've dealt with him before?"

"Without being specific, yes."

"Do you trust him?"

"As far as I could throw this hotel. That's an advantage."

"How?"

"I suspect he'd sell his grandmother into human bondage for the price of a good croissant. It puts me on guard."

I had no words to respond. He picked it up. "Like I said, Matthew, I can book you a flight this afternoon. Or not. The decision is still yours."

I wished that were true. I knew it wasn't. In the words of Robert Service, "A promise made is a debt unpaid." Mary might understand, but in my heart, the promise was also made to Professor Holmes.

CHAPTER TWENTY-FOUR

I HAD TWO last questions before being hustled off to the airport in Bridgetown. "What's the name of this man in Marseille? And how do I locate him?"

"I'll contact him. Don't worry. He'll be in touch with you. You'll be met at the Marseille Province Airport. I know how he does business. Just go where they take you."

"That's not comforting." I remembered how that worked out in New Orleans. "And what do I call him?"

"You don't. He doesn't like to use his name."

"Does he know my name?"

"Of course."

"Then you can send him a message from me. Say it verbatim. 'To hell with that. If he wants to talk, he can find me in Salem, Massachusetts.'"

"Matthew, this is important. We're getting close to pay dirt. It's no time to be touchy about a name."

"I'm not. I'm touchy about a life. Mine. I have no plan to get into his playpen without at least knowing his name."

I could see Wayne squirming between two thorns. I waited. He finally spoke. In a whisper. "The last time I dealt with him, he used the name 'Mr. Yavuz.' It's Turkish. It comes with a piece of advice. A little discretion could go a long way. Healthwise."

*   *   *

My flight arrived at the Marseille Province Airport sometime before midnight. I was looking for someone holding up a sign with my name. None seen. I was beginning to think this "man in Marseille" had flubbed the meeting. Then I became aware of a man of unrecognizable ethnicity in a silk suit that probably cost more than my entire wardrobe. He was suddenly beside me, whispering instructions.

"Mr. Shane, I am Hafiz. If you'll come this way."

Within ten minutes I was through customs and into the back seat of a Bentley, another first.

Hafiz was not a chatterbox. In fact, we drove about twenty miles in a silence that did not seem to invite conversation.

We drove through crowded streets in the direction of what looked like a major seaport. About a block from the water's edge, we pulled up to the entrance to manicured and flowered grounds surrounding a tower of ancient vintage.

The sign at the entrance indicated that the tower housed something called *Le Vieux Port Panier Jardin*. Even in the midnight darkness, from the moment of entry, I felt wrapped in the soft hospitality of a garden inn—actually a bed-and-breakfast, as I later learned. Some undefinable sense of warmth and peace exuded from its old-world simplicity. I was not surprised to find that it was a former convent.

A gentle morning call in perfect English invited me to an unmistakably French breakfast of croissants so light they required fresh butter and jam to keep them on the plate. The fruit could not have been picked more than an hour previously, and the several varieties of fish must surely have been swimming unsuspectingly that morning in the Mediterranean. The coffee, all three cups, was the best since I'd left New Orleans.

How could anything go wrong in this idyllic setting? A phone call in a languorous, non-French accent bade me "Good morning, Mr. Shane." Its deliberate neutrality made me think my question was about to be answered.

The arrangements were simple. Have coffee in the courtyard. And wait. I did. Within half an hour, a man in another silk suit that outdid even the first was bowing before me in a warm, non-condescending manner. Again, the accented English gave no clue to his ethnicity.

Pleasantries having been exchanged, I was escorted to the back seat of what I could swear was yet a different Bentley. This time, I shared the back seat with a lady of the most exquisite Asiatic features I think I had ever seen. She welcomed me warmly in unaccented English, made a brief cellphone call in cultured French, and addressed the driver in what I would wildly guess was Turkish.

We drove first through narrow, shop-lined streets that skirted the aptly named Old Port. The marina that covered half the port was close-packed deck-to-deck with sleek speedboats next to yachts that could sleep half of South Boston. Whatever was left of my sense of foreboding after a breakfast to die for, to use an unfortunate idiom, was lulled into peace by the mellifluous narration provided by my companion.

"You've not been to Marseille, Mr. Shane. A pity your stay will be brief."

That was unsettling on two grounds. She clearly knew more about my past, and future, than I found comfortable. She pressed on without leaving a gap for questions. "This is the *Vieux Carre.* The harbor is well known as the Old Port. It's actually the oldest section of

France. In fact, Marseille is one of the three oldest cities of Europe. The Greeks began building it in 600 B.C."

"I didn't realize this was Greek territory."

I sensed a subdued bristling. "It wasn't. We value our independence, Mr. Shane. We were no more Greek at that time than we were Roman after Julius Caesar's conquest of Gaul."

She looked over at me. "Do you know why the national anthem of France is called 'The Marseillaise'?"

"I've actually wondered."

"Then wonder no more. During the French Revolution, which by the way had beginnings in Marseille, that rallying song that drove the revolution was first sung in Paris by Marseille volunteers."

"That's impressive."

She had a smile that broadcast a quiet national pride. "I was sure an American would appreciate the significance."

I'll admit it. I was captivated. I just let her soft tones wash over me through the circuitous drive. It was easy to be lulled into a sense of security that was belied by the glaring poverty of a number of sections we passed through. We wove through some narrow streets of dwellings that reeked of a crumbling urban decay. They contrasted sharply with the opulence of the Bentley.

We finally reached the outskirts of the city. Even her dulcet voice could not dispel the blast of reality when she handed me a full-face cloth mask with no eye-openings.

"I'm so sorry for the inconvenience, Mr. Shane. I'm afraid from this point on, I must request that you wear this."

It was a bit jarring, but I remembered a ride in the bayou outside of New Orleans when a similar request to wear a blindfold would have given me some hope of living to see a return trip.

* * *

Some miles later, when the mask came off, I think my jaw actually dropped at the lush luxury of ponds, flowering plants, and exotic trees that surrounded the most exquisite mansion I'd seen short of the Palace of Versailles.

My escort and I were let off at the left side of the circular drive. She took us to a walkway that led to a garden setting that must have been fashioned on the Tuileries in Paris.

"Mr. Shane, my father enjoys the fresh sea air in the morning sun. He'll see you in the garden."

"Thank you. Are you staying with us?"

"I believe so."

"Then perhaps you'll call me 'Matthew.' And your name?"

That was a tester. I wondered if the name-game ran in the family. She looked at me with a moment of hesitation that set off a minor alarm. It transitioned into a smile that still held limitations. "Of course, Matthew. My name is Angelique. I see my father's waiting."

She led me to a man of more years than I would have expected with a daughter of Angelique's age. He was seated on one of a cluster of plush chairs under a statuesque willow tree. His eyes were closed, in thought rather than sleep, as I realized when he looked up instantly at the sound of our steps.

Angelique spoke first. "Papa, this is Matthew Shane."

I noticed she stopped short of giving me his name. I also noticed that, while he nodded to a seat beside him, he made no attempt to stand.

Even in that brief moment, I read in his sharp Caucasian features and manner some hint of a life that had survived the blows and come out ahead of his enemies.

"Matthew, sit. You were gracious to come."

He made a slight motion with his right hand. Within seconds, a silver service of coffee appeared in the hands of a formally dressed servant. A cup of steaming rich brew with a clearly Turkish aroma was poured for each of us. I noticed Angelique was sitting within hearing, but not a part of the close conversation.

His smile was warm and comfortable. I read signs of a man who was secure enough in himself to treat this younger man from what must have seemed an alien world with no hint of subordination.

"So, Matthew. For your fourth cup of the morning—coffee, strong, with a bit of cream. No sugar. Yes?"

It felt like a parlor game to let me know that my gracious host had eyes on my every waking moment. And yet, for reasons unknown, I felt somewhat at ease. Without commenting on his powers of surveillance, I accepted with a nod and a smile.

"I know you have a proclivity for getting directly to the point. I admire that. Neither of us has precious time to waste. How much do you know about the excavations of Aztec antiquities around Mexico City?"

I was sure he was aware that I had taken college courses in archeology from Professor Holmes. Some of it centered on the Aztec culture. On the other hand, a refresher couldn't hurt. "A bit. It's been years." I resisted the urge to add, "As you no doubt know."

"Ah. Well. Stop me if I bore you."

"I think that's unlikely, Mr. Yavuz." I thought I'd give the name a test flight. It brought a quick flash in his eyes and an instant glance at Angelique that was hard to read.

"Good. Where to begin. I suppose, the beginning. The people we call Aztecs came originally from the north of Mexico, a place referred to as Aztlan. Whence the name, Aztecs.

"In the thirteenth century, they began a two-hundred-year migration south. According to their tradition, their very deep-seated religion at the time, they were led by their primary god, Huitzilopochtli. Their priests carried his idol in front of them. They believed this god spoke to them through their high priest. He told them to walk until they found a large lake. They were to look for a sign, an eagle seated on a cactus, holding a serpent in its mouth.

"The legend is they finally saw that sign when they came to Lake Texcoco. They built a city there called Tenochtitlan. That was in 1325. It became the center of one of the most advanced civilizations of the world at that time. By the sixteenth century, it was the second largest empire in the New World, second only to the empire of the Incas in South America. Today Tenochtitlan lies buried under the current Mexico City."

He leaned in closer. "That's just history. But for our purposes, it's important to understand why their empire grew. Your Professor Holmes undoubtedly made a point of it."

"You're bringing it all back."

"Ah. Then. Let's focus. This particular god of theirs, Huitzilo-pochtli. He was one of many but one of their two most important. He was known as the god of the sun and of warfare. They believed that this god sustained the world and all the people in it by con-stantly bringing the life of the sun.

"They believed deeply that this god required a daily diet of human blood and hearts provided by the Aztec people. That meant contin-ual human sacrifice. If they stopped feeding this god, or even fed him less than his daily requirement, they believed to their core that the sun would stop sending its life-giving light and warmth. The earth and all the people on it would perish.

"This life-or-death duty to feed Huitzilopochtli a diet of human blood on a daily basis drove the Aztecs to fight constant battles to conquer other tribes and expand their kingdom. Of course, they wanted the heavy tribute they could demand from conquered cities. But the most critical need that drove their conquests was for cap-tured slaves and soldiers of other tribes. These were their primary source of human sacrifices for blood and hearts to keep Huitzilo-pochtli nourished."

I nodded as he spoke, but I had no idea where he was going with this. He leaned in still closer. The intensity of his voice seemed to rise even as he spoke in more hushed tones.

"Matthew, if they were driven by fear to constantly pour the life-blood of captives into the earth to feed this god—and more, the blood of their own people when the supply of captives ran low—can you imagine how deeply they felt this fear, this total commitment, dependence on this god?"

I gave as convincing a "yes" as I could muster.

"It explains so much that we couldn't understand otherwise."

My expression must not have registered the depth of conclusion he wanted. He sat straighter and smiled slightly. "And you're saying to yourself, 'Why is this old man pressing this point?'"

He leaned closer. "Put these two thoughts together. First, think of the flood of riches, from gold to rare jewels, that flowed like a raging river from the cities they conquered into the hands of the priests of this god. They had unlimited wealth. Second, consider the depth of their fear of total extermination if they fell short of the demand of this god for the blood of human sacrifice."

The light in his eyes burned brighter with each thought. Then he said, "Listen to me—there is mention in some of the old codices written by the priests of Huizitlopochtli—mention of a statue. It was designed to bring the ultimate honor, commitment to this demanding sun god. The statue was a representation of a golden eagle, sitting atop a cactus, with a snake in its mouth. You under-stand the significance."

"I do. Go on."

"This statue was large. Perhaps three, maybe four feet tall. That's not clear. What is clear is that it was made of solid gold. It was completely encrusted in the finest gems of the New World. The eyes were of rare jade. The very finest."

"And what happened to it?"

"You're getting ahead of me. I could never really decide if the writings in these codices were just poetic religious thought, or if this piece actually existed. And then—"

The sound of a cellphone broke the moment. Angelique answered it in a whisper. My host paused with a look at his daughter. After a few whispered comments into the phone, Angelique said something to her father in French. Her tone suggested that it was not a trifle. Her father's brow showed lines of either concern or anger. He simply said, "*Tu sais quoi faire. Tu fais-le. Maintenant.*"

My high school French was enough to understand: "You know what to do. You do it. Now."

She nodded. A few more whispered words in the phone and she hung up. She excused herself and left the garden.

My host showed the signs of malaise for a few seconds before returning to our eye-contact. I primed the pump. "You were saying that you doubted the existence . . ."

"Not doubted. Just never knew. I'll be brief. Other matters need my attention. I had occasion to be in Mexico City two months ago. It was known by my contacts that I was there to inquire into relics recently unearthed around the site of the great Aztec temple, the *Templo Mayor*. It was in the former Aztec city Tenochtitlan."

I knew that it was a serious international crime to take items like that out of the country. I followed Wayne Barnes' advice to use discretion. I didn't go there. "Yes?"

"A meeting was arranged quietly through one of my contacts. The leader of the current Aztecs asked to meet with me. My reputation for dealing in Aztec works is not quite as confidential as I'd like it."

"And you met?"

"We did. It was an astonishing meeting."

"How?"

"He engaged me to find and bring back to his Aztec people the very object we've been discussing."

He leaned forward and grasped my arm with a strength that belied his age. "Matthew. This object actually exists."

CHAPTER TWENTY-FIVE

His intensity was infectious. I think he could see it in my eyes. I hardly needed to say, "You have my full attention."

"Did he say anything else?"

He sat back with a smile. "Yes. More details. He said this statue had been kept for centuries deep inside the great pyramid his people built in dedication to Huitzilopochtli. The pyramid was built around 1325 in the center of their city, Tenochtitlan. It's called the *Templo Mayor*.

"When Cortes and the Spanish came in 1521, they wanted to establish Christianity among the conquered Aztecs. They destroyed nearly everything that related to the Aztec religion. That included the *Templo Mayor*.

"Before the Spanish could find it, the then leader of the Aztecs somehow managed to rescue that statue. It was at the very center of their culture. To them it was the most valued object made by human hands. He hid it well. Its secret location was passed on to a succession of Aztec leaders until 1671.

"Around that time, word spread through the Spanish empire in the Caribbean that the sea captain Henry Morgan was wreaking havoc with his raids on Spanish cities. It was also known, at least strongly rumored, that he had Panama City in his sights for his next assault.

"Their leader at that time was dedicated to preventing the statue from falling into the hands of the Aztecs' greatest enemies, the Spanish. They had massacred vast numbers of the Aztecs and enslaved the rest. At great danger, that leader brought the statue to Panama City.

"One night, during the week after Morgan's men captured and destroyed practically everything in Panama City, the Aztec leader had a secret meeting with Captain Morgan. He grew to trust him, perhaps on the theory that the enemy of his enemy was his friend. I think it went much deeper than that after their meeting.

"In any event, the Aztec leader entrusted the statue to Morgan. Morgan made a promise to keep it safe from their mutual enemy, the Spanish, until a time when it could be restored to the Aztec people."

I was weaving what I was hearing together with the account of the meeting of Morgan and the Aztec leader I'd just read about in the logbook of the Welsh seaman, Dylan. The confluence of the two was lighting a fire in my mind. Discretion still dictated absorbing the old man's words without disclosure on my part. At least for the moment.

"What happened to it from there? What did Morgan do with it?"

"Ah, Matthew. This is where you and I add together the pieces that might make the puzzle complete. I heard from the current Aztec leader that Morgan committed himself to the promise. When he left Panama, he had the statue with him. We know he reached Jamaica in safety. He was arrested shortly after his return and shipped off to England in chains. He returned to Jamaica later to assume high office."

"And the statue?"

"Consider the possibilities. It's highly unlikely that he could have taken it back on the ship to England. He was under arrest. That means that before or after his time in England, he most likely secreted it somewhere in Jamaica."

"Might he have sold it himself? He could have taken the profit."

"No. Not possible."

"Why not?"

He sat back and took a deep breath. He looked back at me like a scolding professor. "Think, Matthew. The intrinsic sale value of that statue for its gold and gems, not to mention the rare jade, would have so far surpassed any item on the market, legitimate or otherwise, that it would have been known around the world—maybe not publicly, but most certainly to the people in my line of interest. Then add the immense historic value, not to mention the cultural importance to an entire race of people. A sale like that couldn't be hidden for long. It most certainly would have resurfaced since then."

He looked at me the way Professor Holmes did occasionally. "I think the fact that you could even ask that question indicates that you have a long way to go to grasp what we're dealing with here."

I took the scolding to heart. I was still rethinking my decision to be a receiver rather than sharer of information.

His attention was taken away as we saw Angelique coming toward us from the main building. She said a few words to her father in French that went beyond my high school grasp of the language. I noticed that she had a box under her arm, neatly wrapped in a fine paper.

My host, whose name still seemed shrouded, touched the box and said a few more unintelligible words in French. He switched to English, clearly for my benefit. "Give us a minute, Angelique. We need to finish. Matthew can ride back with you to where he's staying. I'll send a car to take him to the airport tomorrow morning."

Angelique nodded. She gave what I chose to consider a warm smile to me as she sat with us.

Her father's tone took on a serious weight. "Matthew, I'm entrusting you with information that I wouldn't pass on to another living soul. I hope you'll take that into account in being equally open. As I say, we each have indispensable parts of the puzzle."

I decided to yield a little in the discretion department. "Before you say any more, Mr. . . . Yavuz."

That brought a smile that seemed to open the door a crack. "My name seems to be an obstacle. Let's remove it now. In following my peculiar interests as I have for many years, I encounter people who . . . how shall we say . . . would not hesitate to trade my life for a bag of peanuts. As you see, I'm still here, and living well. Why? Because I choose not to be careless with information. That includes my name. You understand?"

"I do."

"Good. Then perhaps you'll understand the trust I'm willing to extend to you when I tell you that my family name goes back seven generations in Istanbul, Turkey. It is Mehmed. It's the Turkish form of Mohamed. So. We're now on even footing, yes?"

"Mm. Yes."

"And yet there's something. Say it. We trust each other completely or not at all. There's no other way."

"One question keeps nagging. Why? I understand enough about your line of 'interest,' as you call it, to know why you trust no one. Practically no one." I smiled at Angelique, who delighted me by returning the smile. "So why trust me?"

He sat back and looked up into the graceful folds of the willow tree next to us. I think he was looking for the right words in a delicate area. When he looked back, his eyes had softened for the first time. "I do my homework, as you Americans say. I know more about you than you could possibly imagine. That's a fact you'll have to live with."

I just nodded.

"I'll say it simply. You've put your life on hold. You've put it in serious danger. You refuse to take the safer, easier way. Why? Simply because you've given your word to two close friends. One deceased, the other his widow. I've known only one other man who would do that. My father."

There was a silent moment that I let rest.

"If I weren't a fair judge of character, I'd have joined my father beyond this life many times. That's my answer. That's why I trust you. That's enough for me. Allah help me if I'm wrong."

I began to say something, but he held up his hand. "I'll simply add this. You have my word. Whatever you may have heard of me from others, I'll make this promise. I'll deal with you as openly, as honestly as would my father. You have to decide if it's enough for you."

Something I saw in his eyes is the only explanation I have for a decision I reached at that moment. Our eyes met. They held each other when I said it.

"Mr. Mehmed. From where we now stand, I promise to be honest with you. Nothing less. You have my word."

He stood for the first time, as did I. We embraced with both arms. I could feel that a bond was formed. I saw a deeper smile on the face of Angelique as she witnessed it. I was pleased to see that she was part of our circle of trust.

He nodded to my chair. We both sat again. "There's more, Matthew. I'll share it, before I ask you to do the same. There is a man in Port Royal, Jamaica. You've heard of him. He's one of what they call 'The Monkey's Paws.' His name is Roger Van Allen. We've shared business deals over the years. Port Royal was always a wide-open trading market for items of antiquity that might run afoul of . . . legal restrictions. It's been true even after the 1692 earthquake and tsunami that destroyed the port city itself.

"Roger contacted me about eight weeks ago. There was an old member of the maritime fleet, an old sailor. He knew about Roger's dealings. He came to him with an item. He said he had gambled on a cockfight in a back-street bar in Jamaica. He won an old, battered sea-chest. Roger was sharp enough to see markings that convinced him the chest might have belonged to Captain Henry Morgan. Roger shipped it to me for a price. I examined it and agreed with his conclusion about the ownership. I bought it.

"Before I found another buyer, I took it apart, piece by piece. I discovered a handwritten paper under the bottom slat."

He had riveted my attention again. "Could it have been written by . . . ?"

"Judge for yourself. The note tells of a meeting between the writer, Morgan, and the then leader of the Aztecs. The meeting was in Panama. It says an object of the highest value was entrusted to him. But more than financial value, it says the object was of the greatest importance as a symbol of the ancient culture and identity of the remaining Aztec race."

I hesitated to interrupt, but he saw my expression. He let me ask, "Are there many Aztecs left?"

"Surprisingly, yes. After Cortes arrived in 1521, the Spanish friars effectively converted the Aztecs to Christianity. They still practice the Christian religion. Over the last five hundred years, the Aztecs, now called the Nahua, have done their best to keep their own language, some of their own customs, alive. In other words, they've struggled to hang onto what still defines them as their own proud race of people."

"How many are left?"

"About a million and a half. They live mostly on farms in rural areas around Mexico."

"Interesting. I'm sorry. Please, go on. Was there more in the note?"

"Fortunately, yes. It says that Morgan feared that some treasure hunter would discover the statue after his death, before it could be safely returned to the Aztec leader. It says he secreted it in an area of the Blue Mountains north of Port Royal, Jamaica. It sounds like the area of the later Maroon settlement called Nanny Town."

"And you believe it's the statue. The bird with the serpent in its mouth."

"What else could it be?"

"Did the note say anything else?"

"It did. For one thing, it mentioned a ship, the *Nuestra Regina*. It spoke of the bravery of the young Welsh captain who drew a Spanish warship away from Morgan's ship so that Morgan could make it back to Jamaica. It mentioned a book, an account of events of their lives kept by the young Welshman in a sealed case. He hoped it would one day be discovered, if it survived the loss of the *Nuestra Regina*."

I could feel my skin crawl with excitement. "Anything else?"

"I'm getting to it. It gave clues to where the statue was hidden. It used words like 'follow the abeng' and 'under the goat's skull.' I'm giving you everything I have."

"Did you understand the clues?"

"No. I knew I needed help in deciphering it all. I needed people with the training, the background to put it together and go after it. I contacted Roger Van Allen in Jamaica. I gave him just enough information to raise his interest. He said that there was a small group of diverse antiquarians and archeologists. Five of them. They met once a year, to play poker, of all things. They were due to meet in a couple of weeks at a convention in Cairo."

"Did you know them?"

"By reputation. Your Professor Holmes was one of them."

"What did you do?"

"I divided the clues I had from Morgan's note into five sections. I had five parchments made up, each labeled with the name of one of the five. I sealed them with sealing wax. I sent them to Roger. I asked him to get each parchment into the hands of one of the five in some way that would not give too much information, but would ignite their interest in getting on board. I stressed secrecy above all. No single one of them was to see the others' clues until they were to be revealed to them all in a particular order. Roger knows me well enough not to break my trust."

I could feel the pieces of this jigsaw puzzle coming together. I could have guessed, but I wanted to hear it. "And he did what?"

I could see a grin begin. "He even amazed me. He contacted the old sailor who brought him the chest. He sent him to Cairo with a story. Roger was part of the group of five. He arranged for the old sailor to walk in during their poker game and spin out a story. As planned, he'd sit in for one hand of poker. He'd toss the passel of five parchments with the clues into the pot, together with a large gold coin. Then he'd manage to lose the hand. I give Roger credit. The drama of it all was enough to get the five on board. They even gave their group a name. 'The Monkey's Paws.'"

He came to a pause and looked at Angelique. She had just stood up. "Papa, time is short."

"I know, dear. One more minute."

He looked back at me. I saw something in his face that again reminded me of my Professor Holmes.

"Matthew. I think you and I might have found something here. Maybe even a trust that goes deeper than wealth. It's been so many years since I've felt it. My father dealt with people on no other basis. Over the years I lost sight of it. The people I deal with are not exactly of the highest character . . . I don't know. Maybe I've become an old fool. If so, I'll regret it. But I like this feeling. I'll mention him again. My father. I can feel him close to me for the first time . . . in a long while."

I left him a few moments in silence. "So, Matthew, I place it in your hands. Shall we play out this game together?"

I was at crossroads. This old man had exercised power I couldn't comprehend to build a personal fortune—an empire—in a dark area outside the laws of many countries. Wayne Barnes had warned me that dealing with him could be dangerous. There was all of that.

On the other side, there was that look in his eyes that brought up memories of the most honorable man I ever knew, my Professor Holmes. I'd promised to be truthful with Mr. Mehmed *in what I said*. But that did not necessarily mean going the next step and affirmatively disclosing information. A lawyer's distinction. I had to decide whether or not to cross that fine line.

I remember that second well. My decision fell into place. The full extent of that decision was about to be tested.

CHAPTER TWENTY-SIX

"WHAT INFORMATION CAN I give you, Mr. Mehmed?"

He smiled. His eyes met with his daughter's. I saw her give a slight nod.

"Two things. As I said, Captain Morgan's note in his sea-chest mentioned the young Welshman and his flight as Captain of the *Nuestra Regina* from the Spanish warship. It also mentioned his logbook. On the chance that there's something useful to us in the logbook, I used that as a clue in Wayne Barnes' parchment. I knew he was a veteran diver in the Caribbean. I even suggested—forgive me for being presumptuous—that he involve you in following up on the clue. You might be wondering why."

"The question has crossed my mind."

"In case the logbook was located, I wanted it in the hands of someone I thought I could trust. Perhaps more than Wayne himself."

I needed to digest that intrigue in my life further. Without rocking the boat, I smiled and nodded.

"And you and he followed up on the clue. May I ask, with what success?"

It was time to commit. "We found the logbook. It was written by the young Welshman from the time he went to sea. It described his extraordinary life under the wing of Captain Henry Morgan. I could give you a brief account. But . . . I have a copy of it with me. I'll give it to you."

I saw the smile broaden. "I'd welcome it. For more reasons than the obvious."

I think he meant it confirmed my decision of trust. "Is there anything else I can tell you?"

"There is. But I think you have only bad news for us. Claude DuCette. The Monkey's Paw in Montreal. I know you tried to visit him at his home. I believe you heard he's dead."

This was pushing my commitment of trust to the extreme. Claude DuCette's life was in the balance. And he had entrusted me with the balance. I needed one more push.

"Mr. Mehmed. I have one last question for you. I hope that you'll be completely honest. It's . . . beyond important."

I could see puzzlement in his expression. "What more could I tell you?"

"The most important answer of all. I'm not a collector. I'm not an antiquarian. I find all of this history fascinating, but it's not really part of my life, as it is for you. My only interest—and I'm sure you know it—is to learn the truth about Professor Holmes' death."

"I know that, Matthew."

"I've had no reason to choose sides. Until now. I have no dream of becoming wealthy through this statue. But I see now there's one thing that might make this whole . . . episode worth the disruption of my life, in addition to finding that answer for Mary Holmes— and for me. It would be seeing that this statue—if it's ever found— gets back in the hands of the people who actually own it—as you said, the people who have need of it for their culture, their identity. The Aztecs."

"That doesn't surprise me."

"Then my last question is where do you stand? What will be the fate of the statue if it comes into your hands?"

He thought a bit before answering. "A year ago, six months ago, the truthful answer, which I would most certainly not have shared with you, was that it would become the centerpiece of my entire personal collection."

"And now?"

"And now, I've come to share Morgan's commitment, your commitment. As far as I am able, I'll see that it goes home to the Aztecs." He raised his open hands. "I can only give you my word for that. I hope we've reached the point where that's enough."

"Almost. That's a major decision. Could I ask what changed your mind about it?"

He paused in thought. He looked over to the eyes of his daughter as if for affirmation. She smiled and nodded.

"I've actually discussed this with Angelique before we met." He paused and looked back into my eyes. "I think I'd never say this to another living soul." Again, a pause. "I said before, there is something in you that so much reminds me of my father."

I started to speak, but he held up a hand. "Let me finish. There's been a trail of death that's followed this thing for everyone who's gone after it for selfish, personal reasons. You know that. Whether it's a curse, which I doubt, or just something that's calling out for someone with an honorable purpose—I don't know. But when I look at you, Matthew, I see my father, standing in front of me, asking me to account. There's only one decision I can live with . . . That's all I can give you. But as Allah is my judge, it's the truth."

If we had not been looking eye to eye, I might not have believed.

I nodded. "Then I have something to share with you. You asked about Claude DuCette. I'll tell you this in the strictest confidence. It's a confidence I pledged with my word."

"It'll go no further."

"Claude DuCette is alive. I found his house in Montreal ransacked. He was afraid for his life. He'd received one of those small cloth sacks the Maroons call a *gris-gris*. It contained a doll with its neck broken. They were also found on Professor Holmes and the three guides in Jamaica. And nearly everyone else who's wound up dead. Claude decided that the safest place he could hide was in the announcement of his death."

"How do you know this?"

"I reached his wife. She convinced him to meet with me. Secretly, of course."

"And what did you learn?"

"Nothing that you don't already know. He told me about the poker game in Cairo. The old mariner who used it to get the parchments into the hands of the Monkey's Paws. He also filled me in on their attempt to find the object in the Blue Mountains in Jamaica. You know how that turned out."

Mr. Mehmed slipped into silent thought. His daughter nudged him out of it. "Papa?"

"Yes, dear. I know. One more minute. Matthew, do you know where Claude DuCette is now?"

I had disclosed enough to be glad that I could say truthfully, "No. I don't. But what could he add?"

"One very important piece. He's the real expert on Aztec history and relics. I was counting on him to authenticate the item, if we ever found it. He could also be the one key to getting it back into the hands of the right person in the Aztec nation."

"If that time comes, I have a way of getting in touch with him."

That brought a smile. "Good. Then it's time for you to be off. Angelique will take you back to where you're staying. One last thing."

"Yes, sir."

We stood. He put his hand on my shoulder.

"I'd like you to do something. I know your life is on hold until this is wrapped up. This might advance the cause."

He saw the question in my eyes. "I'd like you to go to Jamaica. I'd like you to contact Roger Van Allen. He's the last on your list of the five Monkey's Paws."

"I intended to do that anyway."

"Good. I'll contact him. He'll be expecting you."

"And what are you hoping I could get from him?"

"Something I can't get myself. We've had dealings in antiquities over the years. Always at arm's length and without an ounce of trust in each other. You might do better in that department."

"I could try. But what could he add that you don't already have?"

"A plan. That last attempt by the Monkey's Paws was ill-advised. Obviously, the Maroons are still protecting the sanctity of that area called Nanny Town. I have a strong feeling from the note in the chest that's where Captain Morgan hid the statue about fifty years before it became Nanny Town. We need to convince whoever speaks for the Maroons in Jamaica now that we're not there to desecrate what they feel is their sacred ground."

"Is there a chance?"

"I don't know. Perhaps if they understand that we intend to restore an object to another non-English, non-Spanish tribe. Something as important to the Aztecs as they hold their Nanny Town."

My mind was spinning over the wall of impossibility that raised for this Irish/American law professor. "Where on earth would I start?"

"Roger Van Allen. He's a life long Jamaican. He may have knowledge of who can speak for the Maroons."

"He also sounds like just the kind of 'Bakra,' as they call us, they've been fighting for centuries."

"It's worth a try. It has to be better than having five Monkey's Paws go blundering into tribal myths they've never even heard of. That was not a total success."

My silence seemed to give him direction. "Give it a try. You won my trust. Maybe you're the only one who can put this together. What have you got to lose by asking?"

I was answering that question mentally by counting the number of deceased people with little bags of tiny dolls around their necks.

Angelique and I were about to enter the Bentley for the ride back to my B & B by the Old Port. I saw her take out of her purse the cloth face mask that doubled as a blindfold. She looked back at her father and held up the mask. It was a question. Mr. Mehmed simply smiled and shook his head.

*   *   *

Angelique and I rode in silence for the first few minutes until my curiosity got the best of me. "I take it you are not only his daughter. You're also a member of his working staff."

She was looking out the window when she said, "I'm his only staff. My father has many hands and eyes around the world, but he lets no one get close to him. Or to me."

That left a question unanswered. I checked a side rearview mirror. A second Bentley was following about twenty feet behind us. The windows were tinted, but I'd have bet my tenure there were a number of well-armed, well-trained guardsmen inside.

"And yet, he seems to be allowing me into the inner circle. I'm still not sure why."

She turned to me with an enigmatic smile. "Then, if I were you, I'd simply take it as the rarest of compliments."

I did, but it seemed I could hardly remember the last time I got an answer that didn't sound like it came from a Zen master.

As the miles passed on the drive back to my quarters in Marseille, my mind was still grappling with the avalanche of information from

Mr. Mehmed. Our parting words were that he would alert Roger Van Allen that I would be arriving in Jamaica sometime soon. The hope was for a meeting that would accomplish what I still considered a minor miracle—some path to mutual accommodation with the Maroons.

As we drove, I had an unblindfolded view. We penetrated the inner depths of the city through some of the oldest quarters on the way toward the Old Port. In some sections, it was difficult to take in scenes of poverty at the extreme opposite from the estate we had just left.

I noticed, perhaps to my surprise, that Angelique's eyes were riveted to street children kicking anything that could pass for a soccer ball, children with tiny ribs that spoke of a lifetime of undernourishment. Slow-moving adults, whose bodies mirrored the debilitation of the surrounding buildings, showed age that I suspected came not from number of years, but a life of basic deprivation. Most surprising of all, given the grandeur of the home and surroundings she shared with her father, I saw in Angelique's eyes the pain of an empathy that seemed to run deep.

She broke the silence first. "Where you're staying, Matthew. *The Vieux Port Jardin.* Do you find it pleasant?"

I thought back to the garden of peace in the old converted convent. "I do. Very much."

She smiled. "I thought you would. It goes back to a different world."

I was about to ask if she chose it for me, when something in the street up ahead of us caught our attention. A woman, much younger than the other adults, was walking by the roadside with rapid but stumbling steps. She was wrapped, like many others, in ragged layers of cloth. In her arms, she was cradling what appeared to be an infant, completely wrapped in torn rags. She sheltered the child against her body as if to protect it against a fall that could occur with any step.

Our eyes were both locked on the tottering figure as she veered dangerously close to the path of our car. Angelique rapped on the back of the driver's seat. *"Attend, Marcel! Le jeune fille! L'enfant! Prene guarde!"*

The driver hit the brake a moment before the girl's misstep lunged her body into the street. She bent herself to land on her back to protect the child. The pain erupted in a cry. We stopped just ten feet before her. She lay clutching the child in both arms.

Angelique yelled to the uniformed man in the front passenger seat. *"Henri, Elle a besoin d'aide. Le Bebe. Allez vers elle! Vite!"* She was yelling with passion, "She needs help. The baby! Go to her. Quickly!"

He turned and said what I understood as "Your father ordered me not to leave you. No matter what."

Angelique spoke louder. I caught, "We can't leave her. The baby. Help her. It's my order. Do it now!"

Henri got out. He ran to the girl. He bent down to help her to her feet. I could see her cringe backwards away from him. He tried again. She held up her hand to keep him away. They exchanged words I couldn't hear.

Henri's back was to us, but I could read panic in his lurch away from her. The young girl was peeling the cloth wrapping away from the child. She finally held it up to our view. There was no child.

It was a pack of explosives.

CHAPTER TWENTY-SEVEN

THERE WAS A frantic pleading in the voice of the girl. She said something to Henri. She held out what looked like a cellphone and pointed to the car. Henri took the phone. He ran to the window beside Angelique.

She lowered the window to take it. I grabbed her arm while I pulled a handkerchief out of my pocket. "Don't touch it, Angelique. Let me."

I reached across and took it in the handkerchief out of Henri's trembling hand. It jumped to life with a ring. I said in the calmest tone I could muster, "Let me do this, Angelique. Please trust me. I've done it before."

I hit the answer button and put it on speaker. "This is Matthew Shane. You have our attention. What do you want?"

The tone of the voice seemed disguised, and the eastern European accent sounded phony. He spoke to me in English. "Mister Shane. I assume Miss Mehmed is there beside you. Very well. Do you understand that the explosive in front of you is capable of taking the lives of all of you in that car?"

"I understand that. I'll say it again. What do you want?"

"I have just one demand. Miss Mehmed will leave the car. Alone. She will walk forward to the next street and turn to the right. Do you understand?"

"I hear you."

"Good. Then she will do it now. If she does, you will all survive this little venture. If not? None of you will be so fortunate."

"Miss Mehmed is quite shaken at the moment. I'm sure you understand. She needs a minute. I'm going to hang up. Call back in two minutes. We'll go from there."

I hit the disconnect button before he could argue. I wanted him to know he wasn't in total control.

Again, in a calm but no-nonsense voice. "Angelique, do this quickly. Use your own phone. Call the men in the car behind us. Tell them to stay put 'til they hear from you. And mean it."

She did. "Good. Now dial your father. Quickly."

When I heard his voice on the line, I took the phone. "Mr. Mehmed. We've got a situation."

I gave him a quick rundown. I could hear fear, anger, frustration in his voice. "I'll send men. Where are you?"

"Please. Listen to me. We have just a minute. I've handled a number of hostage situations in Air Force security. I know what I'm doing. If you can just trust me."

There was a tense pause. "What can we do, Matthew?"

"First, we understand the situation—I think better than they do. I've dealt with smart ones and dumb ones. These are either dumb or new at the game. Clearly, they want leverage over you. They'll only have that if they have Angelique away from here, alive, and in their control. Right now, they have no power."

"What about the explosive?"

"If Angelique stays in the car, it's useless to them. They could only use it—forgive me—to kill her. It's a blunt instrument. There's no halfway. If they were to do that, they'd have no power over you. And they must know that would bring down the wrath of hell on them. There's nowhere they could hide. Do you follow me?"

"I think so."

"Time's short, Mr. Mehmed. I'm here, and I've been here before. Will you give me permission to work this out? I think I can bring your daughter home."

Another pause. Then a tense "Thank you."

The phone I was holding rang again. "Keep your cellphone on, Mr. Mehmed. You can follow what's happening."

I handed the phone back to Angelique.

Before answering the bomber's phone, I scanned the buildings in the area. I knew what I was looking for. I caught a slight movement in a curtain at a second-story window two buildings away. I leaned forward and pointed it out to the driver and guard. "The controller of the bomb."

The French words must have been similar. They both nodded. I said, "*Bon. Reste ici*"—"Good. Stay here."

I answered the bomber's phone and hit SPEAKER. The voice came back, again in English. "Don't try my patience, Mr. Shane. Miss Mehmed will step out of the car. Now."

"Ah, yes. That's where we left off. I think it's time to reassess the situation. I believe you have a tiger by the tail. Do you understand that expression?"

"What are you—"

"I guess you don't. Let me explain while you think this through. If you were insane enough to detonate that bomb and Miss Mehmed were harmed in any way, there is no place on earth you could hide. And when he finds you—and he would within hours, perhaps minutes—I can't even imagine how deeply you would regret your insanity. That's what the 'tiger' expression means. In spades."

There was just enough of a pause to suggest that he was thinking. "You are trying my patience, Mr. Shane. I warned you . . ."

I let him babble on while I whispered into Angelique's phone. "Mr. Mehmed, the controller of the bomb is in a second-story front room, two buildings down on the right. Get your men around the building fast. But don't let them be seen or make a move 'til we're out of here."

I held Angelique's phone up to the driver and pointed to the building. I whispered, "*Donnez-lui l'addresse*"— "Give him the address."

I got back to the bomb-threat caller as he was winding down his speech. I kept my voice low and calm. "Well then. There you are. It's decision time. You are on the verge of the most painful mistake you could make in a lifetime. Let's see how you handle it."

I disconnected the call.

I said it to our driver in English while Angelique translated rapidly into French. "Start making a U-turn. Slowly! No fast moves."

Angelique grabbed my arm. "What about the girl. We can't leave her. They'll kill her."

I looked at Angelique almost in disbelief. "You want me to . . ."

"We have to. Look at her."

The girl was huddling her body around the bomb in wrenching sobs.

I allowed myself one shake of the head. "Angelique, you are one piece of work. Stay here. Tell the driver to stay put."

I opened my door and got out of the car at a pace slow enough to dispel any notion of panic. I almost closed my eyes. So far, so good. No explosion.

I walked slowly, step by step, up to the girl. With every step, another prayer. I lifted her shoulders back to get her to look at me. Damn, I wished I'd worked harder in French class.

I mimed as well as I could the question—could she hand the bomb to me or was she attached to it? It took a bit, but she caught on. She lifted it off her lap. I mimed, "Lay it on the ground."

She did. It seemed ironic that I needed to keep the bomb within reach of killing Angelique to neutralize the bomber.

I had the bomber's phone in my pocket. I could hear it making an annoying jangle. I took it as a good omen. The bomber was more into making conversation—or threats—than blowing us all to North Africa. How long his patience or good sense would last—that was the gamble. I had no idea of the odds, but it was too late to change strategy.

I lifted the girl slowly to her feet. I could feel her whole body shaking as I walked her to my side of the car. I opened the door. When I turned around to help her into the car, there was a single rifle crack that echoed off the walls of the canyon of buildings.

I could feel the girl's body stiffen. She slowly slipped out of my arms onto the street. Her body went limp. The marksman was true. I was sure she died instantly.

There was no time for regrets. It was like situations I'd been through in Afghanistan. I forced my mind to lock down on one step after the other.

Thinking without emotion, I could count the killing of the girl—and not me—as boosting the odds that my words were giving the bomber second, more realistic thoughts.

I slipped into the car. Angelique was in tears. I took her arm, and said quietly, "Tell the driver to turn around slowly and drive us back out of here. Do it."

She did. The driver got through half a U-turn. There was an eruption of automatic gunfire so loud I couldn't tell what was the firing and what were the echoes. The pavement beside us was spitting chunks of concrete that hammered my side of the car. The driver stepped hard on the brakes.

I yelled above the noise to Angelique, "Tell him to finish the U-turn. But slowly."

The driver, bless him, kept his wits. He followed orders. I grabbed the shoulder of the guard in front and pointed up the street. "*Ou? Ou?*—Where? Where?—The boom-boom?"

Thank God, he caught my meaning. He kept his head up and watched for the next burst of firing. He turned around and yelled to me above the chaos, "*Oui! Oui! Vous avez raison. La! La!*"—"Yes! Yes! You're right! There! There!" He pointed to the same second-story window.

I grabbed the phone out of Angelique's hand. Her father was screaming into it. "What's happening, Matthew? What's happening? Angelique . . ."

I yelled into the phone. "She's still okay. All of us. The Bentley may need a paint job. Listen to me. You have the address of the bomber's building. He's still there. As you can hear. So far it's all noise and warning shots. He might have listened to me. We'll know in a minute. Get your men around that building."

"They're just arriving. I had men close. They're there. Matthew, what—

"No time to chat. Start praying. With God's help, we just might be there soon. Stay tuned."

The car completed the U-turn and stopped.

Another deafening eruption of gun-bursts. This time closer, but still not on us. The bomber's phone was still ringing. I punched the ON button. I tried to be heard over the jack-hammering roar and still sound confident. "Listen to me! Before you commit the dumbest act of your life! His men have your building surrounded. You're in his hands. Right now. Believe me. You don't want to answer for the death of his daughter. Last chance to save your life."

I hit the OFF button.

I said into the live phone with Mr. Mehmed, "Have your men at the building fire off a few rounds to let the bomber know you're there. Right now."

He did. We could hear single shots coming from down the street toward the building. I could only pray that that convinced the bomber that I was not bluffing.

I bent over close to the driver's ear. "Now, brother. Go. *Allez!* Head for home. But slowly. *Lentement!* No sign of panic. We've got control."

Or so we'd like to believe, I thought.

He took me literally. The car crept back in the direction we'd come from at a pace I could have passed walking. The good news was that with each passing yard, we were still alive.

I checked back behind us. I was counting the feet away from the bomb. We finally reached the point where I thought, "Ten more yards and we're clear. Like making a first down."

The thought had barely formed, when my ears were stunned deaf. The rear window was riveted with a blinding cloud of concrete and dust. The car felt encased in a shock of air that seemed to propel it forward. The rear window was scarred and pock marked, but it held.

I rapped the driver on the shoulder. I shouted, *"Allez!* Hit the gas! Full out!"

I don't know if he could understand or even if he could hear me. It could have been his own impulse. He floored it. If that Bentley had had wings, we'd have been airborne.

We were at least a mile down the road before he let the gas pedal off the floor. We came down to cruising speed. It was probably unnecessary, but I yelled, "Head for home, and don't spare the horses."

I checked Angelique. Her eyes were open wide, but the tears had stopped. "Are you all right, Angelique?"

She looked at me and nodded. Her voice was breathless. "Matthew, how did you know that would work? You did it."

I was breathless myself. I said, "Not me." I just pointed up to heaven.

We both settled back in the seat. We let our thoughts slowly catch up with our recollections. I couldn't help replaying the last minute. I could remember the sound and feeling of the explosion. I thought I could actually hear two explosions, the second a little less distinct. Yet that made no sense.

But then, what did?

CHAPTER TWENTY-EIGHT

WE CRUISED PAST two armed guards through the wide-open gate. We swung into the circular drive and pulled up to the front of the Mehmed mansion. Mr. Mehmed was at his daughter's door before the car stopped. When a hug that must have lasted a full minute ended, words of concern passed through two tear-soaked faces.

I was out of the car. The poor Bentley looked like a Campbell's soup can that had been used for target practice. I was just getting my feet back steadily on the ground when Mr. Mehmed came around the corner. He had not wiped the tears when he came to stand in front of me.

His words came from his soul. "Matthew, when you saved my daughter—you saved my life. She is . . . everything. I owe you my life. Nothing less. Please, come into my home."

He had each of us by the hand. He led us up the marble stairs into a mansion that, I suspect, was seldom, if ever, seen by anyone other than his daughter and a small army of trusted servants.

"Matthew, you'll spend the night. I won't hear otherwise. We'll make new plans in the morning."

"Believe me, it would be my pleasure."

He held my shoulder and looked into my eyes—much as Professor Holmes would do. "Your judgment was right about everything. Praise and thanksgiving to Allah."

"We both thank God . . . I was certainly right about one thing."

"What's that?"

"That Bentley will definitely need a paint job."

It took him a second to get my drift. But when he did, he burst into a deep laugh. Angelique joined in, and I gave in to its infectiousness. The three of us were pouring into that laugh all of the pent-up tension that had consumed us for nearly an hour.

*   *   *

Dinner that evening was served in a classic French dining room. The chef's handiwork was clearly equal to the surroundings. By mutual agreement, none of us brought the earlier events of the day into the dinner conversation.

After dinner, the three of us gathered in Mr. Mehmed's study. I couldn't hold the question any longer. "You were clearly the target today, Mr. Mehmed. Through Angelique. What do you think? Was it related to the search for the statue?"

He lit a cigar—unquestionably Cuban—and offered one to me. It complemented an exquisite single malt scotch. I waited for his answer.

"Possibly. But then in my business . . . any number of people could be looking for a sword over my head."

"Another question. This one may not make sense. It's been plaguing me since it happened."

I could see I had his full attention.

"This afternoon, when I thought we were clear of the bomb, I gave the order to hit the gas. Speed off. As we did, the bomb in the street was exploded. We could feel its blast."

"I know. Thank God for your judgment."

"But I could almost swear I heard a second blast, farther away, almost the same time as the first. What could that have been?"

Mr. Mehmed looked from me to Angelique. He addressed himself to me. "You're right. The bomber detonated that street bomb first. It may have been aimed at Angelique. And you. But I doubt it. Everything indicates that you'd talked him out of it. If not, he'd never have let you get that far."

"Then why the explosion?"

He glanced again at Angelique. He hesitated. Then he looked back at me. "These are conscienceless people, Matthew. You knew that the poor girl who had carried the bomb was dead beside the car. From his distance, the bomber might not have been able to tell for sure. She might have known more than he wanted her to tell."

"You think it was to silence her."

"More than likely."

"Then was I hearing things—or was there a second explosion?"

"There was. My men reported it. These people we're dealing with are not careless. I understand their thinking. They had set a second bomb in that second-story room where the bomber was located. I'm sure the bomber was not aware of it."

"I can guess why. In case the first bomb exploded and harmed your daughter, the same device would trigger a second bomb to kill the bomber himself. That was that second explosion I heard. Another witness silenced."

"That would be my assumption."

"You do play with some stone-cold people."

"Look around you. There's a great deal of wealth involved in what I do. It attracts—an interesting variety."

"You could say."

Whether the bombing was connected to the statue or not, I was adding at least two more deaths to the string that seemed to be populating my path to the answer I needed.

"I guess just one final question. Do you have any idea who set up this kidnapping attempt?"

He took another deep draw on the cigar. The clear smoke came out in a slow, white stream. "Yes. And no. You've heard the expression 'When you shoot at a king, don't miss.' This was a bold move."

"Agreed. In spades."

"There are just two criminal cartels in Marseille that would dare to attempt it. One is the Russian mob. The other is the *Union Corse*. The Corsican mafia. They operated the so-called French Connection that trafficked heroine to the United States until it was broken up in 1970. They're still very much around. Very strong. The open port of Marseille lends itself to a flood of criminal activity."

"Which of the two would you guess?"

"My guess. The Corsicans. They're smarter."

"You said, 'Yes and no.' What's the 'no' part?"

"I don't deal with those Corsican gangsters. I want no part of them. They have nothing to do with my business. Including the Aztec statue. I'm sure of that."

"So then?"

"I feel certain they were just hired to pull off the kidnapping. The bomber himself, the one with his finger on the button, he was probably a low-level Corsican soldier."

"Which leaves the real question."

"Exactly. Who hired them? Who's really behind it?"

"Any guess?"

"Not at the moment. I have contacts looking into it."

I knew enough to leave that path unexplored.

Mr. Mehmed raised his hand. Within seconds, a uniformed servant was there to refill my glass of superb scotch. I was not opposed. "So where from here, Matthew?"

"I was just thinking about that."

"May I make a suggestion? Then it's your decision. Horribly involved as you were this afternoon, I don't think you were the target. In fact, they'd have preferred you were not there. Agreed?"

"Yes."

"Very well. Are you still comfortable visiting the Monkey's Paw in Jamaica? Roger Van Allen. I still think he's our key to an expedition with the blessing of the Maroons."

"'Comfortable' is an overstatement. But I agree it's a logical next step."

"Good. You'll stay here tonight. There's an airstrip on the back of the estate. I have a small private jet. I'll have my pilot fly you to Paris. I can make a reservation for a flight tomorrow afternoon to Jamaica. Does that suit you?"

"One deviation. I need to touch base at home. Salem, Massachusetts. Tomorrow is Tuesday. I should be ready to fly from there to Jamaica by Friday."

"Fine. I'll book you a flight from Paris to Logan Airport in Boston. Yes?"

"Perfect."

"And I'll let Roger Van Allen know that you'll be arriving in Jamaica around Friday."

The time must have been somewhere between nine p.m. and midnight when every aching bone in my body settled into a bed that felt like it was made of a cloud. That's the last I remember for the next nine hours.

*   *   *

Morning brought an early rising. Goodbyes to both Mr. Mehmed and Angelique were said with a sincere wish for more time together at the end of whatever the road ahead held for us.

*   *   *

I touched the green, green grass of home around midnight. My condo in Salem looked to me like the Mehmed estate.

I hardly needed to turn on a light. The muscle memory of how to cruise between every room, piece of furniture, and cabinet in the apartment kicked in as soon as I walked through the door.

I hit the button to play back saved phone messages that had been accumulating for nearly a week. I had half-a-brain tuned in to the flow of check-ins from friends, notices from the university, and general spam. The other half-brain guided me without conscious thought to the cabinet over the stove where I stored a small, but selective, store of the wines and whiskeys favored by my drop-in friends. I reached without looking for the green, jug-shaped bottle of the libation I favored for a slow-sipping nightly relaxer before bed, Tullamore Dew.

The first fully conscious sensation I had since entering my condo was a slightly jarring stub of the thumb on the bottle. No big deal. I figured even muscle memory could have its lapses over time.

The second wakening came when I reached for my usual whiskey glass and found that my habitual stacking of glasses in the cabinet was slightly out of synch.

Now I began checking. I would never have otherwise noticed, but little items like lamps, pictures, and small items on shelves were out of line with the dust patterns that had developed over the week. My cleaning service is on a two-week schedule. They would not have touched the apartment while I was away.

By now, I had penetrated even jet lag to full consciousness. It took less than half an hour to take a full inventory. As nearly as I could tell, much had been moved, but nothing was missing. That was some comfort, but given the circumstances of the past two weeks, the sense of vulnerability began erupting into real and imagined fears.

On the forced theory that concern over matters you can't address at the moment is wasted angst, I chilled a few fingers of the Dew over ice and gave in to an enveloping cloud of sleep.

* * *

My first stop the next morning was my office at the law school. There were no summer sessions, so I was practically alone in the building.

I rifled through a mound of mail that hadn't been checked since the morning it began with a call from the dean. I cruised through advertisements and paper spam until I hit a plain white envelope that came through campus mail. It had just my name and office number on it. The lump inside sparked my curiosity. I didn't need a return address to recognize Professor Holmes' hen-scratching.

A quick rip of the envelope sent something tumbling onto the floor. It was a tiny, plain metal key. I took out a piece of lined paper that looked like the notepad Professor Holmes kept on his desk for reminders.

I got chills when I deciphered in his unique hand, "Matthew. Just in case. Tell no one. I'll call tomorrow."

I could have sworn I'd seen that key before, but no memory bells were telling me where. There was a time stamp on the envelope from campus mail. It had been sent the day before Professor Holmes was found dead.

* * *

My next check-in was with Mary Holmes. I could have just called, but I think both of us needed a hug and an in-person visit. Over coffee, we caught up on the events of the previous week. I left out the more adventurous elements. She still asked, "Matthew, are you in danger?"

"Good heavens, no. The most exciting part of my day is lunch."

She seemed relieved. "Are you any closer to an answer?"

"I think, perhaps. At least I know a lot more about the Monkey's Paws."

While Mary refilled our cups, I worked on an "oh-by-the-way" tone. I took the little key out of my pocket. I showed it to Mary, to her mild surprise. "Where did you get that, Matthew?"

"The professor gave it to me a while ago. Do you know it?"

"Sure, it's to our stamp box. It's over here on the shelf. I'll show you. Why would he give you that?"

Mary got up and took a small, metal lockbox out of an overhead cabinet. She put it on the table in front of me, while I searched for a neutral answer. "I'm not sure. Let's check."

I tried the key on the box. It fit the slot, but would not open the box. I passed it off. "Must be to something else. It was a while ago anyway. Probably nothing."

I'm not sure Mary bought it, but we talked about every neutral subject I could think of before I got up to leave. We had the goodbye hug. I almost reached the door before I heard the concern in her voice. "Is that key important for some reason, Matthew?"

I gave her a calming smile. She had enough to deal with without getting deeper into the Monkey's Paws morass. "I doubt it. You know the professor's memory for unimportant details. He probably just wanted me to hang onto it for him."

That part was no lie. But the rest of the truth was that I had seen an identical lockbox in the coat closet of the professor's office.

CHAPTER TWENTY-NINE

As soon as I left Mary, I called Mac McLane. I needed his police presence to get into what was now labeled a "crime scene." He met me at the professor's office in half an hour.

I opened the door to the office closet. There was a stack of books on the shelf I hadn't seen there before. I took down the books. There in the back was the lockbox I had seen once on his bookshelf. It was identical to the one in his kitchen.

I put the box on the desk in front of us. The key slipped into the slot. It turned easily. I looked at Mac. "This may not be the opening of King Tut's tomb, but it feels like it."

"So open it already."

I slipped up the lid of the box. There was a top layer of something like a chamois cloth. Under it lay a sheet of what felt like old parchment paper. It had three even sides. The top edge was ragged, as if it had been torn from a larger sheet.

I felt certain down to my toes that I was holding a piece of one of the five clues given to the Monkey's Paws—the one given to Professor Holmes. Mac and I both pored over the words written in what looked like ancient calligraphy. The words were, "Follow the stream to the cave. Enter with care."

Mac looked at me. "Does that make sense?"

"Not by itself. Sit down, Mac. I've got a story to tell you."

I laid out every detail of what I'd learned in the past week to the one deeply involved person I was absolutely positive I could trust.

"It's half a clue, Mac. Professor Holmes must have torn his parchment in half. Without this, the rest of his clue would be incomplete."

"Seems the boys were not quite as trusting of their buddies as it appeared. Any idea when he did it?"

"I think so. I'm guessing he divided the parchment right around the time he went to Jamaica. Something must have made him suspicious. At some point after he got back, I feel sure one of them searched his suitcase in his attic. I think he found the other half of the professor's parchment. He must have been jolted to find he had only half a clue."

"When did the professor send the key?"

"The university time stamp on the envelope was the day before he was killed. By then he must have known he was in danger. Maybe from one of his buddies."

"Any one in particular?"

"Nothing conclusive. I had a theory that whoever was his roommate at the hotel in Jamaica might have seen him put his parchment in the top lining of his suitcase. Whoever stole it from the suitcase in his attic knew just where to look. Nothing else was touched."

"And that would be which one?"

"Mary said the professor called her from Jamaica. Wayne Barnes had asked to room with him."

"That narrows it."

My wrinkled forehead must have suggested my indecision .

"What, Matt?"

"I told you I spent a couple of days with Wayne Barnes in Barbados. If he took it, he knew he had only half a clue. He also knew how close I was with the professor."

"So?"

"He never mentioned it. He never asked me about it. Why not?"

"If he did mention it, he'd be admitting he'd stolen it. How else would he know it was half a clue?"

"Point taken."

"Then take this point too, Matt. Someone out there, maybe Barnes, might be making the connection between you and the clue right now. People have already died for those things. I don't like the target I see on your back."

Put that way, neither did I.

It seemed like a good moment to mention my sense that my apartment had been thoroughly searched. Searched, but not tossed. Nothing was apparently missing and no harm done. Mac pressed the possibility of giving me police protection. Desirable as that thought was, I had to ask, "Which of your boys is going to follow me to Jamaica?"

All in all, it seemed like a good time to get out of Dodge. Mac's suggestion of having someone at my back was developing a growing appeal. I was actually surprised at the one who rose to the top of my choice of candidates.

Before making a plane reservation on the first thing flying to the Norman Manley Airport outside of Port Royal, Jamaica, I called Maurice Perreault in Bayou Ste. Germaine, Louisiana. I asked if Kwame, his grandfather's closest friend, was there. I was remembering that Kwame had once saved my parts from being the blue plate special for the pack of alligators under the bridge of the old Maroon man in a bayou in Louisiana.

When Kwame joined on the line, I gave them both an abbreviated synopsis of what I'd learned so far. The conversation that followed made it clear that Kwame was still stuck on the belief that it was the old man in the bayou by one of his Maroons, probably Keku, who

caused the baboon attack that led to the death of his friend Rene
Perreault. In a way, I was not unhappy to hear it. I think it helped
induce him to meet me in Jamaica, the religious center of the
Maroons. Since his theory was gathering no proof one way or the
other in Louisiana, he was quick to get on board.

* * *

Our flights got us to Jamaica within an hour of each other. I had
made our reservations at Morgan's Harbour Hotel, where Professor
Holmes and the other Monkey's Paws had stayed during their abor-
tive trek to the Blue Mountain trail.

The first call I made after check-in at ten p.m. was to the last
Monkey's Paw on my list, Roger Van Allen. I caught surprise in his
voice when he heard I was two days ahead of our meeting set up by
Mr. Mehmed.

* * *

Roger met us the next morning in the dining room of the hotel in
the middle of breakfast. With his weathered and tanned features,
well-conditioned build for his age, and bearing that suggested he
suffered no lack of self-assurance, he would be the most suited of all
the Monkey's Paws to play an aging Indiana Jones.

He had no trouble spotting Kwame and me. He was barely seated
at our table when the waiter set a cup of black coffee in front of him.

Introductions were brief. The chat was friendly and general for
the first five minutes. When I interjected a suggestion that we use
the time to exchange information to fill any gaps in our knowledge
of the business of the Monkey's Paws, his smile dimmed. I asked if
there was a problem.

There was a pause. We gave him a moment to put his words together. "Matthew, you've come a long way. I hope you won't regret it."

Those were the last words I wanted to hear. "I certainly hope the same. I'm confused. What do you mean, Mr. Van Allen?"

"Call me 'Roger.' I hope we're among friends here."

"Done. Roger. So what do you mean?"

His eyes were directly on mine. "I hope you understand—I'm not a quitter. Never have been. This is not the first time I've faced difficult odds."

I filled the pause with a non-committal, "Okay."

"On the other hand, I'm no twenty-year-old either. There comes a time in life when you have to look at those odds realistically. I've given it a lot of thought. Here's how it adds up. If we tried again, we'd be facing a trek into a mountain forest that plays perfectly into the hands of an ambush. It's in the control of a tribe that thinks it's such sacred land that some mythical woman will kill anyone—anyone like us—who touches it. I think there may be members of that tribe who'll keep the myth alive by making sure that comes true. You following me?"

"I hear you."

"Well, there were hundreds of the best British soldiers who thought they could buck that belief. They never came back. That's history."

"So I've heard."

"Good. You also heard about our first attempt?"

"Yes."

"Then why would we try again? What's even up there? The vague report of some possible treasure that might or might not have any real value other than historic. That might, as a matter of fact, not even exist."

I just nodded. "Go on."

"So I weigh the odds. For the first time in my life, I have to say it. I'm out."

I was ready for almost anything but that. I still needed to carry on the quest as the only hope of finding the answer I needed for Mary. I also felt that Roger was the best, if not only, link to getting a free pass, if not help, from the Jamaican Maroons. I had one pitch to make. It meant disclosing information so far shared only between Mr. Mehmed and me, but he had trusted me once before.

"I hear you, Roger. Believe it or not, I understand. Unfortunately, giving up is not an option for me. There's a personal reason that has nothing to do with getting wealthy. Would you consider another factor before you opt out?"

"I'll listen to anything you say, Matthew. That's why I'm here."

I leaned forward to plead my case in a whisper to this one-man jury. "If you'll believe me without too much elaboration, I know what the object is."

I could see this took him by surprise. "Would you care to share it?"

I took the deep breath of a diver on the high platform who is not totally convinced he wants to make the leap. It took a second or two, but I could almost hear Mr. Mehmed whisper, *I trust your judgment, Matthew.*

"It's a large statue, maybe three or four feet tall. It's of an eagle with a snake in its mouth standing on a cactus. It's made of solid gold and crusted with precious gems."

I saw a fire come back in his eyes. "It's Aztec then."

"You've heard of it."

"Not the statue. No. But I know that part of the ancient Aztec beliefs. Any archeologist does. It must be worth . . ."

"It is. And more."

"And you know all this how?"

"You're acquainted with Mr. Mehmed of Marseille."

"We've done business. He's the one who asked me to meet with you here."

"Yes. He's now deeply involved in this. Perhaps more than any of the Monkey's Paws. He had a meeting in Mexico with the current leader of the Aztec nation. What he learned went beyond the dollar value. That leader convinced him that this statue exists. It was made long before the Spanish conquest of Mexico. Mr. Mehmed traced the path of the statue from Mexico to some area in the Blue Mountains here in Jamaica. Most likely in the heart of the old Nanny Town."

I could see I had his full attention. "Why would this Aztec tell Mehmed about it?"

"This statue has the most profound importance to what's left of the Aztec civilization. They're struggling right now to keep their unity, their identity as a people, against heavy odds. This statue goes back to their very roots. It was made at a time when their civilization was at its peak power. They were one of the two most advanced civilizations in the new world. They're a Christian nation now, but as a symbol of their pride as a people, it goes far beyond the financial worth of the object."

"I know enough about the Aztecs to understand what you're saying, but what—"

"I can only tell you what I've heard and what I believe. Something happened at that meeting between Mr. Mehmed and the Aztec leader. Mr. Mehmed has committed himself to returning that statue to the Aztec people who actually own it. I might say, who deeply need it."

I could see that he was absorbing every word. I let him mull that over before breaking into his concentration. "Roger, I have no proof. I don't even have the words to express why I believe it. It may run counter to your previous impression of Mr. Mehmed. But for what it's worth, I believe what he told me. Based on that, I'm willing to make that same commitment to find it and return it to the Aztecs. I'm hoping this may put a new light on your decision."

I saw a smile start to creep across his face.

I pressed on. "You're a lifelong archeologist, Roger. Could this rekindle your interest on that basis?"

He held up a hand. "Not quite so fast. What about the others? Wayne Barnes, for example. Is he signed on to this new purpose for the search?"

"No. He may never be. That's something we'll have to face down the road. We can only deal with what we know at this moment."

He said nothing. But he took a slow sip of his coffee and sat back. I added one last shot. "Consider this too. Mr. Mehmed and I are committed to seeing this thing through, as I said, for reasons of our own. Perhaps the others are too, for their own reasons. If we have to attempt the search of that Maroon territory in the Blue Mountains without your help in getting some sort of permission from the Maroons, there'll likely be more deaths. Probably our own."

I could see he was considering my argument.

The smile was slowly coming back to where it was when he came into the room. He pointed a finger at me. "Matthew, you wouldn't play tricks on an old man, would you?"

I leaned back as well. "I have only three words to give you. But you can trust them: I would not."

He nodded slowly. "I see a lot of Professor Holmes in you. I'd trust him with my life. Maybe that's what I'm doing now." He held his hand across the table to be met by mine.

"God help me. I'm back in."

CHAPTER THIRTY

THE ACID SURGE in my stomach at the thought of losing our one link to the Maroon community subsided. It was time to do business.

"I think you'll agree, Roger. The next excursion into the Blue Mountains should be better planned. No more surprises."

"Agreed."

"Before the Monkey's Paws make a move, we need the permission of the Maroon community. Also agreed?"

"No question."

"That's where we're hoping for your help. You know the playing field in Jamaica better than any of us. How do we start?"

He sat back in thought for the minute it took our waiter to refill coffee and withdraw beyond earshot. He was still gazing out at the Caribbean when I gave the conversation a nudge. "What are you thinking?"

"I'm wondering how to break down a wall of distrust of anyone with a skin color that looks English—or Spanish." When he looked back, his eyes fell on Kwame. "I'm sorry. Your name again?"

"Kwame."

"And you're from?"

"Originally? Ghana. East Central Africa."

"I know where it is. Are you Ashanti tribe?"

"No. But our territories are close. My people have a lot in common with the Ashanti. We were both victims of the slavers."

"Are you familiar with the Ashanti religion? I mean particularly their belief in this so-called Obeah woman? The one they call Queen Nanny?"

"Of course."

Roger looked at me with a growing spark in his eyes. When he looked back at Kwame he asked in a more energized tone, "Do you speak their language?"

Kwame could see where this was going. He looked back at me before answering. I just nodded. He looked back at Roger. "Yes. I was raised in a village close to the Ashanti."

Roger had a smile that began to raise a glimmer of hope. "Gentlemen. Stay close to the hotel. I'll get a message to you through the concierge."

He was on his feet and moving toward the door. I called after him. "Do you want my cellphone number?"

He waived off the suggestion on his way out. "Don't trust them. Too many ears."

*   *   *

Kwame and I spent the next day and a half on the grounds of the hotel. We were at the pool, when a waiter found us and handed me an envelope. A note on plain stationary said simply, "Be in front of the hotel at seven p.m."

Shortly after seven, a car pulled up. The driver was a Jamaican. Because of the tinted windows, I couldn't see Roger in the back seat until the driver came around and opened the door. Roger called out. "Climb aboard. We'll have a few words on the way." He looked at Kwame. "You sit here with me."

The level of Kwame's trust of Roger was apparent in his hesitation. We had discussed his feelings that morning about meeting with members of the group he still believed caused the death of his closest friend in the baboon cage. I understood. I did my best to convince him that he'd never know for sure if we didn't follow this path to a conclusion.

Roger gave Kwame a quick beckoning hand motion. I gave him a nod and a shrug, which translated into, "It's what we came for. Let's do it."

He slowly sat in the back seat beside Roger. I sat in front with the driver. We had scarcely cleared the entranceway to the hotel when Roger addressed himself directly to me. "What we're looking for here may well be out of the question. Too many centuries of anger built up on both sides. Our only hope is . . ." He looked over at Kwame. "I'm sorry. What's your name again?"

To move things past Kwame's reluctance to give his name a third time, I interjected, "Kwame."

Roger picked it up. "Yeah. All right. You say you speak their language. I'm counting on that to break the barrier, if anything can. I've used my contacts to locate the one who's apparently their religious leader. He lives in the town that was built by the Maroons after Nanny Town was destroyed by the British soldiers. It's called Moore Town. Are you listening?"

Kwame simply gazed out at the passing countryside. He gave no answer, but looked over toward Roger. Roger continued. "I had to go through intermediaries. It wasn't easy. He's finally agreed to speak with us." He looked back at me. "I told him about your man here. That at least got us this far."

I nodded my acknowledgment, but I could feel the rigidity in Kwame growing by the minute. Roger directed himself to Kwame.

"This'll be delicate. You'll do the talking. Do it in their language. You have to somehow convince him that we're sensitive to his beliefs about what he thinks is sacred land. Play on the fact that we only want to restore something to another tribe. Say it's something as important to their national culture as Nanny Town is to the Maroons. That's something he should understand. Have you got all that?"

There was an uncomfortable five-second pause. Kwame rose a bit higher in his seat. He engaged the eyes of Roger directly. His voice was calm, but I could feel the steel in his tone. "Yes, Mr. Van Allen. I hear your words clearly. I understand your demands. Now let me tell you what I will do. I'll give him the respect the leader of a proud, strong people deserves. This is a people who rose from slavery to defeat the best British troops at their own game for many decades. I won't patronize him, and I won't lie to him. Have *you* got all that?"

Roger's expression was between shock and suppressed anger. He had perhaps never been spoken to by a man of Kwame's background in that tone. I was proud of Kwame, but I was also hoping the train stayed on the track. Roger managed to hold it all in. Perhaps he too wanted to save the moment. "Yeah. Well. Certainly."

Kwame never broke eye contact. "Good. Then perhaps you'll do me the courtesy of telling me the truth. If I tell this man that we intend to restore this statue to the Aztec nation, will I be speaking for you as well?"

Roger looked at me. He could see by my expression that I too was waiting for his answer. Roger looked back at Kwame. "Yes. Of course."

For whatever faith he put in Roger's words, Kwame simply went back to watching the passing scenery.

*   *   *

Just after sundown we passed the sign, "Welcome to Moore Town."
We probably all wondered if those words were meant for us.

Roger gave an address to his driver. Five minutes later we were
parked outside of a wooden building with the illuminated sign
above it, "Moore Town Cultural Center." The power of suggestion
took me back to the steps that led to the home of the old Maroon
man in the Louisiana bayou.

A large man in camouflage shirt and pants walked down the steps
and stooped by the car. Kwame was the first one out, followed by
Roger and me. I took some comfort in the fact that our driver stayed
at the wheel. I resisted the urge to say, "Keep the motor running."

The one-man welcoming committee just looked us over until
Kwame spoke to him in a low voice. I couldn't understand the words,
but apparently, he did. There was a response that was not hostile. It
relieved my tension by several degrees.

He led us up the steps and gave a soft knock on the door. It was
opened by another man of the same proportions. He looked at each
of us with no change of expression until he saw Kwame. He said
something to which Kwame responded. Again, to my relief, they
shook hands.

He invited Kwame to come in. With no indication to the contrary, Roger and I accepted what we chose to consider a silent invitation to follow Kwame.

The inside gave the bare-wood appearance of a meeting room.
There was a long board table in the center with three men of African
descent sitting across from us. None of them appeared to be much
under sixty, but the deeply wrinkled face of the man in the center
appeared well over that.

No words were spoken. Roger and I followed Kwame's lead in approaching the three chairs on our side of the table. Kwame bowed in a respectful way to the old man in the center. He said something softly in what sounded like an African dialect. I thought I noticed a slight melt in the freeze that surrounded our hosts. The man in the center spoke a few words in the same language.

Kwame picked up what was beginning to sound like a conversation. He nodded first to me. I took the cue and bowed as he had. He then nodded to Roger, who hesitated, but finally took the cue with more of a nod than a bow. It apparently sufficed, since the old man held out his hand in what we took as an invitation to sit opposite.

There was an exchange between the old man and Kwame. The only part I could fathom was the word "Kwame." Somehow, I sensed a mutual respect. At one point, Kwame turned to me. He said quietly, "He is asking if I speak for myself or for you two as well."

Before I could give an answer to Kwame, the old man said to me, "You may do me the respect of speaking to me directly. I've spoken the language of the British all my life."

I looked at him and said, "Then I'll begin by saying I'm not British. I'm American. I appreciate your seeing us. My name is Matthew Shane." I nodded to Roger on my left. "His name is—"

The old man held up a hand. He looked at Roger. "I'll hear him speak for himself."

"Yeah. I'm Roger Van Allen. And your name?"

The tension in Roger's tone made me wish I had spoken for him. He was clearly not in his element. It came out more rough-edged than I'd hoped.

The old man looked back at Kwame and said something in the African language. I noticed the level of tension had risen a notch.

Kwame addressed the old man in English. "I mean no disrespect. It would be better if we do this in English. We all have an interest in this meeting. We need to understand the hearts of each other."

"Then we shall speak in English. Tell us why we should allow you to walk on our sacred ground. Do you even understand the meaning of Nanny Town?"

Kwame looked at me to pick up the ball.

I began. "We've come to you in a spirit of—"

The old man raised a hand to cut me off. He looked directly at Roger. "We'll hear it from you."

My mind froze. My doubt that Roger could hide his colonial feelings long enough to plead a convincing case was raging. I under-stood the reason he was chosen. The old man was insightful enough to know that he'd get the truest reading of our sincerity, or lack of it, from Roger.

I gave Roger the subtlest look of concern I could muster. He began as I might have feared. "All right. Here's the story. There's something we need to find. It's located somewhere in the place called Nanny Town. We know how you feel about it. Ever since the escaped slaves, the Maroons, built the town—"

He was cut off by the old man who rose to his feet. He spoke in a low tone, but there was no mistaking the force of his words. "You're wrong, Mr. Van Allen. It would be well for you to understand why you're wrong before you say another word."

I think Roger just held his breath. I know I did. The old man went on. "That word, 'Maroon,' is British. It was meant to be derogatory. You should already know that, since you were born in Jamaica. It meant to the British something wild. An escaped slave. It's a word we would never have used to refer to ourselves. But our ancestors gave a new meaning to the word by defeating the British at every turn until their king was forced to resort to a peace treaty nearly three hundred years ago."

Roger held his silence. The old man leaned forward on the table to address Roger more directly. "Let me also be clear about your words 'escaped slaves.' Our ancestors were never slaves. Never. They were taken from their villages in Africa by men with guns. They were forced to do crushing labor. They were subjected to indignities by the Spanish, then the British. But they never surrendered their minds or their souls. They were never what you call 'slaves.' When they threw off their chains and settled in Nanny Town, they gave the British a taste of how free men can resist their subjugation."

The frigid silence was palpable. The old man sat down without breaking eye contact. Roger was clearly flummoxed. The best he could raise for a response was, "I see."

The tone of the old man was now soft but, to my fear, just as resolute. "Do you? The thoughts of a lifetime do not change in one conversation. I think we both know what's in each of our hearts."

The finality of those words nearly sank my heart. Those two frozen attitudes were not likely to melt, no matter what I said or how I said it. I was looking into a pit of defeat when Kwame touched my arm. I looked at him. He gave me the slightest nod toward a dark corner of the room to our right.

I looked over. I had been so focused on the old man at the table that I was nearly unaware of someone sitting in the shadows in a rocking chair. I recalled noticing that the only distraction of the old man's attention since we entered the room was an occasional quick glance in that direction.

It was desperation time. With nothing to lose, and apparently nothing to gain from more silent obeisance, I stood straight up. My complete focus was now on an elderly woman, dressed in what I took to be African tribal clothes sitting in a rocking chair.

Without asking permission, I walked over to her. Bowing had gotten us nowhere. I simply began. "May I speak to you directly?"

There was a sharp focus in her eyes. "Why would you want to do that?"

"Because I believe you're the person in charge. What I have to say is important. It needs to be heard by an open mind before we leave this room."

I could feel the heat of the eyes of the old man on my back. I somehow knew that he was back on his feet and fuming. He started to say something that I'm sure would have killed any of the hopes we brought with us.

Before he could speak, the woman stood. She raised a hand to the man at the table. I could hear his words—whatever they were—catch in his throat.

The woman, probably twice my age, held my eyes with hers. She walked slowly with a wooden cane to the other side of the table. The old man in the center slowly backed away. The woman took his seat. She signaled me to come back and sit opposite her.

"You have something to say to me, Mr. Shane. Something important, you say. And what might that be?"

There was something in the calm of her tone that opened a crevice of hope.

I took one long breath before launching into the most important plea I'd made in my lifetime—in or out of court.

CHAPTER THIRTY-ONE

"I DON'T ASK this for myself, nor for any of us here."

"That remains to be seen, Mr. Shane."

"I'll explain. There's a people much like yourselves. They built an empire on their beliefs and their unique character, which was their strength. Like yourselves, they were subjected to crushing domination by the Spaniards. Also like yourselves, they never surrendered their souls or their character."

The woman's eyes held mine with every word. "You're speaking of the Aztecs or the Incas."

"It could be either. In this case, it's the Aztecs. Today they live in villages scattered across southern Mexico. They've adopted the Christian religion. They also cling to the ancient customs that made them one unified people. Their strength is in that unity. I'm sure you of all people understand."

Our eyes were still locked. "Go on, Mr. Shane, but be careful. We've heard patronizing words from many of your race."

"Then you'll be the judge of my honesty. There's been a long course of events going back centuries. The lives and deaths of many people have been involved. It finally brought me here to speak with you. And yes, I do have something to ask of you. I won't diminish it with words. I understand the weight of what I'm asking."

"Then ask."

I knew there was only one thing that could survive her judgment. She'd know it in an instant—undiluted honesty. I said it simply. "There was an object, a large golden statue. It was made centuries ago by the Aztecs to pay the deepest honor to the god they then believed sustained all their lives. Their greatest fear was that it would be discovered and desecrated by the Spanish. In a moment of trust, their leader put it into the hands of a man who committed himself to safeguarding it until it could be returned to the Aztecs. His name was Henry Morgan."

I paused for a moment. She nodded. "Go on."

"Captain Morgan hid the statue somewhere on your sacred ground now called Nanny Town. It was long before Queen Nanny led your people. He left a document giving vague clues to the location."

"And you're here to ask me what, Mr. Shane? I want to hear it in your own words."

"I'm asking two things. The first is the most serious. I need your permission to walk on the sacred ground of Nanny Town. And yes, I do know the gravity of what I'm asking. The second is your help in understanding Captain Morgan's clues to find the statue. I'll just add this. You can judge what I'm about to say. My sole interest is in returning the statue to the current leader of the Aztecs. The Aztecs are a Christian people now, but this statue still represents their uniqueness as a nation capable of building one of the great civilizations of the ancient world. Based on their leader's own words, it could be an essential element right now in sustaining the identity and unity of these very dispersed people. I guess even more to the point, if anyone on earth actually has ownership rights to the statue, it is the Aztec nation."

It was all I could say. I sat down opposite the woman whose eyes never left mine.

"You don't waste words, Mr. Shane. We've heard many long speeches from men of your race. They simply covered up lies."

I began to speak, but she held up her hand. "I believe you're an honest man, Mr. Shane. But you're only one. What about these men with you? And any others who are not here to speak for themselves?"

Kwame stood to save the moment. "My name is Kwame. I'm from Ghana. My people have lived in peace beside the Ashanti in Africa from a time unknown. You can judge my words as well. I'll do nothing that will bring dishonor or desecration to the sacred land of the Ashanti."

The woman nodded. I detected a softening smile toward Kwame. The smile faded when she looked into the eyes of Roger. "And you."

Roger somehow managed a tone of humility that could possibly pass for honesty. "I agree with my friends."

The woman looked back at me. "As I said, I'm inclined to believe you, Mr. Shane."

Before I could speak, she stood and raised a silencing hand. "I'll be in contact with you. Arrangements will be made."

Again, she stopped me from speaking. She looked from me to each of the others. "Take these words to heart. You're taking on a serious responsibility here. You'll be closely watched. Eyes will be on you long after you leave Jamaica. We know that each of you can only control your own actions. But know this well. If any of you, or your comrades, break the word you've given here, consequences will follow. By now you should understand my meaning."

I simply said, "We do."

*   *   *

Kwame and I were back at the hotel before midnight. Roger went his own way after our drop-off.

Regardless of what the time might have been in Marseille, my first call was to Mr. Mehmed. He seemed greatly relieved when I reported the few words the Maroon woman had said to us. "I thought you could do it, Matthew. What about Roger Van Allen?"

"He came through in the end. It got us to first base."

"That's an Americanism. Meaning what?"

"It means we're only partway home. Somehow, we have to keep the others in line. Roger and Wayne Barnes in particular. Then there's Claude DuCette. There was a clear command, probably to us all—do not get greedy. Even beyond Jamaica."

"We'll take precautions."

"Meaning what?"

"We'll talk about it later. What's the plan?"

"I wait here for word from the Maroon woman. I'll be in touch."

I could hear him talking briefly with someone there before he was back on the line. "Matthew, this comes from both me and Angelique. Please, take care of yourself."

He could probably hear the smile in my voice when I signed off.

* * *

Kwame and I were at breakfast at the hotel the following morning. A note came to the table that brought us to the front desk. We saw a man there who had been at the Cultural Center the day before. He addressed himself to Kwame in his own language. They spoke briefly and the man left.

"What is it, Kwame?"

"A week from today. Early morning. We meet at the same building in Moore Town."

"Anything else?"

"Yes. Just you and me."

"No Roger? None of the others?"

"That's the message."

I had serious doubts about how that would play with the three remaining Monkey's Paws—Roger Van Allen, Wayne Barnes, and Claude DuCette. Nonetheless, what was done was done. Another American expression: half a loaf is better than none.

*   *   *

My first call was to Roger Van Allen. I knew it in my gut. The woman's message limiting permission to enter Nanny Town to Kwame and me would set off a firestorm. It did. He'd have none of it. His first reaction was to send her a message making his own demands. I read that as a disaster for us all.

I finally talked him down to just allowing me to make his case to her directly. He set up the contact. She agreed to speak with me again. Kwame and I made the trip. We met in the same room. This time, we actually sat down to a cup of tea.

The conversation was civil. In fact, pleasant. Kwame and she exchanged words in the Ashanti language, and we spoke a bit in English. At one point, she said, "You've come a long way again, Mr. Shane. I assume you received my message. Is there more to say?"

I spoke softly, and with the respect she must have expected. "I'm most grateful; we both are. I don't undervalue your permission to walk on sacred ground. We'll act with complete respect."

She nodded. "As I shall expect. What else?"

"There are others for whom this is the end of a long journey."

"Shall we be specific? You mean your Mr. Van Allen."

I'm sure she read my facial expression, which must have confirmed her first opinion of him. "Yes. I'm riding two difficult horses here. The first is the challenge of finding the object. I have to try. I've given my word to return it to the Aztecs. The second is Mr. Van Allen. He's been part of this quest from the beginning. He is most insistent on being present at the conclusion."

Her expression was sharply focused. "His insistence is of no consequence to me."

I started to speak. She raised her hands. "And what of your own insistence, Mr. Shane?"

"I don't presume to insist. You've already been quite generous. I'm embarrassed to ask for more. I'll simply say that if you could find it possible to allow us to include Mr. Van Allen, Kwame and I would do everything in our power to see that our pledge of respect extends to his conduct."

"And you believe you can control Mr. Van Allen's . . . ingrained attitudes."

"In honesty? No. No more than any of us can control the thoughts of anyone else. But we'll do everything in our power to see that no disrespect is shown by his actions."

She sat quietly before speaking. "I understand his motive in insisting. This object apparently has great value. But what's your interest in including this 'difficult horse,' as you say?"

"Rough as he appears, he's been a lifelong respected archeologist. He's spent a career seeking out objects of historic value. Kwame and I have no idea what we'll find, or how to find it. His expertise might be invaluable."

She took a moment of thought before speaking. There was no lightness in her tone. "I'll grant what you want, Mr. Shane."

She stopped me in the midst of a "Thank you."

"Take my words seriously and convey them to Mr. Van Allen. You'll be closely watched. Anything . . . anything, Mr. Shane, that appears to violate your promise of complete respect, by any of you, will be dealt with swiftly. I know you don't share our beliefs. But believe my words."

*   *   *

My relief was mixed with a healthy dose of uncertainty when I conveyed the message to Roger. His reaction was undiluted enthusiasm.

*   *   *

There was actually a third "difficult horse" to deal with. I had to run the plan by Wayne Barnes. Come hell or high water, I was not going back to the Maroon woman with another request. Also, since Wayne was still at the top of my list of suspects for the theft of Professor Holmes' clue from his home—and heaven knows what else—I would not miss having to look over my shoulder for him during the trek to Nanny Town.

I made the call. Wayne was, as anticipated, more than a bit crusty about not being allowed to go the final mile. With a good bit of "take it or leave it" in my tone, we reached a compromise. Given the complete control of Nanny Town by the Maroons, he agreed to wait for us at the bottom of the trail leading to the ridge of the three Blue Mountains. He knew from the previous attempt by the Monkey's Paws that it was the only way into or out of Nanny Town.

*   *   *

The final duck proved to be the easiest to get in a row. I sent an email to the address I had for Claude DuCette in Montreal. There was a measure of disappointment in his reply, but he was also content to remain safely among the apparently dead. The deal was that if we actually found and brought out the statue, he would meet us in Port Royal. As our expert in all things Aztec, he would render an opinion on its authenticity. One thing I felt I could count on was that his sole interest was, most likely, in the archeological value of the piece.

*   *   *

That afternoon, Kwame and I caught separate planes, his to New Orleans, and mine to the comfort of home in Salem, Mass. Everything in my apartment was as I left it. Apparently, whatever my uninvited guest found, or didn't find, took any further search off their to-do list.

Dinner at O'Neill's Pub, with accompanying liquid solace from the fine Irish houses of Jameson and Guinness, followed by a full night's sleep, rewound my springs. I started the next morning by inviting Mary Holmes to breakfast at The Ugly Mug Diner on Washington Street. The hugs and shared memories were reason enough, but I took the opportunity to ask if Professor Holmes ever mentioned his feelings about any of the other Monkey's Paws. I didn't mention the word "trust," but she caught my meaning.

Her first response was that it was the one part of his life that he almost never discussed with her. A little later in the conversation, she interrupted whatever I was saying. "Matthew, you asked about Barry's feelings about the others. You know he trusted everyone. But there was a phone call a few days before he left for Jamaica."

"From one of the Monkey's Paws?"

"I'm not sure. I think so. I never listened to his phone conversations with colleagues, but something in his voice this time . . ."

"What?"

"I don't know. If it were anyone else, I'd say fear. But we both know Barry didn't know the word. I'll say … distress. Enough to get my attention. I asked him about it when he finished. He just smiled and said everything was fine. I think it was the only time in our lives I didn't believe him."

That set off instant recollections of Wayne Barnes asking to room with Professor Holmes in Jamaica, followed by the pinpoint search by someone of his suitcase when he got home, and the professor's precaution of splitting his parchment clues and getting one half into my hands. It also brought thundering back the hovering realization of Professor Holmes' murder.

CHAPTER THIRTY-TWO

THE WEEK PASSED more quickly than I might have liked. Almost before I knew it, I was back on a plane to Port Royal.

Kwame and I met again at Morgan's Harbour Hotel for a late dinner. We were into desert when Roger joined us. He was staying at the same hotel for the night so we could start an early morning drive. According to the old Maroon lady's cryptic message of a week previous, we were to meet at the same building in Moore Town.

I filled Roger in on Wayne Barnes' agreement to wait at the hotel in Port Royal for whatever discovery we might be bringing down. Claude DuCette's name never came up since it was assumed that he, like Professor Holmes and Rene Perreault, was among the dead. I let the assumption ride.

We were into second coffees when Roger broached the issue I was reluctant to face. "It's cards on the table time. Damn the secrecy instructions on the parchments. We have to lay out all the clues if we're going to put this expedition together."

With some intuitive reluctance, I agreed. We knew that Claude DuCette's parchment, the first one opened, told the Monkey's Paws to meet in the lobby of the hotel for that first disastrous expedition. This time, we'd be following the instruction of the old Maroon lady to meet at the cultural building in Moore Town.

Wayne Barnes' parchment had instructed him to locate the wreck of the *Nuestra Regina* and search for the logbook left by the Welshman, Dylan. Wayne and I had done that in one eventful dive. The logbook identified the object as the statue entrusted by the then Aztec leader to Captain Henry Morgan. It confirmed that Morgan brought it back to Port Royal in Jamaica. Wayne Barnes and I and Mr. Mehmed were the only ones to have read the logbook. Roger Van Allen never asked me to show it to him. I wondered why, but as they say, let sleeping dogs lie.

Roger's clue apparently had given him a lead to someone in the Maroon community in Moore Town. It enabled him to arrange the original meeting to get us permission from the old Maroon lady to set foot on Nanny Town soil without losing our lives. That, too, was done.

That left the parchment clues given to Rene Perreault and Professor Holmes. I was the only one Rene Perreault had entrusted on his deathbed with his clue, "Follow the abeng." It seemed necessary to disclose it to Roger to move the game to the next level. Roger's reaction was similar to mine. "What the hell does that mean?"

That left only the clues given to Professor Holmes. This is where it became dodgy. I knew the clue in the half-parchment Professor Holmes had torn off and sent to me in campus mail. It read, "Follow the stream to the cave. Enter with care." What stream? Those mountains were probably laced with streams. It seemed useless without the clue in the other half-parchment. As far as I knew, the professor had never divulged that second half to anyone. On the other hand, that was the half-parchment that was apparently stolen from the professor's suitcase in his attic after he returned from the Monkeys' first attempt. If Roger divulged the clue, he would seem to be admitting to the break-in and theft from the professor's home.

I could have called Mr. Mehmed in Marseille. He was the one who put all of the clues onto the parchments based on the writing

of Captain Henry Morgan found in the bottom of Morgan's
sea-chest. On the other hand, since Roger did not know that, I
thought I'd play it for leverage.

"We could be at a deadlock here, Roger. I can give part of Professor Holmes' clue. He sent me half of his parchment. It won't tell us
much without the other half. Can you add that?"

There was a pregnant pause. I gave it a nudge. "It's your play,
Roger. We can call it a stand off and never find this thing. Or we can
both turn our cards face up. With no questions asked."

He leaned in closer. "Let's do it. Actually, I got a call from Professor Holmes a few days after we got back from that first trip. He was
afraid he might . . . I don't know, come to some harm. I think the
Nanny Town curse had him spooked. He wanted to tell me the clue
in case something happened to him."

That unloaded more questions than it answered. Of all the Monkey's Paws, why would Professor Holmes pick Roger to trust with
his clue? And why only half a clue, while he sent the other half to
me? For that matter, why not send both halves to me?

In a display of more trust than I had in my heart for Roger, I
reached for my paper napkin. I tore it in half. I handed one half to
Roger and took out a pen. "Let's go for it, Roger. I'll write the professor's clue I have here. You write the clue he gave you there. Shall
we trust each other that far?"

He smiled, and then shrugged. "What the hell. Here's to a big win
for both of us."

"You mean for the Aztecs."

"Yeah. Of course."

We both wrote on the napkins. I folded mine and tossed it onto
the table between us. He held on to his while he looked me in the
eye. His expression was hard to read. "I could just grab your clue and
run. I'd have the whole show to myself."

I matched his look. "I know. But you won't."

"Yeah? Why not?"

"Lot of reasons. For one, you'd never get past the old Maroon lady in Moore Town alone. Without her help, those clues could be in Swahili. Shall we stop playing games?"

That smile, more like a grin, was back. "You'd be a hell of a poker player."

He tossed his half napkin over to me and picked up mine. As if in synchronized motion, we opened them together. His read, "Under the goat's skull."

*   *   *

We were up before dawn. By sunup, Roger, Kwame, and I were on the road to Moore Town. Just before noon, the Maroon woman met us at the Cultural Center. We gathered around the same table.

After the exchange of formalities, I took the lead. "We appreciate your seeing us. I find we need your help right from the beginning. We have three clues to locate what we're looking for. We have no idea what they mean."

She looked into the eyes of each of us. I think she was reassessing her decision to allow us to go on her sacred ground. According to her belief, only her permission could protect us from some predestined death.

At my earlier suggestion, Kwame and Roger kept silent. Her eyes came to rest on mine. "And you, Mr. Shane. You're still ready to take responsibility for any breach of trust . . ." She looked at the others. "By any of you?"

Her words laid a heavy load on my shoulders, but I was in this deep. I said it simply. "I am."

She just nodded. "Then what are these words you don't understand?"

I said, "This came from the writings of Captain Morgan. They were written when a smaller number of your Ashanti people were living where Nanny Town was built later. The words are: 'Follow the abeng.'"

She smiled and glanced at one of the other older Maroons in the room. "When people have little, Mr. Shane, they use what they have with intelligence to survive. When our Ashanti forebears escaped the chains and guns of the Spanish, and then the British, they took refuge along the ridge that joins three peaks of the Blue Mountains. Needless to say, they were hunted by their captors. Can you imagine their life?"

"To be truthful, no."

"That's an honest answer. They were constantly pursued by the Spanish, then the British, to take them back into captivity. Their punishment for escaping, to set an example, would be beyond anything you or I could imagine. In those Blue Mountains, they could hide when the soldiers came after them. But they were spread out across three peaks. They needed a system of warning. You understand?"

"I do."

"And for that, they relied on what we call the abeng. For us, it's taken on a spiritual significance."

"What is it?"

"It's a simple cow horn with a hole drilled in the pointed end. The idea came over with the Ashanti from Ghana, Africa. For those who know how, it can make many sounds. It can be heard at a great distance. In the times of slavery, abengs were used to relay signals from one peak to another, across the three peaks. Using different tones, they could announce the approach of the Spanish or British soldiers. They could tell how many there were, and even what weapons they carried, six hours ahead of their arrival. Our Queen Nanny used the warnings to set up ambushes along the trail. British writers have since called the abeng our greatest weapon against their army."

"That clue is beginning to make sense."

"Yes, Mr. Shane. I believe it's telling you to follow the path of the voice of the abeng to where it ended in our Nanny Town."

"And to do that, I'm afraid I have to ask yet another favor. Could you provide us with a guide who knows the path of the abeng?"

"Oh, you'll be guided, Mr. Shane. I have no intention of sending you onto our sacred ground unaccompanied."

She glanced at Kwame, and more particularly at Roger. Thank God, they both stuck to our plan of silence on their part.

I pressed it one step further. "Then perhaps the guide can also help us with the clue after that."

"Which is?"

"'Under the goat's skull.'"

She smiled and nodded. "I suggest you follow your first clue to the end. Ask your guide at that point."

"Is it a location?"

She just stood slowly. "I believe you should begin now. It will take you two days of walking. It's not an easy trip. I'll provide two guides with supplies, food, and blankets. You'll need to spend tonight on the second peak. It's too treacherous to walk at night."

We followed her lead and stood.

"I'll also provide you a mule for carrying the statue back. From your description, it will be a heavy burden."

"Thank you. You've been very considerate."

"Don't thank me until you return, Mr. Shane. I think your path ahead may not be as uneventful as you seem to think. I've granted your requests, but..."

"But be careful of what we ask for. Is that it?"

"I wish you well, Mr. Shane."

* * *

We drove to a spot called Garbrand Hall. We were met by two tall, apparently well-conditioned Maroon men who identified themselves to Kwame in the Ashanti language as our guides. Provisions and blankets for the night ahead were loaded on a mule.

With as little delay as possible, we began a trek on a narrow path through a tree-covered rise. Six hours later, it brought us to our stop for the night. We were told that we had ascended some two thousand feet. Our guides laid out a campsite at a place called Island Head.

My legs were foreign enough to that kind of sustained exertion that the stop arrived just before a painful exhaustion. Whatever unidentified fare our guides cooked over an open fire was so welcome that I made a note to ask for the recipe—if we survived the trip.

The next morning, muscles that were still stiff from the previous day's climb were called out of makeshift bedding to face another day of trekking. With each mile of advance on a trail across what appeared to be three peaks, the dense tree-packed sides of the path seemed to crowd in closer. It was easy to understand how guerilla ambushes by the Maroons could have left the trail strewn with the bodies of British troops.

Perhaps it was the previous day's conditioning. With occasional stops, my legs held out to our camping stop at full sundown. We were told by our guides that we had reached the outer boundaries of Nanny Town. It was most certainly the power of suggestion that gave me an awed sense that the eyes of something, someone unseen, were on our every move.

Our campsite was on the edge of a precipice that dropped two or three hundred feet. After we'd eaten, I asked Kwame to translate a question to our guide. "What was the meaning of 'Under the goat's skull'?" And more to the point, "Are we getting close?"

I watched our guide as Kwame asked the questions. There was a ripple through my stomach when the guide simply pointed to a massive stone outcropping just above us. It stood silhouetted against a three-quarter moon. From pointed ears and horns to the chilling grin that might have been supplied by my imagination, the rock form was a stunning suggestion of the goat's skull.

I urged Kwame to ask about the final clue—"Follow the stream to the cave. Enter with care." Our guide was a man of few words, but few were needed. He pointed over the precipice below the stone goat's skull. The light of the moon traced a zigzag path that led down to where moonlight reflected off of the coarse ripples of a rushing stream.

The pieces were rapidly coming together. I was driven, as were we all, to attempt the descent by what light the moon provided. Kwame explained our guide's caution against the snags, sudden drops, and root snares that could mean instant disaster before sunrise. My wearied legs added the final argument for a night's rest until dawn. Everyone agreed.

I had no sooner eaten and crawled into the nest of blankets our guide provided when I fell into a sleep deep enough to resemble a coma. Whatever dreams were inspired by the grinning rock sculpture of the goat's skull above us left me somewhat shaken with an undefined dread when I woke. I came out of that sense of foreboding slowly to the sounds of a rapid exchange in Ashanti between our guide and Kwame.

Almost immediately, Kwame was beside me with his hand shaking my shoulder. I forced my eyes open and propped up on an elbow. Kwame was whispering rapid words in my ear. "Your friend. Roger Van Allen. He must have sneaked out before dawn. He took the mule."

He pointed to the edge of the cliff where the path down began. My mind was stunned awake and grasping the full meaning of his words. "He's gone."

CHAPTER THIRTY-THREE

KWAME AND I and our two guides grabbed a quick, cold bite and packed up camp. Within twenty minutes, we were on the trail that wound down toward the stream. The winding descent went considerably faster than the previous days' climb. It was partly gravity, but mostly the driving urge to catch up with our abandoning partner, Roger.

The trail was as treacherous as our guides had suggested. Nature had done its best to reclaim the open path. Branches and tangled vines on both sides nearly joined across the trail. They tugged at our arms and legs with barbs. Rains had laid bare jutting roots that snagged our feet at any unguarded step. How Roger had made the descent leading a mule in the dark of barely lit pre-dawn hours was unimaginable. Yet his footprints and the prints of the mule continued to lead us down at the best pace we could make.

We hit the bottom of the path within two hours. It led straight to the rushing stream we had seen from above. There was no difficulty picking up Roger's trail on the near bank. He was clearly following the last clue sent by Professor Holmes to me—"Follow the stream to the cave. Enter with care."

Any thought of a rest at the bottom was trumped by the drive to overtake Roger. There was no way of telling how many hours' head-start he had on us. We moved on at a pace that nearly matched the gurgling rush of water over moss-covered rocks. There was no need to track footprints and hoofprints. We knew Roger was following the flow downstream.

Sometime around noon, we met a wall. The trail was blocked by a daunting barrier of slashed branches and uprooted bushes laced together with vines. The tangled mass was as tall as our arms could reach. Roger's footprints led directly to the base of the obstruction.

Kwame pointed to the fresh cuts of the tree limbs. "Your friend, Roger, knew we'd be coming after him. He wanted to slow us down. It worked."

If there were any previous doubt that Roger was in business for his own profit, that killed it. We needed time to clear the obstruction he had obviously put in our path. By then, the smothering heat of the sun in the crevasse had multiplied the effect of our exhaustion. Even with four of us working, we had lost at least an hour before we were back on Roger's trail. Our two Maroon guides gave us strips of some kind of dried meat to chew for a shot of energy as we plodded on.

I lost track of time. I could only tell that, as the sun got lower, the urge to overtake our defecting partner was losing its power to drive us at a sustained pace. I could see even Kwame's footsteps becoming more plodding.

When the sun fell nearly below the rim of the canyon wall behind us, the temperature dropped rapidly. The sweat that had been drenching our bodies was now chilling every sunbaked inch of skin.

Without any of us saying it, I knew we all dreaded the thought of another night of stagnating delay in the darkness of that crevasse. We agreed to push on for as long as any speck of sunlight lit the path.

In another half hour, I was on the verge of giving in to my internal chills and the unnerving sounds of whatever predators were coming out for the evening hunt. A crackling fire built right there on the trail seemed like the best of all possible ideas.

Just before I called a halt, our lead guide stopped. He turned and tapped Kwame's shoulder. He whispered a few words. I came up alongside. "What, Kwame?"

He signaled for silence. He pointed to a place ahead where the water seemed to roil with increased sounds of rapids. We pressed on until I could just make out a bend of the stream. Just after the bend, the water rushed through an open mouth in an out-jutting of the mountain's rock wall.

The words of the professor's clue flashed back. "Follow the stream to the cave." The opening was just tall and wide enough for one of us to enter at a time. The last part of the clue squelched my overwhelming urge to just step into the water and wade in: "Enter with care."

Kwame and I stood as close to the opening as we could get on the dry path. There was not a glimmer of light. We both listened for any sound over the gurgling of the stream. There was none.

I felt Kwame's arm on my shoulder. I looked up to see him pointing to the mule, grazing on the other side of the stream. It was a safe bet that Roger was inside the cave.

I knew Kwame and I were both weighing the alternatives: spending the night on the ground until dawn's light, or wading right in to meet whatever was waiting for us in the black recess of the cave. Flashlights would have been a nice luxury, but, to our regret, we had never contemplated traveling after sundown or before sunrise.

Our guides had stopped twenty yards behind us. I could sense they were dealing with every rational fear that had my own nerves on edge, plus every unhinging threat their Maroon myths and beliefs could conjure. It was clear they had ventured as far into Nanny Town territory as we could expect.

I finally made a suggestion that moved Kwame and me off of dead center. We each felt around for a four- or five-foot stick. We wrapped one end with dead vines. Kwame had matches that we used to light the vines to make torches.

By the light of the fires, we spoke in gestures. We silently agreed that I'd take the lead. Kwame would follow close behind.

I took a firm grip on the burning branch and said a short but fervent prayer. I stepped into the stream. My first prayer was granted. The bottom was solid and flat enough to let me keep my balance.

A succession of short steps through the opening brought me into a pitch-black chamber of rock walls. The torch picked up a four- or five-foot ledge to my right. I was able to step up onto the dry path.

I signaled with the torch. Kwame followed until we both stood on the path inside. Our combined fires were barely enough to cast a dim light around a rock chamber about twice the size of my bedroom in Salem. My eyes followed the rushing sound of water ahead. I could see the stream coursing out through an opening in the far stone wall. It was large enough for the flow, but not large enough for a man to pass through.

I'll admit it. My senses were raw with fear. In spite of it, a thought crowded into my consciousness. Could we be standing where Captain Henry Morgan secreted a priceless object of the ancient Aztecs? Perhaps Professor Holmes had instilled more of the archeologist's fire in me than I ever realized. Maybe that was what moved one foot slowly ahead of the other, deeper into the blackness.

Kwame was at my back. We inched our way along the ledge. The fires on our sticks were beginning to dim as the burning roots were consumed. My eyes, and probably Kwame's, were straining to pick up any outline of either Roger or the statue before the flames died completely.

By now, every nerve was strung tight as a fiddle. My imagination was fighting my mind for control. I thought I caught the outline of a bulky form. It was partly submerged in a pool of still liquid that stretched across the path. My mind was saying it could be Roger—possibly even the statue. My imagination was countering. It could be something—waiting for us to come close.

I turned and tapped Kwame on the shoulder. I pointed to the form. He nodded. That told me it was real. I stared for a few more seconds. My focus now was to catch any flicker of movement. For what little comfort it gave, there was none.

I heard Kwame whisper, "Let's keep going. It's right there."

My mind was silently screaming, "I know. But what is it?"

I willed each foot to take a step closer. And another. If it was making a sound to warn us off, the rushing water was drowning it out.

We were now within five feet of it. In the dying seconds of our light, my eyes strained harder to get one vision of what it was. Then I was suddenly seeing it. And I was wishing to God I hadn't.

It must have struck Kwame at the same instant. We backed off several fast steps before plunging back into the steam. Our legs moved faster than I thought possible to carry us out of that cave.

Once out, we jumped on the bank and ran back about ten yards. We both just stood there numb. It was a minute before either of us spoke. When we did, we realized that we had both seen the same thing. It was Roger's still form. His eyes and mouth were wide open, but he was seeing and saying nothing. There was something else we both saw around his body.

It was clear. Roger had followed the clue to the inside of the cave. His focus must have been locked on finding the statue when he had walked into the still pool—into a nest of striking water moccasins.

With our guides, we trudged back to the place where the mountain path came down to the stream. We had no choice but to camp there for the night. There was not an ounce of energy left in our bodies.

The guides built a fire there on the path. When Kwame and I reached some level of equilibrium, we shared what we believed we'd seen. We agreed on the two most pressing points. The venom of a cluster of strikes had taken Roger's life.

That meant that a third member of the Monkey's Paws had given his life in the quest. Only Wayne Barnes and Claude DuCette were left.

We were adjusting slowly to the other stark realization. We were still too numbed to fully absorb the finality of what we had just seen. At the end of the pursuit of the five parchment clues, there was no golden statue.

* * *

In the morning, we re-traced our way up the path. It was a tired, shaken, empty lot of us that finally found our way down the mountain trail to our starting point at Garbrand Hall. As agreed, Wayne was there waiting for us. He could tell by my expression there would be no joyous celebration that evening. I gave an account of what we'd found, and hadn't found, within five minutes.

In his life as a treasure-hunter, Wayne had surely followed quests that had ended in the equivalent of empty caves, but perhaps none like this. The drive back to the hotel in Port Royal was like the return trip of the team that had lost the Super Bowl. There was nothing more to say.

When we reached the Port Royal hotel, it was all I could do to climb the stairs to my room. Each foot weighed a ton. I could hardly wait to collapse every bone and muscle on the bed. I felt I owed one phone call before I succumbed to heaven-knows how many hours of sleep.

Mr. Mehmed answered on the second ring. I poured out a some-what coherent version of the previous two days' episode. When I finished, he had just one question. "Matthew, are you all right? You sound terrible."

For the first time, I focused on his question. It was not just extreme tiredness. My entire body was radiating enough fire to heat the hotel. My muscles were not just tired. They ached like an abscessed tooth. I could feel myself drifting more into unconscious-ness than normal sleep. Whatever had grabbed hold of me in that valley was wringing me out.

I heard Mr. Mehmed ask again louder. "Matthew, are you all right?"

I could only give him the truth. "No. I don't think so. I must have caught something."

His voice was becoming more distant. "Matthew, stay where you are. I'll have someone look at you. Then I'll have someone take you to the airport. My plane will be waiting. What room are you in?"

I heard the question, but I had no strength to answer it. I could just feel my body slump down on the floor beside the bed. My lights went out.

*　*　*

Time seemed frozen. My only senses of being alive were a raging fever and a constant replaying of the most hideous imaginings from my time in the cave.

I had no idea how much time passed, but I remember at some point, a partial parting of the clouds. It was my first awareness of a world beyond myself. I felt something cool and moist wiping my fore-head, then my whole face. It was like an oasis in a parched desert.

I thought I was hearing a voice in the distance, or perhaps next to my ear. I struggled to bring it closer. It was the sweet, soft voice of Angelique. I tried to say, "Thank you," but I don't know if the words ever got beyond my throat. And then the darkness folded over me again.

*   *   *

I again had no inkling how long it had been, but the time came when I could open my eyes. What I'd been telling myself was an illusion was actually real. Angelique was beside the bed. I could hear her call her father. Within minutes I saw Mr. Mehmed's smiling face beside hers. How I got to the Mehmed home, I had no idea. But neither did I care. I was just basking in their presence.

I could feel a weak smile blooming across my face. I thought I saw Angelique catch a tear. Mr. Mehmed said, "Welcome back, Matthew."

My smile was now a grin, but the best conversation I could manage was a soft, "Hello." They both burst out with an emotion-releasing laugh.

CHAPTER THIRTY-FOUR

THE DAYS THAT followed in the care of Mr. Mehmed and Angelique brought me back from the depths I had fallen into over the previous week. The exhausting descent to the cave and an apparent run-in with a malarial mosquito were the final nails in what could have been a coffin.

It was a few days before I could stand and dress and begin taking part in the life around me. The days after that were among the best memories of my lifetime. They were filled with long walks around the Mehmed estate with Angelique and long dinners and evening chats with them both.

On one of our walks, about two weeks into my recovery, I raised the courage to say to Angelique that I had never enjoyed anything in my life as much as my time with her . . . and her father. She smiled in a way that stoked the fire in my heart.

Before we arrived back at the house, she looked at me and said, "My father is also enjoying this time with you. I think he always wanted a son. I do my best to please him, but . . ."

I said, "Angelique, you must know he loves you beyond measure. You're his life. He said so the last time I was here."

She smiled. "I know. I'm sure of it. But . . . a son."

* * *

That evening after dinner, as had become our custom, Mr. Mehmed and I spent time in his study with a drop of very fine scotch. For the first time since I'd been flown there, the discussion turned to what originally brought us together. I was the first to break the barrier. "Have you had any success finding out who hired the Corsicans to kidnap Angelique?"

"Not yet. It takes time to work these things out diplomatically. I've finally arranged a meeting. Day after tomorrow. He's one of two leaders of the Corsicans. I'm told he's most likely the one to have made the deal. You can understand why he's not anxious to meet with me."

"And what will you say to him?"

He took a deep draw on his cigar before answering. "Some of these people are not encumbered with your sense of honor. With them, business is business. That usually means money. Nothing else."

"So you'll offer him more than he was paid by whoever hired him to do the kidnapping."

"A good deal more. Enough to insure a truthful answer."

He looked at me. "You're smiling, Matthew."

I'd reached the point of being comfortable enough to ask the question. "You're a powerful man, Mr. Mehmed. I would have assumed that once you had a name . . . perhaps a more direct approach."

He smiled. "Ah, yes. There was a time. You'd certainly know that if we'd met earlier."

"And now? If I may ask?"

"You may, Matthew. You and Angelique. No one else. As you might know, I lead a very isolated, very private life."

"I know. I don't mean to overstep."

He shook his head. "No. I want to answer. It's good to express it. In strict confidence. There are those who'd take advantage of what they'd see as a weakness."

I nodded in affirmation of that confidence. He took a few moments to find the words.

"I've come to realize a person can change, even the habits of a lifetime. I find myself thinking differently these days. I've mentioned my father. I believe he's pleased. When we finally meet again in the next life, perhaps it will be with pride, and love. On both sides."

I started to speak, but he added, "I should say, Matthew, you've had something to do with it."

Before I could answer, Angelique joined us. The conversation turned to the lighter events of the day.

*   *   *

The next morning after breakfast, Mr. Mehmed asked me to join him in the garden where we first met. Coffee was brought to us as soon as we sat down. I waited for him to open the conversation.

"How are you feeling now, Matthew?"

"Thanks to you both, better than I can ever remember."

"Good. Then I want to assure you, you're more than welcome to stay with us as long as you can." He leaned over with a smile. "I know nothing would please Angelique more."

"Nor would anything please me more."

He gave me time to answer the question he was really asking. "You know I made a promise to Professor Holmes' wife. It's still not accomplished. I thought when we followed that last clue, I might have found the answer I needed."

"I know."

"Then you know I still need proof that Professor Holmes didn't take his own life. And the name of whoever committed the murder."

"Where does it take you from here? Your search seemed to reach a dead end."

"So I thought. It's just in the past day or so I finally realized something. It's not a dead end."

I could see his attention sharpening. "When we reached the bottom of that trail, we followed Roger Van Allen's path downstream without question. As you know, we found nothing. I was so defeated that I never considered the alternative. What if we had turned upstream instead of downstream? The parchment clue was ambiguous. That could be the direction Captain Morgan took."

"Does that mean you're going back?"

"I have to. I've got to see this thing through. Remember, you made a commitment to the leader of the Aztecs. If I find that statue, we might both be able to clear our debts."

I heard deep concern in his voice. "How can I help?"

* * *

I spent the rest of the morning on the phone. My first call was a shot in the dark. I reached Marvin, the desk clerk at Morgan's Harbour Hotel in Port Royal. He remembered my recent visit that ended in my being carried out to an ambulance. His concern for my recovery seemed genuine.

I made a reservation with him for another stay beginning the following day. I made it for three people, just in case I could talk Kwame into another adventure and also get Wayne Barnes to join us. I also assured Marvin that I'd be there in person to slip a generous tip under the counter for a bit of confidential information.

"I'd like you to check your register for a date a couple of weeks ago. You had a guest. Professor Barrington Holmes. Someone roomed with him. Could you tell me who it was?"

There was a pause. "I'm sorry, Mr. Shane. I'm afraid they won't let me give that information. I could lose—"

"A minute after I arrive tomorrow, there will be an envelope in your hand with an expression of my gratitude that will surprise you. It may even shock you. Am I understood?"

I could almost see him looking around the lobby for other ears. There were apparently none. "I heard what you said, but if anyone . . ."

"They won't, because you're not going to say a revealing word. I'm just going to say a name. I'd like you to simply tell me if the weather there is sunny or rainy—understood?"

A slight pause. "I think so."

"Excellent. I'll say the name Wayne Barnes."

I remembered that Mary had said the professor called her when he got to the hotel. He said Wayne had asked him if he could share a room with him. I just needed to confirm it.

There was another pause. I assumed hopefully that Marvin was checking the hotel register. He was back on. "I'm sorry, Mr. Shane. We're expecting a very rainy day."

If Marvin had understood my code, that meant it was not Wayne. I might have been doing him an injustice. I played what was now more than a hunch. "Another name. Roger Van Allen."

Marvin came back. "Ah, the sky is clearing up. It's going to be a bright sunny day."

The puzzle was beginning to come together. Roger must have changed rooms with Wayne after they'd arrived so he could room with the professor. That meant, if my logic was working, Roger was the one who probably knew that the professor's parchment was in the zippered compartment of his suitcase. He could easily have had someone steal the parchment from the suitcase in the Holmes attic. Still not conclusive, but interesting.

My next call, to his obvious surprise, was to Mac McLane in Salem. "Matt, where the hell have you been? More important. Where are you now?"

"Hi, Mac. There's a lot to tell. Last question first. Would you believe, Marseille, France?"

"From you? I'd believe anything. Why there?"

"Long story. Can you talk?"

"Shoot. All the details."

I poured out the whole saga since we'd last been in contact.

"And where does that leave you, Matt?"

"Still up a creek. Literally. I can't prove anything. But if I had to bet the farm, my money'd be on the late Roger Van Allen. I think he was behind it all. The death of Rene Perreault in New Orleans, the ransacking of Claude DuCette's home for his parchment clue. Most important, the murder of Professor Holmes."

"So what's your next move?"

"I have to go back to Jamaica. I need to see what's at the other end of that stream."

"Alone?"

"I hope not. Wayne Barnes might join me. Maybe the man I told you about. Kwame."

"Do you trust Barnes?"

"I think so. I thought he was the one who roomed with Professor Holmes in Jamaica. I was wrong. It was Roger Van Allen. I'd bet a bundle Roger had one of his people search the professor's suitcase in his attic for the parchment."

"I hear you."

"That reminds me. You might be able to plug a hole. Roger told me the professor called him from Salem a few days after they got back from that first Jamaica try. He said the professor gave him his clue over the phone. It was 'under the goat's skull.' I'm inclined to doubt it. I still think he searched the professor's suitcase. Could you check the professor's phone records to see if he actually made that call?"

"I'll see what I can do."

"Good. I'll tell you something else. After Wayne Barnes and I dove for that logbook on the *Nuestra Regina*, someone came after his yacht in a speedboat. Guns blazing. He was sure he was the target, not me. I believe he was right."

"Are you thinking Van Allen?"

"Right. Probably one of his men. I'd bet he was trying to eliminate one more Monkey's Paw. One less to share the prize. No proof, but the pieces fit."

"And your friend the professor? What about the baboon blood? The cottonmouth venom that killed him. The little Maroon voodoo doll we found in his pocket."

"You mean the *gris-gris*. It all ties together, Mac. It's a cluster of clues that all point to the Maroons. If someone wanted to do away with a one-fifth share of the treasure, and lay the guilt on a tribe about two thousand miles away . . . "

"You're still thinking Van Allen."

"It's reasonable. He's from Jamaica. He knows more about the Maroons than anyone else. I've been more convinced than ever since he skipped out on me to grab the statue for himself. He even took the mule to haul it out."

Mac's silence meant he was looking at it from all angles.

"Yeah, I know what you're thinking, Mac. Still no proof. That's why I'm going back."

* * *

My next call was a brief one to Kwame. He was relieved to hear that
I was still on the planet. He was less thrilled to hear what I was pro-
posing. Except for the malaria, he had suffered everything I had on
the last trip. A return engagement was not appealing. I made a pitch
to his weak spot.

"I know you're still convinced that the old Maroon man in the
bayou ordered the death of your friend, Rene Perreault. I still think
you're wrong. Why not play out one more scene? It might give us the
answer."

"Because I have no reason to think I'm wrong."

"If I give you one, a good one, will you come along one more
time?"

"I don't know. Try me."

"Think of the day of Rene Perreault's death. Notice I don't call it
an 'accident.' You still believe it was the old Maroon man's son,
Keku, who closed that gate after Mr. Perreault went into the cage."

"Nothing says otherwise. Probably on the order of the old man to
carry out their beliefs about the curse."

"And you remember I had the police check the gate and the latch
for fingerprints."

"Yes."

"And they found?"

"No prints."

"Right. None at all. Why?"

"Keku must have wiped them clean."

"Again, why? How would it help him?"

I could hear his breathing in the silence. I was hoping he was
reaching the same conclusion I had on the day of the incident. Keku
had been using the latch to tend to the baboons every day. It was his
job. His fingerprints would be expected to be there. There was no
reason for him to wipe them off. On the other hand, anyone else

who deliberately shut that gate would have a reason to wipe them clean.

"Kwame, what do you say?"

"When do you want me to meet you in Port Royal?"

* * *

My last call was to Wayne Barnes. I made the pitch for one more try, this time going upstream. I added as an incentive that this time we wouldn't have to look over our shoulders for betrayal by Roger.

"True. But are you forgetting something?"

"I hope not. What?"

"Roger was our connection with the Maroons. How do we get permission to go to Nanny Town? A lot have tried without it. The survival rate is not impressive."

"I know. There's one chance. I think I may have established a tentative relationship with an elderly Maroon lady there. She seems to be in charge."

"How tentative?"

"Good question. Roger's sneak play might have blown it. I won't know 'til I try. I'd like to have you there for a quick start if I can get through to her. What do you say?"

He thought for a second before committing. "As they say in golf, 'never up—never in.'"

"Meaning?"

"Let's do it. What have we got to lose?"

I thought of my last view of Roger. I had a clear answer to that question.

CHAPTER THIRTY-FIVE

WAYNE AND I met at the hotel in Port Royal for dinner the next evening. Kwame came in an hour later. With no contact information for the elderly Maroon lady, the best we could do for a plan was to drive out to Moore Town the next morning and ask around.

It turned out to be more simple than I'd thought. We had barely entered the town and parked outside of the Maroon Cultural Center before our presence was known. Two Maroon men were at the doors of our car. It seemed the better part of discretion to let Kwame do the talking in the Ashanti language.

Within ten minutes we were following hand signals to enter the building. The Maroon lady was seated at the same table, pointing to three chairs across from her. Her tone, if not laying out the red carpet, was at least less hostile than I expected.

"And so, Mr. Shane, like the proverbial bad penny, you keep showing up. Are you thinking of taking up residence in Moore Town?"

I smiled at her unexpected use of the "bad penny" idiom. "Not at the moment. But it's not for lack of your patience or hospitality. This is our third meeting. I wonder if I might have a name I could call you."

She had a small, undecipherable smile. "Why? Do you plan to continue these meetings indefinitely?"

"Perhaps someday we'll meet on a more social basis. For the moment, your assumption is right. I need your indulgence one last time. It's difficult to ask. Mr. Van Allen's actions the last time brought dishonor on me as well as himself. I'm sure it was an offense to the sanctity of your Nanny Town. I can only pray that you'll accept my sincere apology."

I'd have continued, but she stopped me. "There's no need to apologize for something beyond your power to prevent. Mr. Van Allen made his own choice. I think you'll agree it was not without its consequences."

For the first time, the thought occurred that perhaps Roger's entry into that deadly pool of water moccasins was less accidental than assisted. The legend of Queen Nanny's reprisal for any disrespect to her special territory might have had a helping hand. Either way, Roger had made his own bed. My better sense told me not to press the issue.

I simply nodded.

"My name is Amaris. I admire your persistence. What is this next request?"

I explained that there was one stone left unturned—the upstream path to whatever we might find there. I saw her look at the unfamiliar face at the table. I introduced Wayne Barnes, who had the good sense to show more respect for our hostess than Roger had.

"And do I assume your mission is still to return what you find to the people who own it?"

"Yes. The Aztec people of Mexico."

"Nothing else?"

"Nothing." I left my own personal quest for an answer to Professor Holmes' murder unspoken. No need for complications.

She stood, which was a signal for us to do the same. "Be here tomorrow morning."

I thanked her. She started to leave, but turned and looked into the eyes of each of us. "I trust you'll take to heart the lesson of Mr. Van Allen."

*   *   *

As planned, the next morning the three of us were up with the sun. We arrived in Moore Town within a couple of hours, better equipped for having taken the trek once before. We were met by two different Maroon guides. Again, they supplied a mule to carry out what we would make one last effort to find.

The climb to the ridge across the three Blue Mountain peaks was as arduous as the last one, but this time cooler weather favored us. It was just sundown when we camped at the same site in view of the outcropping called "the goat's skull."

Just before dropping off into a welcome sleep, I filled Wayne in on the next day's trek down the zigzagging trail to the stream below. It seemed a good moment to take one final attitude check. I asked if he was still on board with the intention to return whatever we found to the Aztec nation.

"We talked about this, Matt. I told you. I'm in."

"Just checking."

"Then let me ask you something. I've been into archeology all my life. Just finding a piece like this would be the top end of my career. But what's in all of this for you?"

I thought about the right words. "You knew Professor Holmes."

"Sure. He was one of our Monkey's Paws."

"He was the closest friend I ever had. He was my substitute father. His loss left a hole I'll never be able to fill."

"I understand."

"Well, not completely. To add insult to injury, the police labeled his death a suicide. I knew the professor well enough to know they were wrong. I made a promise to his widow, and I guess to myself, to prove otherwise. That's what pulled me into this hunt. I have to see it all the way."

"I hope you find what you're looking for, Matt. But wasn't that put to rest when they found that Maroon doll on his body? Remember, he'd touched on Nanny Town ground without permission. Maybe one way or another the Maroons were keeping that Nanny curse alive."

I could have gone into my latest conclusions that Roger Van Allen had been behind nearly everything that was being laid on the Maroons, but it had been another physically exhausting day. The demand of every muscle and tendon for a night's sleep won out.

*　*　*

We were up just before the sun. Camp was broken. We were on the trail by the first rays of sunlight. By noon we were at the stream. A few strips of jerky set us on the path upstream without spending time on a noon meal.

Two hours went by, three hours, four hours. I was getting an increasingly sinking feeling that the cave mentioned in the last parchment clue was simply not there.

It came like a flash of renewed spirit when we rounded a bend in the stream. There it was. The mountain beside us took a curve to the left. The stream seemed to flow directly out of a craggy opening in the wall of solid rock straight ahead.

It was like a gaping mouth just large enough for a man to enter, bent over at the waist. I had a shivering wave of *deja vu* when I recalled what lay inside the last rock opening I'd entered. It was mixed with a revived anticipation of possibly finding the pot of gold.

This time it was Wayne who opted to take the plunge first. The stream bed held solid under his first couple of steps. He ducked down and disappeared into the blackness. This time we had the foresight to bring flashlights. I waited outside for his signal with the light.

It was a long three or four minutes waiting for the on/off flashes of light from inside. That was my cue to follow.

During those minutes I couldn't stop my mind from racing back through the flow of disasters that led to what could now be a finale. I was replaying an avalanche of the words I'd heard over the past three weeks. It all froze when I was suddenly struck with one of those brain bursts that jar you to your toes.

The next second, I was pulled back by Wayne's call. "Get in here, Matt." I had barely a few seconds to pull a few thoughts together.

Kwame and our guides had waited around the previous bend in the stream to feed and water the mule. I was alone when I stepped into the stream. I ducked under the jagged top of the opening and made my way inside. It was pitch black, except for the narrow cones of light from our two flashlights.

Once inside, the cave opened up enough to stand erect. Wayne was waiting twenty feet ahead on a dry bank to the left of the stream. He was slowly edging to his left to shine his light over a sharp drop-off into an abyss.

"Over here, Matt. Look at this."

Booming echoes of his voice brought streams of dirt and jagged pebbles from more points above us than I could count. It gave me the creeps. Wayne was so fixed on what he was seeing below that I doubt he noticed the dirt shower.

When I stood beside him, we shined our two light beams down over the edge. They were catching a ledge about twenty feet down into an abyss. The lights were reflecting off a large undefined object resting on the ledge.

Wayne looked at me. "Could that be it?"

We were both nearly breathless. "One way to find out. There's a long rope in the pack on the mule."

I was the closest. I went back and bent through the opening. Kwame and the others had caught up.

"What did you find, Matt?"

"I don't know. Quick. Throw me that rope from the mule pack."

I was about to duck back into the cave, when my cellphone came alive. I'd have skipped the call, but I saw who it was.

"Mr. Mehmed. I may have news."

His tone was tense. "Where are you, Matthew?"

"We found the cave. I'm here with Wayne. I'll get back when I know. Gotta go."

I handed the phone to Kwame. Wayne was yelling like a madman to get me back in the cave with the rope. He was making more dirt and rock spills from the roof of the cave. I could still hear Mr. Mehmed's voice through the phone as I ducked back in. "Matthew! Matthew. You've got to hear this!" First, I had to silence Wayne before he started a total cave-in.

When I was back in the cave, I threw the rope to Wayne. He found a massive boulder to the right of the stream. He made a loop in the rope and threw it around the rock.

Wayne looked at me. "It's about twenty feet down."

"You want to go for it?"

My light picked up ripples of sweat on his face. "I can't, Matt. I can't do heights. You go."

By now, I could feel the grime of dirt from the ceiling covering my head. "We better make it fast."

Wayne threw the free end of the rope over the side of the ledge. I put my light in my belt and slithered over the side of the ledge with both hands on the rope.

"Give me light down here, Wayne."

I could see the flashlight shaking in his hands as he tried to look over the ledge. The beam was hitting the outcropping twenty feet below. The light was vibrating too much to make out what was sitting there.

I let inches of the rope at a time slip through my hands to lower myself down. I finally felt my feet touch the shelf. I eased onto it gently to be sure it wouldn't break loose under my weight.

I could feel something massive and solid beside me touching my knee. Now my own hands were shaking. I took the flashlight out of my belt. I played it upward on Wayne's face. He looked as if he were on the verge of a heart attack. "Look at it, Matt! Is that it?"

I was almost frozen to the spot. The thought was racing through my mind. *In one fraction of a second, with just one turn of the light-beam, I might be the first one to see what spilled human blood for over five centuries. This could be the end of the quest that has totally derailed my life.*

It took every ounce of willpower I could summon. I remember closing my eyes for a second and whispering, "Dear God . . ."

I pointed the beam of the flashlight and opened my eyes.

Whatever I'd prepared myself to see—whatever anyone had said about it since that first meeting of the Monkey's Paws—I was not ready for what I saw there beside me. Even in the weak beam of an old flashlight, the blinding brilliance of light reflected from thousands upon thousands of jeweled facets set in the purest gold, standing higher than my waist, was . . . mind-numbing.

I could hardly speak. Wayne was yelling for an answer. I could feel the fall-out of dirt and stones from the ceiling even there, below.

I looked up. I tried to keep my voice soft. "It's here . . . This is it . . . We found it."

I couldn't hear what he said. I saw him edging his head as far over the ledge as his fear would let him. He was shining his light below, but his hand was shaking too badly to focus it.

Another wave of ceiling rocks forced my mind back to the pressure of time. I grabbed the rope and looped it twice around the statue under what appeared to be the great wings of an eagle. I secured it with the best knot I could tie.

I said it almost in a whisper. "I'm coming up, Wayne."

With confidence in the fact that the rope had held to the rock for my descent, I started a hand-over-hand climb to the top ledge. I was finally able to pull myself up over the top. Wayne was standing back from the edge. He was looking at me as if I'd come from outer space.

He was spitting it out. "What is it? Is that it?"

I was still catching my breath. I said it between gasps. "Yes. I'm sure. Stop talking before you start a cave-in. Move softly. Untie that rope from the rock. Hand it to me."

It took his shaking hands twice the time it would if I had done it myself, but I needed him to focus and quiet down. He handed me the end of the rope.

"Stay here, Wayne. We have to pull it up slowly. We need the mule."

He just nodded. It seemed he was slowly getting a grip. I carried the rope outside the cave opening. It reached to where I could secure it to the harness on the mule.

I told Kwame in a few words I'd found it. I told him to hold the lead-line of the mule. I'd give him the word when to have the mule pull on the rope and when to stop.

I turned to go back into the cave. Kwame grabbed my shoulder and pulled me around. I knew he was shaken, since he didn't ask anything about what we'd found. "Matt, you can't go back in there."

"Why not?"

He held my phone up close to my ear. I heard Mr. Mehmed's voice. "Matthew, can you hear me?"

"I have to get back in. No time. I'll tell you later."

"Please! Wait! Just listen to this!"

What he said might have jolted me into a state of panic, if my earlier brain burst had not braced me for it. I knew Mr. Mehmed was stunned by my lack of reaction. There was no time for an explanation. "It's all right, Mr. Mehmed. I can handle it. Maybe. Just stay on the line. Listen."

"Matthew, be careful!"

Since that was not in the cards, I just said, "A prayer would be most welcome. Right now."

CHAPTER THIRTY-SIX

I TURNED TO go back into the cave. Kwame grabbed me. "Matt, you can't do it."

"It's all right. I know what I'm doing. You know what you have to do. Keep listening for my signal."

I ducked back inside the cave. Wayne was standing there waiting for me to make the next move. By now, my nerves were on ice. I knew I had to act quickly and quietly before we were both wearing tons of rock from the cave ceiling.

Wayne seemed to have settled enough to do what was needed. I told him to watch over the ledge with the light to see that the rope on the statue was holding. He edged over just close enough to see it.

Two quick tugs on the rope told Kwame to start the mule pulling forward. The rope went taut. I could feel the strain as the mule put its shoulders into the pull.

Wayne yelled back. "It's moving! It's off the ground!"

"Quiet, Wayne. Just watch. Let me know if it slips."

I could feel the rope inching forward under the strain of the mule. I knew either the weight of the object or scraping of the rope on the rock ledge could snap the rope in an instant. Every inch was a partial victory.

In spite of my warning, Wayne kept calling out every foot of the rise.

"Keep it quiet, Wayne. Just let me know when it's three feet from the top."

I was forcing myself to take a breath with every foot the rope moved. It seemed forever. Wayne finally yelled. "It's just three feet down."

I turned back to the open mouth of the cave. I said it just loudly enough for Kwame to hear me. "Right there."

He remembered my signal. Kwame stopped the mule. It just held its ground.

I turned back with my light on Wayne. I expected something, but not quite what I saw. He stood facing me. There was a look of cold steel in his eyes. There was a gun in his right hand.

His voice was more steady now. "Tell him to get that mule moving. Pull that thing up over the edge. Do it now."

I locked eyes with him and bent down slowly. I'd been waiting for him to make some kind of move. I took my right hand from behind my back and held the six-inch blade of a knife against the taut rope.

His eyes went from ice to shock. I could see the gun shake in his hand. "What the hell are you doing?"

I whispered in a forced calm. "That depends on you, Wayne. Nothing moves 'til we've had a few words."

"Like hell! Get that mule moving! Now!"

He emphasized the "Now" by cocking the hammer of the gun. I froze my nerves. I countered his threat by moving the edge of the blade on the rope. I severed a few strands.

"Dammit! Are you crazy? Stop it!"

"Put the gun down at your side, Wayne."

He stood motionless. I cut a few more strands of the rope. He hissed, "All right. All right."

The gun came down to his side.

"Now let's talk."

He just stood there. I could see a fire kindling in his eyes. I had to move him in as few words as possible. The ceiling was spurting pebbles every time we spoke.

"Tell me about the death of Professor Holmes. How did you kill him?"

He just stood there. His eyes were blazing now.

"You're crazy. Why the hell—"

"Not so crazy, Wayne. Just finally awake. You planted every clue you could think of to point me to the Maroons. Maybe too many. For a while, you had me thinking it was just Roger Van Allen. He was the Jamaican. I know it now. He might have planted the clues. But you were the smart one. You pulled the strings, didn't you, Wayne?"

"The hell I—"

"You're wasting time." I looked up at the trickles of dirt. "And we don't have much time. I know you did it. I finally got it. You said last night that a *gris-gris* was found in the professor's pocket when he died."

I could see his eyes squinting.

"You couldn't have known that unless you had it planted. That was never made public."

"That doesn't mean . . ."

"Then how about this. I got a call from Mr. Mehmed in Marseille. Remember him? I'm sure you do. He's the one who had all the clues from Morgan's note in his sea-chest. In fact, he's the one who put the clues into the five parchments."

"So what?"

"A Corsican gang leader in Marseille was hired to kidnap his daughter. Never trust a gangster if you're not the highest bidder,

Wayne. The Corsican told Mr. Mehmed you're the one who hired him. Sounds like you wanted to squeeze all five clues out of him as a ransom for his daughter. I wonder where in this world you thought you could hide from Mr. Mehmed."

That had him stunned, but I needed words.

"I need to hear it, Wayne. And damn fast, or we'll never leave this cave. I want to hear that you planned the murder of Professor Holmes."

His breath was becoming rapid. Beads of sweat mixed with ceiling dirt were reflected in my light beam. But no words were coming out. I was becoming as desperate as he was. I bent down and touched the knife edge to the rope.

"I'll hear it now, or I'll send this thing to the bottom of that pit. I know you just want it for yourself. One last chance."

I sliced a few more strands. Nothing. I sliced a few more. I had no idea how long I could keep it up without a snap. But neither did he.

He was still holding the gun. It must have given him hope of walking off with the prize.

His eyes were like blazing coals. The gun came up in a sudden move. His arm was extended right at my face. "Back off! Drop the knife. Now!"

I matched the fire in his eyes with a deliberate calm. "I don't think so. Look at your hand. Look at that gun shake. How's your aim? You think you can kill me before I can swipe that rope with the blade?"

It had him thinking. "All I need is a word. Admit you killed Professor Holmes. That's all I need. I'll back off."

He took two more panting breaths. "Roger Van Allen killed him. He planted the Maroon clues. He knew about their curses. He did it."

"Halfway there, Wayne. You set it up, didn't you? You were the brains. I need to hear it."

I knew I was on thin ice, but I sliced a few more strands of rope. They snapped with a sound that drove him over the edge.

"All right. It was my idea. I planned it."

"To eliminate one share of the prize."

"Yes. Now back off. Get away from that rope."

I took one deep breath. I was savoring that moment. I finally had what I'd needed from the moment I'd heard of the professor's death.

I knew that Kwame was just outside as a witness to what I'd heard. I still had the knife on the rope. I'd never have that moment again. I pushed it one more time. "You had Claude DuCette's house searched, too, didn't you? You were after his clue."

"Yeah. Now drop the knife."

"And those guides on that first expedition here. You had that done too. Right?"

"Yes. So what? This is the last warning."

"Almost there. One last thing. Tell me about the death of Rene Perreault in New Orleans. It was your man who closed that gate to the baboon cage, not Keku. Isn't that right?"

"So what? What do you care?"

"You laid the blame on Keku with another one of those *gris-gris* planted on Mr. Perreault. Then you had Keku killed. No witnesses, right?"

Silence.

"Right? This rope can't take much more."

"Yes! So what? He was a crazy old coot with those damn animals. Now—"

That was as far as he got. In an instant, I was knocked on my side by an elbow from behind. Kwame forced his way past me. He grabbed the knife out of my hands.

He stumbled over my legs. He scrambled to his feet with the blade raised. His face was strained with rage. He yelled something in another language.

I knew he was about to lunge for Wayne to avenge the death of his friend Rene. Wayne knew it too. He swung the gun-arm from me to Kwame.

The rest is like a blur. It flashed past in an instant. A gunshot with a million echoes numbed my ears. I felt Kwame fall backward over my legs. I heard a rumble from above.

Without looking back, I grabbed Kwame's arm. With a strength that came from somewhere, I got to my feet. I dragged him like a sack out of the cave entrance. Once clear of the cloud of rock-dust blasting out of the cave, I dropped down on the ground beside his limp body.

I just lay there until the blinding dust-cloud subsided. My hearing must have been coming back. I could hear Kwame's voice. "You okay, Matt?"

I waited 'til I saw that I could stand. "Yeah. Good."

I turned and saw a growing splotch of red just above Kwame's right knee. Apparently, Wayne's aim was better than I thought.

I tore off a strip of cloth from the bottom of my shirt to make a tight band above the wound. I rolled him over to see that the bullet had passed completely through.

"I think you'll live, buddy."

"Thanks. I plan to." He nodded back toward the cave. "What about him?"

I walked back and looked inside the cave opening. The pall of rock-dust had settled enough to let a flashlight beam penetrate the space. It looked as if several feet of ceiling rocks had been blasted loose by the gunshot. All I could see where Wayne had stood was a three-foot pile of rocks.

I made a decision. This was the last time I ever wanted to come back to Nanny Town. I crawled over the pile of rubble and made my way to the edge of the drop-off. The statue was still hanging by the rope about three feet below the ledge.

I came back out and checked on Kwame. He must have been in pain, but he was awake and alert. I had him translate directions to the two Maroon guides.

I found the second rope on the mule pack. I crawled back inside with it. I made a large noose, and managed to lower the loop down over the wings of the eagle statue. I lay a blanket over the ledge under the rope.

This was it. If it worked, it worked. If not, that thing that had brought so much death would fall to an unfathomed depth forever.

I brought the end of the rope out of the cave and secured it to the mule harness. Kwame followed my directions. I crawled back into the cave and gave two pulls on the rope. Kwame understood. He gave the word in Ashanti to one of the guides to start the mule pulling.

The statue moved, first with a jerk, and then slowly, inch-by-inch, until it reached the ledge. There was little I could do but watch. It caught on a lip of rock.

I could feel the mule struggling against the taut rope. I slithered around until my legs hung over the edge. I gripped the rope to prevent falling over. I reached inside myself for all the strength I could muster and kicked out at the side of the statue with both feet. It swung out just enough for it to clear the lip.

The mule was able to move forward. I could feel the rope slip through my hands as the statue rode up over the blanket onto the ledge. It came to rest on the flat surface.

I gave the rope two tugs. Kwame got my signal. He had them stop the mule until I could pull away the blanket and wrap it around the statue. Another tug on the rope, and I could just guide its slide over the fallen layers of cave ceiling.

I can still remember the look on Kwame's face when I took off the blanket and he got his first sight of the statue.

There was just one more thing to do before the Maroon guides and I raised it onto the mule backpack and we started the trek back to Moore Town. Mr. Mehmed was still on the line. Kwame had filled him in on the shooting and given him a play-by-play of the recovery of the eagle. I finished it by sending three or four pictures of what all the ruckus had been about.

I knew Mr. Mehmed had seen a thing or two in his lifetime. I could still hear an audible gasp when he first saw the pictures.

His first question was, "Are you all right, Matthew?"

I could answer that in one word. "Yes."

His second question was more difficult.

"Was it worth it?"

I took a minute. The best answer I could give was, "Let's talk about it over a good cigar and scotch."

CHAPTER THIRTY-SEVEN

Our Maroon guides made a call. Within an hour, a helicopter was landing beside us to fly Kwame to the hospital in Kingston.

Before they could move him, he called me over beside him. With the loss of blood, I think it took all the strength he could muster to pull himself up close to my ear. "After all of it, Matt. I have to say it to you. You were right. I was blind. I owe that old Maroon man in the bayou an apology. I'll do it. As soon as I can . . ."

"First, get that wound healed. I think Rene's grandson, Maurice, will need your help with the animals."

He nodded. "You, Matt. What about for you?"

I had no answer. That would take some thought. "I'll be in touch with you, Kwame. We've been through too much to lose the friendship."

I think it was the first time I saw Kwame smile. He just lay back on the pallet. Our hands were joined until they lifted him aboard the helicopter. The roar of the blades covered whatever his last words were, but I knew we'd be speaking again.

* * *

The two guides and I managed to wrap the statue in a blanket and secure it with rope. We loaded it onto the mule. I was nearly as tired as the last time, but somehow the trek back to Moore Town seemed easy. From there, I drove a rental car to Norman Manley Airport outside of Kingston. In my last call to Mr. Mehmed, arrangements had been made to have his plane fly the statue to his landing strip in Marseille.

I would have been on that same plane, but there was one visit I had to make first. When Mary Holmes opened the door, I could see the light in her eyes. It was like the return of a long-lost son. The hug lasted until I could free the catch in my throat to say two words—"It's over."

She knew what I meant. There were no words right away, but I could feel moist drops wetting both of our cheeks, whether from her eyes or mine I don't know. It didn't matter.

There was time at her kitchen table to fill in all of the details that I had been careful to keep hidden for so long. They poured out of me without interruption. When I finished, there were more tears, but there was something else. I could see a calm look in her eyes that hadn't been there since that first word of Professor Holmes' passing.

I stayed in town to keep in close touch with Mary for a few days, just to be sure that she was beginning to put her life back together.

*   *   *

I used that time in Salem partly for a brief meeting with the dean of the law school. I was still in limbo over the direction my life would take. I needed a spate of time to let things settle into place.

I had never taken a sabbatical. I had amassed more than the time to qualify. The dean listened, almost in awe, as I narrated how I spent my summer vacation. Since he could have my courses covered, he was quick to grant a sabbatical for the fall term, with options open for any decision I might make from then on.

*   *   *

My next flight out seemed preordained. I landed at the airport outside of Marseille in the early evening. The reunion of the three of us—Mr. Mehmed, Angelique, and me—was like the emotional closing of a chapter of my life that I never dreamed of living, and the opening of a new chapter that I could never have foreseen.

I learned at dinner that Mr. Mehmed had been in touch with the leader of the Aztec nation. He said that he had greeted what Mr. Mehmed revealed to him first with disbelief, and then with overwhelming anticipation.

When the leader got back to Mr. Mehmed, he reported that there was to be a three-day festival on Lake Texcoco where the city of Tenochtitlan was originally built. It would be a festival of reuniting and celebration to receive back the emblem of their great Aztec civilization.

I used my email contact to give the news to Claude DuCette in Montreal. Nothing on earth could have prevented him from coming out of the shadow of death to be at the festival.

*   *   *

It was the last night of the festival when Angelique and I had our first real chance to be alone. The question of my immediate plans took top billing. I'd given it enough thought to make a commitment, but I needed to hear it from her first.

"Matthew, what now? Will you be leaving?"

I might never have said it before all that I'd been through. Something inside of me, perhaps the courage to chance saying it, gave expression to the words. "Angelique, the last thing in the world I want to do is to leave you . . . ever again."

I held my breath, but it was only for an instant. She was in my arms. I could just hear the words, "Then please, Matthew. Don't ever leave me again."

*   *   *

The weeks that followed seemed to fly like lightning. Once back in Marseille with Angelique and Mr. Mehmed, I felt a fresh burst of life in their company, without a looming cloud of potential danger ahead.

Mr. Mehmed had an air of what Angelique could only describe as a joy she'd never seen in him. He seemed to relish the idea that our relationship might result in the son he'd always wanted. Angelique and I were working on plans for that.

I still longed for those deeply meaningful conversations I once shared with Professor Holmes. My consolation was that the truthful memory of the finest man who ever touched my life was intact. I could almost sense the pride his archeologist's soul might have felt in what was accomplished—the restoring of a historic piece of a once-great nation's pride.

BOOK CLUB
DISCUSSION QUESTIONS

1. What do you think would have happened to the remaining members of the Monkey's Paw had Matthew Shane not stepped in to prove that his mentor's death was not suicide?

2. Without Matthew Shane's pursuit of the truth, do you think that the ancient Aztec treasure would ever have been discovered? Returned to the Aztec people?

3. Do you think there are actually groups like the Monkey's Paw who pursue ancient or even modern ultra-valuable treasures? Do you know of any specifically?

4. Were you surprised that the King of England enlisted the pirate fleet of the English sea captains for his own navy in his war with Spain?

5. Did you consider Captain Henry Morgan a hero or a villain—or a combination?

6. Had you previously heard of the Maroon Nation of escaped slaves in Jamaica? Throughout the world, do you think there

are many of these secretive enclaves? What about within the borders of the U.S.?

7. Professor Holmes had a profound influence in Matthew Shane's life. In your own personal life, would you be able to designate an individual who would command that amount of respect and commitment?

8. What was your assessment of Mr. Mehmet and his position in Marseille?

9. What do you predict for the future of Matthew and Angelique? Happy ever after? Or dark clouds ahead?

PUBLISHER'S NOTE

We trust that you enjoyed *Deadly Depths,* John F. Dobbyn's seventh crime novel. The prior six novels comprise the Knight and Devlin Series. While all the novels stand on their own and can be read in any order, the publication sequence is as follows:

NEON DRAGON (Book 1)

Amid the flash and din of Boston's Chinese New Year's celebration, a man is murdered. Young lawyer Michael Knight is surprised when he's asked to represent the accused murderer—the son of a prominent judge.

"Dobbyn's writing is fast, smart, and exotic. With his hero, the aptly named Knight, Dobbyn has proven that the spirit of Perry Mason is alive and well and has developed a deeper conscience."
—*The Strand*

*   *   *

FRAME-UP (Book 2)

Gold-Medal Winner of the *Foreword* Book of the Year Award
A deadly, high-stakes art fraud case leads Michael Knight from the seediest parts of Boston to the sophisticated Amsterdam inner sanctum of international crime.

"*Frame-Up* is the best kind of legal crime fiction, where the real stories come not from legal minutiae in the courtroom, but from human beings caught in the legal system's fuzzy moral contours."
—Alafair Burke,
New York Times best-selling author

BLACK DIAMOND (Book 3)

Michael Knight and Lex Devlin find themselves in the crosshairs of two warring mobs—the Boston Irish mob and the mob from the old sod. And with a horse race at stake—all odds are off

"Knight has a sharp wit and a gift of gab that he uses to exploit the enmity between and within the rival gangs—it's difficult to believe that anything terrible could happen to a clever lad flashing so much good old Irish blarney."
—*Publishers Weekly*

DEADLY DIAMONDS (Book 4)

"Blood diamonds" have found a route from Sierra Leone through Amsterdam, Ireland, Boston, and into the laps of Michael Knight and Lex Devlin.

"*Deadly Diamonds* takes you from mob strongholds in Boston to the diamond pits of Sierra Leone, in a plot twisty enough to leave skid marks on the page. A great read!"

—Lisa Scottoline,
New York Times best-selling author

FATAL ODDS (Book 5)

Gangs fueled by the almost limitless profit from the illicit trade of exotic and endangered species of wild animals captured in the rain forests of the Amazon face off with Michael Knight and Lex Devlin.

"*Fatal Odds* does everything right: a nail-biting plot to keep you turning pages, characters that shine brighter with every twist and turn, and a ripped-from-the-headlines authenticity that will leave you shocked. Here is a novel that expertly mixes thrills and smarts."

—James Rollins,
New York Times best-selling author

HIGH STAKES (Book 6)

The legacy of the actual prince of Romania—Vlad Dracula—reaches into today's most violent criminal organizations. Three violent gangs—Russian, Chinese, and Romanian—all after a Stradivarius—Michael Knight in the crosshairs.

"This rapid pace adventure delivers equal quantities of action, history, secrets, and conspiracies. Definitely an entertaining romp."
—Steve Berry,
New York Times best-selling author

If you liked *Deadly Depths*, we would be very appreciative if you would consider leaving a review. As you probably already know, book reviews are important to authors and they are very grateful when a reader makes the special effort to write a review, however brief.

For more information, please visit the author's website:
johndobbyn.com

Happy Reading,
Oceanview Publishing
Your Home for Mystery, Thriller, and Suspense